A HANDBOOK

HARRY FERGUSON

BLOOMSBURY

First published in Great Britain 2004

Copyright © 2004 by Harry Ferguson

The moral right of the author has been asserted

Wall to Wall Media Ltd would like to thank the following
for their help in making the programme: Team Dynamics
International Ltd, Hidden Technology, K9 Electronics,
Diligence, Adolfo Dominguez, Hobbs, T.M. Lewin, Vitra.
Photographs on pages xvii, xviii, xix, xx, xxi, xxii, xxiii, 83 (top),
170 (top and bottom)
© Martin Thompson 2004

Bloomsbury Publishing Plc, 38 Soho Square, London W1D 3HB

Extract from *Kim* by Rudyard Kipling. Copyright © Rudyard Kipling.
Reprinted by permission of AP Watt Ltd on behalf of The National Trust
for Places of Historic Interest or National Beauty. Extract from *Tinker
Tailor Soldier Spy* by John le Carré. Copyright © John le Carré 1974.
Extract from *The Looking Glass War* by John le Carré. Copyright © John
le Carré 1965. Extract from *The Spy Who Came in from the Cold* by
John le Carré. Copyright © John le Carré 1963. Reprinted by permission
of David Higham Associates.

A CIP catalogue record for this book
is available from the British Library

www.bloomsbury.com/harryferguson

ISBN 0 7475 7523 1

10 9 8 7 6 5 4 3 2 1

All papers used by Bloomsbury Publishing are natural,
recyclable products made from wood grown in well-managed
forests. The manufacturing processes conform to the regulations
of the country of origin.

Typeset by Hewer Text Ltd, Edinburgh
Printed in Great Britain by Clays Ltd, St Ives plc

CONTENTS

Introduction

From time to time, God causes men to be born – and thou art one of them – who have a lust to go abroad at the risk of their lives and discover news – to-day it may be of far-off things, tomorrow of some hidden mountain, and the next day of some near-by men who have done a foolishness against the State. These souls are very few; and of these few, not more than ten are of the best . . .

Kim
Rudyard Kipling

What does it take to become a real spy and can any member of the public be trained to do the job or is it a skill which is restricted to a select few of the public-school educated elite? These were some of the questions which we set out to answer early in 2004 when we began filming for the BBC 2/BBC 3 TV series *Spy*.

In November 2003 a website was created which apparently had facts about how to combat the common garden mole, but actually contained a hidden website for *Spy*. Advertisements were placed in the press and on the radio and business cards were left in pubs and clubs asking for those interested in becoming a spy to contact the website. Applicants had to answer detailed questions about their powers of persuasion, stamina and control of personal relationships. Over 5,000 people applied. This number was reduced to a shortlist of several hundred who were invited to regional interviews where they were filmed and questioned in greater depth. The final few were invited to a selection weekend where they were given a series of physical and mental tests and, finally, eight were selected to take part in the series.

Unlike other programmes about espionage, *Spy* was never going to be about explosions, seducing beautiful women and dry martinis. Instead we wanted to look at the real work of modern spies. And to ask the question: in the world of computers, the internet and twenty-four-hour surveillance by spy satellites do 'old school' spies have a role to play in the world any more?

Eight members of the public, four men and four women from a range of educational, social and ethnic backgrounds were selected to take part in a training course based on the real techniques used by intelligence services around the world. Many of the exercises were copies of real intelligence service training exercises and the targets were members of the public who had no idea that they were the subject of espionage techniques. The recruits were trained and assessed by real intelligence officers and at the end of the course the best recruits were sent on a mission abroad against real security forces.

A basic training course for an intelligence officer lasts at least six months in the UK, two years in the United States. Our recruits had their training crammed into just eight weeks. Even so there were many techniques and lectures which it wasn't possible to show on television. This book aims to fill that gap and give you a better idea of all the training the recruits received.

A Note About Secrecy and Sources

In designing the course we were faced with an immediate problem: although we had a range of experience from several different intelligence organisations both at home and abroad, we were all agreed that we must not divulge secrets and all information must be 'open source'. So could the programme be made at all? The first thing we had to do was to find out exactly how much was already in the public domain. As former operational officers, we were surprised at what we found. Espionage these days is an international affair with Western intelligence services more reliant on each other than ever before. A great deal of previously sensitive information has been made available, much of it in the United States which often has a much more mature approach to freedom of information than we have in the UK.

Another factor which helped us was the way that the 'spying game' has changed in recent years. In an age when a satellite phone signal can be intercepted and a missile launched from a drone destroying the user of the phone within four minutes, terrorists have quickly learned that Western intelligence services have complete control over technical devices. Phones and the internet can be intercepted, bugging devices have become so small as to be almost undetectable and any country where terrorists work openly can be isolated and even invaded (Afghanistan) in order to drive them out. To combat this, terrorists have reverted to the old techniques of espionage: fewer face to face contacts, disguise, cell networks, brush contacts, dead letter boxes and couriers. The old skills have become relevant once again and the intelligence services are having to relearn them.

Finally, a Warning

You have to be trained to do this. People don't like being spied on. Reading a book on spies doesn't give you the skills any more than reading a book about surgery makes you a doctor. I hope this book gives an idea of the issues which surround the subject of espionage and perhaps even inspires you to apply to the real intelligence services, but – and I mean this – don't try this at home!

Harry Ferguson
July 2004

The Trainers

This was the team chosen to design and run the course, each an expert in his or her own field. Their task was not only to train the students, but also to select the winner – the one candidate they felt had the right qualities to become a real life spy.

Harry Ferguson

After graduating from Oxford University, Harry served as an officer in MI6 for several years where he specialised in profiling, counter-espionage and intelligence analysis. After leaving MI6, he joined the Investigation Division of HM Customs and Excise as an undercover surveillance officer working against gangs smuggling materials such as heroin and components for weapons of mass destruction. He is currently a full-time writer.

Mike Baker

Mike worked for fourteen years as a covert field officer for the CIA specialising in counter-terrorism, counter-narcotics and counter-insurgency operations. During this time he was noted for his outstanding performance and achievements. He is currently Chief Executive Director of Diligence LLC, an intelligence and security company formed by former members of the CIA and MI5 which provides security personnel and expertise around the world.

Sandy Williams

Sandy is an intelligence and surveillance expert whose background currently remains classified.

Dr John Potter

John is a psychologist specialising in leadership, teamwork and stress management issues. He served for eight years as a Senior Lecturer in Military Technology and Military Psychology at the Royal Military Academy, Sandhurst, and is currently Associate Professor to the Centre for Leadership Studies at the University of Exeter. He also works as an international management consultant and trainer to a range of blue chip clients throughout the world.

The Recruits

Over 5,000 people applied to take part in the series. After a lengthy process of tests and interviews, these are the eight who were selected:

Austin

(19) Single. Works in the media industry. The youngest of the candidates and the only one from an Afro-Caribbean background. He was intelligent and physically very fit, working out regularly at his local gym and playing football every week. He was proud that he had overcome the disadvantages of a tough upbringing to achieve success in his own life, but also that he was trying to put something back by working with disadvantaged young people in his local community. He was exactly the sort of 'new Briton' that the intelligence services would like to attract. But would his youth, desire for the good life and occasionally confrontational attitude work against him?

Jennie

(27) Single. Project manager. A family-oriented woman who admitted that she sometimes struggled away from home. Her sense of justice and ability to keep important secrets were seen as strengths, but there were worries that she might be too ready to show her emotions and that she had a low threshold for the more detailed work which she could consider boring. It seemed likely that stronger personalities in the group might edge her out, but would her good social skills get her past that disadvantage?

Simon

(35) Married with three children. Works in the food industry. Simon was an instantly likeable character from Northern Ireland with the 'gift of the gab' and a seemingly inexhaustible supply of stories. A strong family man, he was clearly well grounded and appeared to have an intelligence which his life to date hadn't fully exploited. But he was also a man of strong political views and this might prove a source of friction with others. Furthermore his lack of ambition thus far in life might continue to be a feature of his character. When the going got tough, would he be too laid back for his own good?

Max

(35) Single. Carpenter. Although Max shared a flat with a woman, he was in fact gay, something he claimed to have successfully hidden from his workmates for over ten years. The programme was to be his 'coming out' statement. He was another candidate who was clearly intelligent but hadn't necessarily achieved as much in life as he might. He tended to worry that other people were better than him and this low self-esteem was likely to hold him back on the course. He was intimidated by the thought of what the course might contain, but was determined to face it. Would he have the ruthless streak necessary to succeed against other very strong candidates?

Gabriel

(24) Single. Management consultant. The poster boy among the applicants. His easy-going manner and clean-cut looks combined with his intelligence and sense of humour made him an early favourite. Physically fit and well travelled, at first glance he appeared to be exactly the sort of white middle-class male that the intelligence services would recruit at a moment's notice. But it also seemed that he could be naïve. If the group turned against him, he might quickly crumble and drop out. Would he have the tenacity to make the most of his obvious advantages?

Nicola

(24) Single. Insurance underwriter. She had always wanted to be a spy and was keen to see what the work was really like. She was intelligent, creative and could be a lively contributor in a social group, getting involved in everything easily and helping to bring others into the action. The biggest question mark was whether she had the necessary strength of character. She had shown that she was a confident performer amongst people with whom she felt comfortable, but if the group started getting really competitive it was feared she wouldn't have the enough self confidence to cope.

Suzi

(57) Single with two children. Music agent. Suzi was described by one of the selectors as 'a woman of experience'. She had been married twice and had to bring two children up alone. She had overcome a physical disability through the intensive study of ballet. Despite these challenges, she had found time to travel widely and she was clearly a woman of strong feelings and opinions, interested in others and keen to find out more. The problem was that her strong-willed nature might prove too much for other trainees. Would she be smart enough to mask her very powerful character?

Reena

(28) Single. Works in market research. In television terms, Reena was the most experienced of the applicants, having worked as an occasional presenter for some cable television stations. She was clearly a woman of drive and ambition who admitted that she saw the course as a way to further her long-term goals. She was very sociable and could be charming, but she clearly liked to be best. Would the other applicants turn on her because of this and amidst several other strong characters within a pressurised environment how would she react?

The recruits gather at the *Spy* training school, not realising that they are already under observation.

The trainers compare notes.

1 Capabilities

It's a great game of chess that's being played – all over the world – if this is the world at all, you know. Oh what fun it is! How I WISH that I was one of them! I wouldn't mind being a Pawn, if only I might join . . .

Through the Looking-Glass
Lewis Carroll

At some point in their lives almost everyone has wondered what it would be like to be a secret agent. What would it be like to spy on people without being spotted, to break in to secret bases past guards and security devices to steal documents or plant bugs, to manipulate others so that people would trust you with their secrets and even their lives? What sort of character does it take to assassinate terrorists who would otherwise slaughter thousands of innocent people? Only those who have done the job know if it is as exciting as it seems in the movies or whether it is actually just a rather boring Civil Service post, but we have all wondered . . .

At the end of this book you will find details of how to apply to become a real spy. But before that you need to know what being a spy involves and whether you have what it takes. The best way to judge this is to consider the choices that the experts had to make before the series was even filmed.

The panel of espionage experts advising the producers had each worked for a range of different intelligence and security services, but they knew that the qualities required are much the same the world over. The trouble is that very few candidates have all the necessary qualities. They could only take eight trainees, so what kind of people were they going to be looking for?

Based on their experience as both assessors and trainers, they decided that candidates for the series had to have five key qualities if they were to stand a chance of making the grade:

- Resourcefulness
- Observation skills
- Nerve
- Empathy
- Discretion

Resourcefulness

This is probably the key quality required in an intelligence officer. For a spy it has three meanings:

1. The Ability to Improvise

There are certain unwritten rules about the life of a spy, one of which is that you almost never have the right blend of skills and equipment you need and you will usually only find this out at the last moment. In the film *The Ipcress File*, based on the book by Len Deighton, the spy Harry Palmer has been captured and is being brainwashed by a shadowy foreign security force. He has to find a way to keep track of how long he has been held prisoner and to resist the brainwashing techniques which are being used against him. All he can find is an old bent nail but he uses this both to scratch a line on the wall for every day he is held prisoner and to ram into the palm of his hand every time the brainwashing begins. The pain helps him to resist the interrogations. This is the sort of desperate improvisation a spy may have to rely on at any time.

In the series, the ability to think up ideas under pressure was tested very early on in the 'balcony exercise'. Before they had been given any sort of training, the recruits were given just half an hour to come up with a way to get access to a flat and to be seen a few minutes later drinking a glass of water on the balcony with the owner. They were given no equipment or money and no briefing on who they could expect to be living in the apartment.

Based on a real exercise reportedly used by the Israeli intelligence service Mossad, this task represents the basic problem of gaining access to a restricted area which all spies encounter in their day-to-

The Balcony Exercise

How to do it: Suzi is handed a glass of water
on the balcony by the owner of the flat.

How not to do it: Gabriel is led away by the police.

day work. Pre-series tests had shown that it could be done, even in these days when we are all supposed to beware of door-to-door callers. But when the recruits arrived at the target location it was discovered that the occupants of the flats had recently been warned about the danger of bogus callers. The prospects for success had suddenly fallen dramatically.

Astonishingly, four of the eight candidates were successful. Two were, perhaps unsurprisingly, Nicola and Jennie, young, attractive women who do not appear to present a physical threat. Each of them had chosen fairly plausible stories about wishing to photograph the neighbouring flat or being in the early stages of pregnancy which were enough to get them through the door. Suzi, older but equally friendly, was also successful. But the fourth success was more surprising. Austin is a well-built young man and should have come across as just the kind of threatening stranger who would normally be refused access. However, he quickly dreamt up a story that the briefcase the production company had given him contained £10,000 in cash and that a radio station would only give him the combination if he could get onto the balcony of a selected block of flats. The story worked, but it also represented a tendency for the dramatic which the trainers knew Austin was going to have to curb if he was to proceed much further on the course.

2) The Ability to Be Creative

Much of a real spy's time is spent recruiting (or at least trying to recruit) agents – people who will provide secret documents and other intelligence. As you will see in a later chapter, this process, known as **profiling**, often means creating specific scenarios by which people are manipulated into working for you. The spy effectively becomes the story writer for other people's lives.

Furthermore, when working 'undercover' a spy also has to devise a background story to support their cover. Much of this will be done by specialist departments in the particular intelligence service, but a great deal also has to be devised by the spy to suit their own particular abilities. To be able to create these 'legends' convincingly requires a particular brand of creativity. Without it, a spy can never be effective.

The Ability to Work Alone

It may seem hard to believe now, but in the early 1980s much of South America was covered by just a single MI6 station operating out of Buenos Aires in Argentina. That station was manned by just one officer. There were two reasons behind MI6's thinking:

1) The area was the CIA's backyard so there seemed little point in simply replicating their coverage;
2) In any case, the area was a sleepy backwater (drugs trafficking was not seen as a priority intelligence target at this time). What threat to the UK could possibly come from this area?

In 1982, Argentina invaded the Falkland Islands. Hundreds of good men on both sides subsequently lost their lives in the fighting. Because of the lack of precise intelligence, the UK had been caught almost completely by surprise.

After the war, in the hunt for scapegoats, a lot of criticism was directed at the MI6 station and the lone officer running it. The Falkland Islands Review Committee under Lord Franks commented, 'Changes in the Argentine position were more evident on the diplomatic front and in the associated press campaign than in the intelligence reports.' Stephen Dorrill, an accomplished commentator on MI6's activities has similarly remarked, 'Much of [Buenos Aires station's] reporting consisted of little more than what was in the local press.'

Of course it is always easy to appear wise after the event and no one can really blame the officer involved. Even so, one wonders just how many lives might have been saved if the right intelligence agents had been recruited in the years leading up to the conflict.

After the example of the Falklands and particularly in an age when the 'war on terror' can flare up almost anywhere in the world, no spy can afford to sit back comfortably in his sleepy posting and think 'nothing will ever happen here . . .'

3) The Ability to Work Alone

A spy's life is lonely. Most missions in the field are accomplished by one person working alone. There may be a headquarters team to help the spy plan and train, but ultimately he or she is the only one responsible for either the success or failure of the mission. For security reasons they cannot even tell close colleagues about projects they are working on. They can't share their troubles or their triumphs. Like Mata Hari or Sidney Reilly, their only reward may be to end up one day in front of a firing squad in a distant land – or even worse.

A spy therefore has to be able to motivate himself. You may be in a foreign country, alone, pretending to be someone else every hour of the day, but you cannot sit back and relax. Even though the country you are based in may seem to be a forgotten backwater you must recruit your agent networks and support facilities *now* because there will be no time when the crisis actually strikes.

In the series we replicated this need to work alone in several ways: the students were separated from their families for the entire series and were only allowed to tell one person why they were going to be away for seven weeks. Once on the course, the students were all in competition with one another and at various stages were encouraged to spy on and even betray each other, so there was no one for them to confide in as the pressure mounted. As well as being trained and tested every day, they were given additional homework which they could complete 'if they wished'. Sometimes this finished work was just thrown in a litter bin in front of their eyes, clearly an utter waste of time. But other parts of it were vital to the successful completion of later exercises. There was no way of knowing which was which. They were even given language tapes in Arabic to study in every spare moment they had. Only those who drove themselves to complete all the work would be successful. It's a tribute to those on the course that they all worked so hard to complete every task.

Mata Hari (1876–1917)

She is one of the world's most famous female spies, yet she was hardly involved in espionage at all. Her real name was Margaretha Zelle. In 1895, aged only nineteen, she married an older soldier, Rudolph MacLeod. He abused her, raped her and carried on affairs with a string of women. Seeking comfort, Margaretha conducted a series of affairs with other military officers. In 1899, tragedy struck when someone poisoned their children. Although the daughter lived, their son died. It was most likely a servant seeking revenge against her abusive husband.

Margaretha filed for divorce and, since MacLeod's behaviour had been so outrageous, she won her case and custody of their daughter. But MacLeod refused to pay support and began a vitriolic campaign against her. Her position became impossible and, desperate for money, she handed the daughter to MacLeod and headed for Paris.

In Paris she enjoyed great success as an exotic dancer named Mata Hari (from the Malay word meaning 'eye of the dawn'). Between 1905 and 1912 she was one of the most successful and notorious cabaret acts in Europe. In May 1914 she performed in Germany where she fell for an army officer. It was later claimed that he had recruited her for the German intelligence service at this time and that she had spent four months in a spy training camp. She left Germany two days before war broke out and returned to France where, because of her German lover she was immediately placed under surveillance. In 1916 she met a French counter-espionage officer called Georges Ladoux. He asked her to spy on the Germans and she agreed. A plan was hatched to send her via Spain and Britain into neutral Holland from where she would try to seduce high-ranking officers.

In fact, the plan went wrong when she was deported from the UK as a suspected spy and she returned to Madrid. Whilst there she had yet another affair with a German officer. She tried to get intelligence from him, but

cont'd

he quickly suspected her and fed her old or false intelligence. A coded message was sent from Madrid to Berlin. The French had broken the German diplomatic cipher and intercepted this message which led them to conclude that she was a previously recruited German agent.

She returned to France, but in February 1917 was arrested on a charge of espionage. She was held in solitary confinement under appalling conditions and interrogated repeatedly. She never made any admissions. Finally it was decided to place her before a military tribunal in July. The lawyer appointed to defend her was a senile seventy-four-year-old expert in corporate law. He was not allowed to question any of the witnesses. She was quickly tried and condemned to death. As justice it was a farce. Her prosecutor, André Mornet, is famously supposed to have remarked forty years later, 'There wasn't enough evidence to whip a cat'. She was executed by firing squad on 15 October 1917.

To this day many questions remain. The Germans knew that the cipher they used to transmit the message from Madrid to Berlin had been cracked by the French and was likely to be intercepted. So were they getting rid of an agent who was no longer of use or by putting the French on to Mata Hari were they protecting some other agent? Or had they realised that Mata was working for the French and enjoyed the joke of tricking the French into executing one of their own agents?

Observation Skills

There are two types of observation which a successful spy must master:

1) Intelligence-Gathering Observation

A spy may only get a moment to glance at a technical drawing for a missile or to remember the face of a terrorist glimpsed through a car window. In fact a spy needs powers of observation which are almost photographic. And it is not just the ability to see and hear details which is important – you must be able to *remember* all the details you see and hear. It may be some time before you have the chance to record the intelligence.

A spy travelled abroad to conduct an interview with an agent who was a scientist in a highly sensitive weapons programme. The scientist's position was so delicate that it was considered too dangerous for a member of the local intelligence station to meet him. To evade any possible surveillance the interview was conducted in a moving vehicle. Obviously the officer couldn't drive, conduct her anti-surveillance manoeuvres and write notes at the same time. However, she couldn't openly use a tape recorder because she knew the agent was very nervous about talking to a spy and the sight of the recorder might make him clam up completely. So the officer had the technical division of her service equip the car with a hidden recorder so that it would secretly record the conversation. At the last moment, she decided that she had better have a back-up in case the main system failed so she also took a personal tape recorder. The interview lasted almost half an hour and the information was absolutely crucial. She had to get it back to her headquarters as quickly as possible.

But when she got back to base she found that both tapes had failed to record anything. For some reason the secret microphone in the car had only picked up engine noise. The tape on her personal set had jammed. With her headquarters desperate for the information as quickly as possible, she had to compile the entire interview from memory. She did it and a raid on the facility was successfully completed a short while later.

The skills in observation necessary for a spy have remained the same for hundreds of years and are beautifully illustrated in Rudyard Kipling's story *Kim*. The youth Kim is training to be a spy and is

9

challenged by his trainer to put himself up against a smaller boy who has been in training for some time:

'Play the Game of the Jewels against him. I will keep tally.' The child dried his tears at once and dashed to the back of the shop whence he returned with a copper tray.

'Gently – gently,' said Lurgan Sahib and from a drawer under the table dealt a half handful of clattering trifles into the tray.

'Now,' said the child, waving an old newspaper. 'Look on them as long as thou wilt, stranger. Count and, if need be, handle. One look is enough for me.' He turned his back proudly.

'But what is the game?' asked Kim.

'When thou hast counted and handled and art sure that thou canst remember them all, I cover them with this paper, and thou must tell over the tally to Lurgan Sahib. I will write mine.'

'Oah!' The instinct of competition waked in his breast. He bent over the tray. There were but fifteen stones on it. 'That is easy,' he said after a minute. The child slipped the paper over the winking jewels and scribbled in a native account-book.

'There are under that paper five blue stones – one big, one smaller and three small,' said Kim, all in haste. 'There are four green stones, and one with a hole through it; there is one yellow stone that I can see through, and one like a pipe-stem. There are two red stones, and – and – I made the count fifteen, but two I have forgotten. No! Give me time. One was of ivory, little and brownish; and – and – give me time . . .'

'One – Two –' Lurgan Sahib counted him out up to ten. Kim shook his head.

'Hear my count!' the child burst in, trilling with laughter. 'First, are two flawed sapphires – one of two ruttees and one of four as I should judge. The four-ruttee sapphire is chipped at the edge. There is one Turkestan turquoise, plain with black veins, and there are two inscribed – one with a Name of God in gilt, and the other being cracked across, for it came out of an old ring, I cannot read. We now have all five blue stones. Four flawed emeralds there are, but one is drilled in two places, and one is a little carven –'

'Their weights?' said Lurgan Sahib impassively.

'Three – five – five – and four ruttees as I should judge it. There is one piece of old greenish pipe amber, and a cut topaz from Europe. There is a carved ivory from China representing a rat sucking an egg; and there is last – ah ha! – a ball of crystal has been set in gold leaf.'

He clapped his hands at the close.

'He is thy master,' said Lurgan Sahib, smiling.

Kim clearly made a mistake in his initial count. Notice how the child's descriptions are so good that even we would stand a good chance of picking the stones out of a box of assorted jewels. Then compare them with Kim's. But in the story Kim practises until he learns how to beat the child at the game every time, whether it is played with jewels, kitchen utensils or photographs of strangers. Then his spy master considers him ready to go out into the world for further training.

Kim's game is still used by the British army in training its undercover operatives. The only major difference is that the army's trainee spies are challenged to memorise military equipment or the faces of known terrorists and always under stress conditions when they are exhausted and disorientated. Sometimes the old ways are still the best.

Today there are all sorts of technical devices which a spy can use to replace the old skill of observation and many modern spies make use of them: pens which can scan and record many pages of text, micro-sized cameras which can be smuggled in by agents, digital microphones no bigger than a button. But they have two important drawbacks: they might be found if you are stopped and searched and they will always let you down when you most need them.

So a spy must learn to use her eyes and not only to spot details but to remember them. Very few of us are born with a photographic memory, but like all abilities, speed reading and memory can be massively improved with training. As with many espionage skills, the successful spy drives herself to practise, practise, practise.

2) Defensive Observation

A spy must not only remember information, but must also have an eye for small details which could be the first sign of trouble: the agent who hesitates for a moment over a certain question, a momentary glimpse of an earpiece indicating that a surveillance team is following him or the almost imperceptible change in an office or room which reveals that a covert entry team has been there and placed a bugging device.

To illustrate this in the series the trainees were constantly tested at random times. In Programme Two, a fake fire alarm was staged and the trainees were asked to describe the guards who had sounded the alarm. Objects were constantly moved in the training rooms to see if the trainees spotted changes which could have signified that a bugging device had been placed. There was even an exercise staged at the London Eye where the trainees were expected to note descriptions of suspicious characters involved in certain activities. The improvement by the end of the series was remarkable and the three trainees who made it to the final exercise had mastered this skill thoroughly.

It takes discipline to constantly watch for small details. Most people look but don't see. They are generally poor witnesses when something dramatic happens and in court cases eyewitness identifications are notoriously unreliable. As a spy you *must* train yourself to see.

Nerve

A good spy must be able to see an opportunity, assess risk, then act without hesitation: that brief moment to look at a document left on the desk, the split second to ask a chance contact if they'll come to a later meeting, the nerve to sit tight and be patient when waiting in a hostile environment for an agent who is fifteen minutes late.

The recruits had to spot five suspicious characters amongst the crowds at the Millennium Wheel. Some of the targets were more obvious than others!

As well as their own eyes, the recruits had to be trained to use technical devices, which can mean staring at a monitor for hours on end camped in the back of a van. Technical devices can be invaluable – *if* they work.

In the 1990s an undercover team was sent to cover a major arms fair at a military base in South East Asia where it was believed that a group of international arms dealers were going to finalise a deal to import a consignment of illegal weapons. With another officer, one of the team followed a suspect as he travelled around the naval base and found that a major meeting was being held in an office in a high security area at the edge of the base. The main entrance to the office was up a flight of stairs on the exterior of an administration building. A guard was posted at the door, watching the crowds passing below him.

There was no time to set up a bugging operation and the number of possible exits meant it was no use waiting until the end of the meeting. There were a large number of strangers wandering around because of the fair, but as the officers stood there wondering what to do next the guard saw them and became suspicious. One of the officers decided that there was one chance. He walked up the stairs to the office, showed his visitor's pass and asked for directions to another part of the base. As the guard was giving directions the officer had a few seconds to look over his shoulder through the glass door and see who was sitting round the table at the meeting. From the descriptions he provided from that brief glimpse the team was able to identify several of the arms dealers involved and later to seize the consignment as it was unloaded from a freighter.

If the officer hadn't taken that split-second opportunity, the operation might not have been successful. It was a risk – the security guard might not have fallen for the rather weak story that the officer was lost, but that's the sort of instant assessment every undercover officer has to make.

A spy must continue to think and act even when the pressure is on. This is not a matter of courage. All of the recruits on the course showed that if they had enough time to think, they were prepared to

Right alongside her target, Nicola held her nerve
and was the only team member not 'burned'.

overcome their fears and act. To have nerve is to possess a different quality, the ability to remain cool and continue thinking even when everything seems to be going wrong. For the recruits, this quality was tested many times in the various exercises and not all of them did so well.

Nicola was on a surveillance exercise when the target she was following ended up standing right next to her on not just one but two separate occasions. Even though Nicola felt sure that the target must have spotted her, she held her nerve and continued to act normally. In the end she was the only member of her surveillance team who was *not* spotted.

By comparison Simon was placing a surveillance device in a house when a neighbour came to the front door. Simon failed to realise what was going on and he was spotted by the neighbour. The situation might have been saved. He answered the door with a story that he was there to fix the stereo and it is possible that this might have been believed, but, under pressure, he stopped thinking and was still wearing the plastic gloves he had been given to prevent fingerprints. The neighbour saw them and realised something was wrong. The entire operation was compromised and the team had to pull out shortly afterwards without achieving any of their objectives.

Possibly the most spectacular failure of nerve was by Gabriel, on the very first exercise, the balcony mission. When his story about feeling ill failed to get him access to the flat and he had the door closed in his face, Gabriel seemed to lose the plot completely. Forgetting that the most important point of the exercise was not to draw attention to himself, by repeatedly knocking on the door and calling through the letter box, he so scared the occupants that they called the police. It was fortunate for Gabriel that it was so early in the course and he was given another chance.

Interestingly it was the female recruits who tended to perform best in this respect. Suzi was typical of them in this regard. On one exercise designed to test the recruits' abilities to gain access to restricted buildings, Suzi was supposed to keep the staff of an expensive restaurant occupied whilst her partner Austin went into a restricted area and copied a document. It was only expected to take a few minutes, but in the end Austin waited for almost half an hour for just the right moment to make his move! Suzi could have panicked. She could have left the restaurant and abandoned Austin.

Simon heads towards the door of the target premises on the OP exercise to deal with a nosy neighbour, forgetting that he is still wearing the plastic gloves. His inability to think under pressure led to the collapse of an entire operation. The gloves gave him away.

Despite being unprepared, Suzi successfully distracted staff for more than thirty minutes as she waited for Austin to make his move. A classic example of a spy holding her nerve under pressure.

But she kept her head and continued to play her role of a woman who had come to book a special dinner party, and did it so naturally that the staff admitted later they had no suspicions at all. She was definitely exhibiting the sort of nerve a spy requires.

Empathy

British intelligence services used to have a reputation for only selecting officers who were 'club types' – the sort who could mix in good company, enjoy a drink at the bar and get information from people like themselves with the right sort of connections. Today the game has changed. Intelligence officers need to be able to work with a wide range of people across the full spectrum of race and social class. These days new recruits to all intelligence services are taught about the psychology of persuasion, reading body language and neuro-linguistic programming (NLP).

These are key skills for those thinking of applying to the modern British intelligence services. Application forms for MI5 ask candidates to give examples of how they have managed to persuade people to do things they might not otherwise have done. Most spies are responsible for running agents: they must persuade people to work for them, pass secret information and perhaps even risk their lives. They can only do this if they have the ability to understand others and manipulate the relationship so that the right opportunities arise. This is not something which can be done crudely – nature has equipped human beings with a whole range of ways of detecting insincerity and manipulation.

All of the recruits were picked because it was felt that whatever their age or background they had personalities which could encourage trust in others, and it was an ability which was repeatedly tested in ever more complex exercises. At first it was simply a matter of getting strangers to give them a piece of information or to look after an envelope for them. By the end of the course the recruits were able to work undercover alongside strangers for a number of days and persuade them to complete illicit tasks such as acting as a lookout during a break-in or lying to a spouse for them. These are the empathic skills which all real spies have to possess.

Jennie at the sports-centre reception desk with her
recruitment target. Her excellent social skills
enabled her to persuade the receptionist to
cover for her while she enjoyed her 'illicit affair'.

Although this man said that he had 'absolutely no time to talk',
he was soon drawing Nicola a complex map thanks to her
empathy skills.

Discretion

It goes without saying that all spies must be able to keep secrets. But for real spies it is even more complicated than that. Not every piece of information which should be withheld has a nice clear 'SECRET' label on it. Spies are constantly assessing how much they can tell other people about their lives and work, whether it is agents who work for them or other intelligence officers who work alongside them.

All the recruits were instructed to leave their old lives behind as soon as they were summoned to the training course. They were not supposed to bring any reminders of their old lives with them, were to act as if they were completely different people. This would seem like a simple instruction, but almost all the recruits failed to follow it. Some responded to their real names when they arrived at their hotels for the first night. Others had photographs, credit-card slips and other identifying documentation in their clothes and luggage. Possibly the worst offender was Simon who had brought photographs of his children and was nearly in tears when it seemed as if these might be torn up. The trainers quickly realised that his family was to be a major vulnerability for Simon and one he would either learn to master or fail the course.

Discretion was constantly being tested throughout the series. As the course progressed their shared experiences and their isolation from their families meant the recruits bonded closer together. Sandy was in charge of this aspect of the training and came down hard on anyone who broke the rules of secrecy, because in the outside world they would be endangering not only themselves but those they worked with. She was always watching for documents or belongings which were accidentally left lying about and anyone who revealed personal information to the other recruits received a particularly bitter reprimand. Most of the recruits suffered at her hands over the first few days and it was hardly surprising that she soon became known as 'the bitch in the wig'!

But this is an important lesson which all spies have to learn and possibly one of the hardest. The worst part is that you can't share knowledge of your position or success with others, which can be especially difficult when you meet old friends who are

Every recruit had to learn that secrecy meant leaving their families behind. Simon, who was very attached to his family, found this hardest of all.

On the very first day of training Mike discovered family photographs hidden in Simon's luggage. Simon could not come up with any plausible explanation.

enjoying high-flying careers. The temptation to let someone – anyone – know what you really do can become overwhelming. Furthermore, it is a natural part of human interaction to tell others about yourself and your family. This tendency to confide can be one which is difficult to suppress but, once the discipline is learnt, experienced officers never lose it. One thing the trainers all noticed about each other was that although we had been out of the job for some years none of us told the others much about our current work or families. It was an aspect of training which was to prove fatal to the chances of some of the recruits.

All the recruits failed the very first test in discretion on their initial morning at the *Spy* training school. The trainers decided to replicate an old German army trick which was employed against British prisoners of war. The Germans had found that many British prisoners refused to do more than give their name, rank and number as they had been instructed to do. Rather than waste a lot of energy subjecting each of these men to individual interrogation, the Germans used a more subtle method.

Prisoners were allowed into a detention room in twos and threes. At first they were wary of each other, but gradually they exchanged one or two words about who they were and where they were being held. The Germans found that this communication had a snowball effect and that as new prisoners were introduced and saw other prisoners talking, so they felt free to talk themselves. By bugging the room, the Germans were able to collect as much information in an hour as they might have gathered in a week of conventional interrogation.

When the recruits arrived at the *Spy* school they obviously expected some sort of process to start, but the trainers gave them nothing. The only person they saw was Sandy and she would say nothing at all to them, no matter what they said, no matter how long they stood and stared at her. Austin tried to outstare her, but Sandy was far too good for him and he eventually gave up. The recruits found that they were allowed to wander throughout the school and explore where they liked. This confused them. They couldn't work out what was going on. The first two who arrived were cautious and barely said anything apart from a few nods and murmurs. But by the time recruits four and five had arrived, they were all talking freely as a way to break the tension. They soon found the coffee machine and by the time all eight students were together it was like a party. They were all happily giving each other their real names, home addresses and family details. Microphones placed by the trainers recorded all of this valuable information. It seems that the old tricks still work – the students had all failed their first test.

Other Qualities

Linguistic Aptitude

If you are considering becoming a real spy, one thing you can do to improve your chances of recruitment is sharpen your language skills. To speak another language fluently implies a certain level of intelligence and experience. But furthermore, facility with language often reveals sensitivity to the customs and culture of others. What made T.E. Lawrence such a remarkable spy and leader of the Arab resistance was his complete immersion in their customs, their dress, their whole way of life. Finally, knowledge of other languages is often essential if a spy is successfully to recruit agents. Imagine if the positions were reversed – if someone tried to recruit you would they be more likely to do it by speaking English or a foreign language?

A knowledge of the usual stand-bys such as French, German, Italian or Spanish is a help of course because in some parts of the world these are a standard second language and they indicate a mind which can adapt to new languages. But a potential spy will have more than this: Russian used to help a great deal, but the world has moved on. Today Arabic is at a premium, as are the languages of Asia and the Indian sub-continent. But you never know where the next emergency will occur and knowledge of Turkish, Polish or Uzbek may be exactly what is required.

If you join MI6 or the CIA today, you will have to undergo a 'linguistic aptitude test'. The services are not so interested in how many languages you speak as in how readily you absorb new languages. To reflect this essential quality we gave the recruits Arabic language materials to learn from and told them that it might be vital in a future exercise. This exercise also tested their ability to work on their own initiative since it was up to them how much or how little time and effort they devoted to it. For

The recruits learned to hate their silver briefcases
almost as much as Sandy, 'the bitch in the wig'.

The secret contents of a silver briefcase.

some of them, being forced to examine this new language and culture became one of the most rewarding parts of the course.

The British intelligence services recruit about twenty speakers of Arabic, Persian, Turkish, Urdu and Pushtu each year. But they find it difficult to recruit enough people especially considering that the recruits need to be UK citizens and have a good knowledge of the politics of the region. Although there were 737 postgraduates of Islamic and Middle Eastern studies in England and Wales in 2003, only twelve of these were British. So if you're thinking of applying to become a spy in the future, start learning one of these languages now.

Stamina

Being a spy, living under cover, constantly watching everything which is said or which happens around you is psychologically draining. There are some secrets which you cannot share with anyone, not even family. Although there are people who have the intelligence and other skills which are necessary to become intelligence officers, not all people can live this secret life. On the training course this constant pressure was replicated in a number of ways. The recruits never knew when they were being filmed or having their conversations recorded. They were told that there were secret cameras and microphones hidden at all locations and they could never be sure if something they did or said would later be shown in public. And they were kept constantly on the edge of mental exhaustion – even when they weren't at the *Spy* school they were given boring, repetitive homework such as memorising long lists of facts about obscure pieces of military equipment, knowing that they could be tested on them at any time. This work was on top of planning operations, planning cover stories and all the other training work they had to complete.

With the recruits' minds exhausted, the training team began to turn the emotional screws. The only people they were allowed to grow close to during the course were their fellow trainees. Then at a certain point in the training they were pitted against each other and encouraged to spy on and even to betray each other. Many of them could not stand the strain. All of them thought they were being secretly followed at some time or other. Simon missed his family desperately and was nearly in tears on several occasions. Gabriel

Arabic was the language the recruits were
expected to learn as part of the course, but a
real spy must be prepared to learn any language.

The recruits soon learned to trust no one – not even each other.
Nicola and Gabriel try to trick Max into confessing to a breach of
the *Spy* school's rules in a hotel bar.

seemed to become obsessed with Sandy's opinion of him and whether she was setting him up for betrayal, even at one stage threatening to slap her. Even Jennie, initially the strongest of the recruits, was breaking down in tears by the end of the course and threatening to quit because she could not take the mental strain any longer.

This is what is meant by stamina. Living a secret life sounds glamorous until you actually do it. Keeping secrets from others is draining, as is constantly monitoring everything for possible traps or surveillance. The sense of paranoia can become overwhelming. Add to that a sense of responsibility for agents who have been killed or captured when an operation goes wrong and the emotional cost can break anyone. It is a rare person who can stand this kind of strain for an entire career and we were determined to test the recruits as far as we could. That was when we knew those who could and could not become spies.

Questions of Morality

You wanted an eleventh Commandment that would match your rare soul! Well, here you have it . . . We sent him because we needed to; we abandon him because we must. That is the discipline you admired.

The Looking Glass War
John le Carré

Can someone with a conscience become a spy? We live in an age when the intelligence services are accused of many different crimes: the CIA of assassinating President Kennedy and concealing activities at Area 51; MI6 of assassinating Princess Diana; Mossad of being behind the 9/11 attacks in the United States. Of course all of this is so much rubbish, but espionage does have a reputation as a job where normal morality does not apply – after all, if something is done in secret, then who cares what you do?

So a lot of people believe that if they became a spy they would be asked to act immorally. And the truth? The bottom line is that intelligence services will do whatever has to be done. If that sounds too vague then consider this: would you kill someone else if you

The recruits were abducted, hooded and interrogated
by a team consisting of former special forces personnel.

Although chilled to the bone,
terrified and deprived of sleep, Jennie managed
to resist the interrogators' attempts to break her.

knew that you would definitely save 5,000 men, women and children? How about 500,000? Or 5 million? The point is that the intelligence services never know how great tomorrow's threat will be nor even what the balance of moralities will be in the next operation. All any spy can do is take each operation as it comes and pray that he or she makes the right decision.

With familiarity comes contempt and it would be easy for spies who become accustomed to manipulating the lives of their agents to harden to them as people. Often intelligence services will test the moral sense of potential officers by presenting them with operational choices or tasks which are morally dubious. This is not, as one might think, because they are looking for the unfeeling robot who will do whatever he is told like an obedient soldier. That sort of person will never become a successful agent runner. The services are looking more for the officer who is prepared to express doubts and to hesitate before placing agents in danger.

On the course the recruits were required to betray each other. The final six were split into two teams of three and within each team two were asked to trick the other one into providing evidence which would be sufficient for them to be dismissed from the course. One such team was Austin and Jennie who were pitted against Simon. Austin readily agreed to undertake the mission because he knew that sometimes spies have to put personal feelings aside and get on with the job. But Jennie was quite different. She hesitated for a considerable time before signing the document and eventually broke down in tears. She knew what succeeding on the course meant to Simon, who had wanted to be a secret agent since he was a small boy, and how he would feel when he found that his friends had betrayed him. Neither Austin nor Jennie were doing anything wrong, but in a recruitment situation, Jennie would probably score more highly in most intelligence services because she had the strength and the sensitivity to have doubts about the mission she was being asked to undertake. That's the sort of person who can become a good spy because she cares about the people she works with and who work for her, and that creates trust.

A Note About the Recruits' Training

We wanted to test the recruits against people in the real world rather than actors to show that the techniques they were being taught actually work. At the same time we needed to create a safe and controlled environment for the recruits to try out these skills without putting any members of the public at risk. To achieve this we adopted the following procedure: the recruits were tested against members of the public who were completely unaware that they were the subject of an exercise, but who were told about what had happened immediately afterwards. Where buildings were infiltrated, permission was sought from management beforehand although staff remained unaware. When filming in people's homes, the owner was informed that a TV programme was being made and of the general nature of the exercise, but not that espionage techniques were involved, nor of the exact date. Clearances were obtained from those who took part in the training and this system allowed us to achieve the maximum level of realism and tension required.

2 What Does a Spy Actually Do?

Now, there are five sorts of spies: there are native spies, internal spies, double spies, doomed spies and surviving spies. When all these five types of spies are at work and their operations are successfully clandestine, it is called 'the divine manipulation of threads'.

The Art of War
Sun Tzu

Of course, the answer to what a spy actually does seems pretty obvious: they gather intelligence. But what procedures does a spy go through to get that intelligence?

People either imagine a spy abseiling down the side of a tall building before karate-chopping a guard, then delivering a box of chocolates to a young woman in a negligée. Or they go to the other extreme and imagine that spies are little more than low-class diplomats, hanging around in the right places, reading lots of dull paperwork and keeping their ears to the ground for the right snippets of information.

The reality is that in any intelligence service there are two types of officer: **field officers** who actually live and/or work abroad and **desk officers** who supply most of the administrative back-up for active operations. Desk officers are often field officers who are being rested or retrained before returning to active duty, although some officers will spend their entire careers working as desk officers because, although they are highly intelligent or talented, they do not have the nerve or the skills necessary for working in the field. Desk officers will work in one of the headquarters buildings of the intelligence service, usually in a department which has a particular responsibility such as profiling, security or intelligence analysis.

Field officers working in a foreign country are usually grouped together in a **station**. A station is a team of intelligence officers with the responsibility of spying on a particular country. A station may be either **declared** or **undeclared** (clandestine). A declared station is one where the intelligence officers are known to the host country and there is a liaison of the host's intelligence service. For instance the MI6 station in the United States is a declared station and the CIA and MI6 cooperate closely together. A station in a hostile country will remain undeclared and the officers working there must take special precautions to keep their identities secret. Almost all Mossad stations around the world are undeclared. The senior intelligence officer is known as the **head of station**. They will usually work from an embassy or some other suitable location with secure communication facilities. For countries which have particularly harsh operating conditions the station may be based outside the country with station officers travelling, either covertly or overtly, into the country whenever they need to conduct an operation. Not all field officers are attached to a station. Some may be working so deeply under cover that not even the station is told about their mission, protecting them if the station is penetrated by an enemy agent or bugging device.

But wherever they are working, there are usually nine main parts to a spy's work:

1. Running Agents

Many kinds of agents are employed to provide intelligence necessary for any espionage operation and a good station will have a range of them available for different operations. The main types of agent are:

Intelligence Agent

This is what people typically think of as a 'secret agent', someone whose job is to produce secret information for his handler.

Confusion Agent

An asset used to confuse the counter-intelligence and security agencies of another country.

Access Agent

Doesn't produce intelligence, but can set up meetings with or provide introductions to people who might become agents. Access agents are usually highly thought of in local society so that if they hold a party or other function then any potential agent who is invited will attend.

Double Agent

Pretends to work for his own service but in fact is passing secrets to another intelligence service. A double agent who has been caught by his service and is persuaded to pass misleading intelligence is known a **re-doubled agent**. A **triple agent** is one who works for three different services.

Agents of Influence

A trusted contact of the intelligence service who is highly placed in the target country whether in politics, the media, one of the professions or some sector of industry. Although not producing intelligence, they are in a position to perform tasks to aid the intelligence service. A newspaper editor might place a certain story, a politician might agree to support a change in the law and so forth.

Used in foreign countries there is little argument against this type of agent. However, there have been allegations that intelligence services recruit this kind of agent in their own countries to promote the interests of the intelligence service rather than the country. In the UK, the former editor of the *Daily Telegraph*, Dominic Lawson, was accused of assisting MI6 largely because he had a relative who was an MI6 officer. This allegation was strenuously denied and never substantiated, but every intelligence service around the world is bound to have a range of media and political contacts. It is a fine line between being a 'trusted contact' and an 'agent of influence'. They are sometimes referred to as 'honorary agents'.

Illegal Agent

More often known simply as 'illegals'. They are intelligence officers living in the target country under non-official cover (see Chapter 3).

Because they never have contact with the station in that country they are much harder for security forces to detect.

Facilities Agent

Provides material help to the intelligence service in the target country. A telephone engineer might be able to place bugging devices, another agent might keep a safe house for agents on the run or own a garage to provide untraceable vehicles at short notice.

Principal Agent

Handles a network of other agents and acts as a handler instead of the intelligence officer. This type of highly competent agent is very rare.

Provocation Agent

More commonly known as an *agent provocateur*. An agent recruited within an organisation, not only to provide intelligence, but to urge the organisation spied upon to more illegal and extreme acts in order to help trap those involved when the authorities move in.

Sleeper Agent

Placed in the target country but does nothing and has no contact with the intelligence service until 'activated'. A sleeper agent is almost undetectable by the host country's security forces.

Whenever a spy joins a new team there will be a stable of agents already in place. Each agent will need to be seen regularly, and at every meeting there are various tasks which may need to be accomplished:

Debriefing. The most important part of the meeting: getting the latest intelligence from the agent.
Briefing. Letting the agent know her next mission and the intelligence the service would like her to provide.
Reward. This can mean paying the agent either a salary, a set amount based on the value of her last intelligence report or just an

amount to cover expenses. Some agents, such as those driven by political or religious principle may refuse payment altogether. For these people reward means letting them know how valuable their work is and the effect it is having.

Equipping. Giving the agent any material she may require for her next mission such as film, specialised cameras or bugging devices.

Training. All agents need regular training both in new equipment and in procedures such as counter-surveillance or secret writing. Where possible they are taken out of the country for this, perhaps under the pretence of going on holiday. But in some closed societies this is not possible and the training has to take place during agent meetings.

Welfare. Probably the second most important stage after debriefing. The officer takes time to monitor the agent's morale and checks to see if there is anything they need or if there has been any change in their family background. From this information a good officer will sense when problems are forming and take early action to deal with them.

And all this has to be achieved in conditions of complete secrecy. Other field officers may be involved in providing security measures such as counter-surveillance. Even desk officers can be called out to meet an agent and some networks will be run for security reasons by a desk officer who will only rarely visit the country to meet agents face to face. It is this relationship between the intelligence officer and her agents which is at the heart of a well-run intelligence service. It is almost always the agents who run the risks. It is almost always the agents who have the most to lose if the relationship is discovered. A good spy is like a good general who cares for the welfare of those under her command but who knows that there may be times when lives may have to be put at risk.

2. Spotting Potential Agents

Field officers will be constantly on the lookout for people who might become agents. This is known in the trade as **profiling**. Once a suitable target has been identified, reports will be sent back to HQ where specialised **profiling teams** will start to examine the background of the target, assessing their suitability and access for intelligence work. If the target seems promising and the operation is authorised by senior managers, the process of recruiting the agent will begin. This is known as **cultivation**. A cultivation may take a few months, though in difficult cases it may take several years. Often it doesn't work out, but the process should end in **recruitment**, when the target finally becomes a fully conscious agent of the intelligence service.

What is the difference between a spy and an agent?

The operatives which people generally think of as spies generally fall into one of two categories: either they are **intelligence officers** or they are **agents**.

An **intelligence officer** is a man or woman who works for an intelligence service such as the CIA, MI6 or the KGB. They are highly trained in all aspects of espionage, but their main purpose is to recruit and run agents. This is the sort of person referred to in this book as a **SPY**.

An **agent** is a person recruited by an intelligence officer to collect intelligence or support the spying operation in some other way. They are often just ordinary people who either disagree with their country's policies or are otherwise persuaded to work with the intelligence service of another country.

Although it is often the agent who does the actual work such as photographing a document, stealing a piece of equipment or placing a bugging device, there are times when a suitable agent cannot be recruited and then it is the intelligence officer who must put herself forward, carry out the operation and take the risk of getting caught. It is hardly surprising that the general public often get agents and intelligence officers confused. This is not helped by the fact that some US organisations refer to their intelligence officers as 'agents'!

3. Paperwork

Whether a field officer or a desk officer, a spy spends a great deal of time either writing or reading seemingly endless piles of paper. For every agent meeting a detailed document known as a **contact report** has to be produced. This will include a note of everything discussed at the meeting, whether there were any problems and a note of the agent's current state of mind. The meeting may have produced one or more **intelligence reports**. These have to be written up in a way which disguises the source and then they are sent back to HQ where the report is assessed for accuracy and then disseminated to customers in other government departments. **Profiling reports** have to be written about potential new agents. **Security reports** have to be written about the activities of officers from other services who are known to be working in the area. Every spy needs to be aware of the latest local developments by reading **local press**, **diplomatic reports** and even **academic**

To replicate the real life of a spy the recruits were continually given paperwork exercises which ate into their spare time and kept them under constant pressure.

studies. He also needs to be aware of political events in the world at large in case they affect events in the country where he is working. In fact for every spy working abroad there are at least three back home sorting through the all the bits of paper the work produces.

Anyone who joins an intelligence service expecting a healthy outdoor life is going to be sadly disappointed . . .

4. Evaluation of Intelligence

Every intelligence service around the world is given a list of requirements they are expected to fill each year. Every field officer needs to be aware of the requirements for his station and also needs to be able to judge whether what he has been given by an agent is reliable. Back at HQ, reports officers will spend a great deal of time comparing the report with other information, both overt and covert, to see if they agree with the field officer's view. The report will then be given some sort of quality rating with the best reports going directly to senior government officials.

Every intelligence post abroad will have a target for the number of reports of a particular grade which it is expected to produce during the year and desk officers have to be careful since field officers have been known to try all sorts of tricks to fill their quota, even putting forward information which is really just guesswork by their agent in the hope that it might be accepted.

It is important to get this part of the job right; ultimately it is on intelligence reporting that the service will be judged. The poor reporting from the CIA and MI6 before the war in Iraq and the subsequent enquiries show what can happen when a service gets it wrong.

5. Liaison with Other Intelligence Agencies

All intelligence services have allies and at home there will be a great deal of trading of both intelligence reports and expertise between allies, including joint training. In the field, liaison can be more difficult since enemies will be watching to see if they can spot intelligence officers. Despite this risk, there is often a considerable amount of cooperation between field officers from allied services. No station ever has enough personnel and the sharing of information on local targets is a great help.

At the same time, no one trusts their allies completely. So when officers get together in the field there will be information they don't talk about and on occasions they may even mislead each other to deflect attention from a current operation. It takes strong interpersonal skills to keep good relations with allies without giving too much away.

The recruits were always in competition with each other and were encouraged to betray each other. Yet they also needed to cooperate on many of the missions. Max proved a skilful manipulator, never giving too much away and always seeking to collect information on the other recruits which he passed on to the trainers.

6. Covert Diplomacy

A crucial aspect of a spy's role is talking to people that their government can't be seen talking to. It was MI6 which opened negotiations with the Provisional IRA leading to a ceasefire (see overleaf). In Afghanistan in the 1980s during the Soviet occupation, intelligence officers from the UK and the USA liaised with Afghan guerrillas covertly providing weapons and training which eventually broke the Russian stranglehold. Intelligence services never know who they might be required to contact. Twenty years from now it might be necessary to open a dialogue with Osama bin Laden or other senior officials of al Qaeda.

However, allowing intelligence services to establish covert relationships can be dangerous. Intelligence officers used covert channels to supply weapons to Nicaraguan guerrillas during the Iran-Contra scandal in the USA in the 1980s and the discovery of it almost brought down the US government.

7. Covert Action

This is the real James Bond stuff. Break-ins to steal documents or plant bugging devices, training guerrillas, even assassination. Usually special military forces or technical experts will be flown into the country for this work. But on certain occasions there will be reasons why they can't be used and that is when the Intelligence Officer has to go in herself. All officers in all services are trained in weapons, burglary skills, explosives, etc. The amount and seriousness of the training tends to

MI6's covert role in the Northern Ireland peace process

Michael Oatley was a senior MI6 officer who was posted to Northern Ireland in 1973. He had been expecting a posting somewhere more exotic and knew absolutely nothing about the Irish conflict. But rather than being a weakness this turned out to be one of his greatest strengths, for having no preconceived notions about the rights and wrongs of the situation he decided to learn as much as he could about all sides in the conflict in his search for a solution.

Oatley was posted as the deputy to Foreign Office official James Allan. One of Allan's responsibilities was to supervise secret meetings between the various parties to the conflict, often including both republican and loyalist paramilitary groups. This was extremely delicate work and Allan and Oatley had a hard time convincing the various groups to trust them. The thing which most surprised Oatley was that although the Provisional IRA was responsible for much of the killing in Northern Ireland, no one seemed to be making an effort to understand their motives. He later said, 'If I was going to spend two years or longer in Northern Ireland, I ought perhaps to try and concentrate on seeing whether my particular skills and background could enable me to find a way to influence the leadership of the IRA or to make some kind of contact through which they could be influenced.'

The problem was that whilst many experts could see that some sort of dialogue was needed, the British government could not be seen to be talking to terrorists. This was a perfect task for MI6 which at the time was an organisation so secret that the government would not even confirmed that it existed (the UK government finally admitted to the existence of MI6 in a House of Commons statement in May 1992). The government was able to task MI6 to explore ways of making contact

cont'd

without asking too many questions about exactly what its spies were doing.

By the end of 1974, Oatley, with the support of many others, was able to create three secret channels to the Republican terrorist groups. One was through a British businessman in Northern Ireland who happened to be a friend of a member of the IRA's ruling Army Council; another was with a retired Commander of one of the Provisional IRA's Operational Brigades; the third was an even more secret contact who, whilst not a terrorist himself, had close links with them and was trusted enough to be able to pass messages across. It was not Oatley's job actually to say anything through these contacts but merely to establish the links so that they were there if the government wished to use them. Nor did this mean any decrease in effort by the regular security forces to bring the terrorists to justice. In fact during the time when these contacts were being established, the security forces were enjoying their most successful period to date.

The combination of pressure from the security forces and the possibility of talks on a secret channel helped to bring about the situation where the Provisional IRA declared a ceasefire during the Christmas of 1974. Oatley and Allan then had a series of meetings with senior IRA figures which were arranged through the secret contact and a permanent ceasefire was declared in February 1975.

Oatley moved on to a new posting in March 1975 and the ceasefire broke down a few months later. But the incident shows how powerful covert diplomacy can be when governments are unable to act openly for fear of public and media reaction. The trust which Oatley had built up continued to be useful in the following years. His final meeting with a Republican representative was shortly before his retirement in late 1990. The purpose was to 'hand over' the covert liaison to a new senior officer. The link established twenty years before was still proving useful.

vary between services. The CIA and Mossad take such training particularly seriously. This sort of work makes up less than one per cent of a spy's duty, but is by far the most dangerous, and the most exciting.

8. Living a Cover Role

Never forget that all of the tasks above have to be accomplished by the spy whilst holding down another full-time job. You might think that of all the things a spy has to do this is the task to which he devotes the least amount of time, but whether it is cover as a diplomat, working as a businessman or wandering around as a tourist, the cover has to be perfect because if detected by the enemy's security forces then none of the other tasks matter.

This is an important part of **tradecraft** – all the skills which a spy uses in her work. Living under cover without detection is probably more important than being able to conduct a brush contact.

The highest level of tradecraft is known as '**Moscow Rules**' because it was thought that Moscow, the heart of the Soviet empire, presented the most difficult operating conditions for a spy. In fact it worked both ways and, because of the extreme conditions most Soviet diplomats worked under, they had to be so cautious that it might well be called 'Washington Rules'. But the truly highest level of tradecraft is when all the defensive and offensive moves of the spy become second nature and she is able to do it all naturally without anyone else realising that anything unusual is going on.

9. Counter-Espionage

The greatest prize for any intelligence service is to recruit an agent in a foreign intelligence service. That one officer can provide almost all the secrets of the other organisation, effectively crippling it for years to come. To this day British intelligence services cannot shake off the spectre of the 'Cambridge spies' such as Kim Philby or Anthony Blunt and in the United States, CIA traitor Aldrich Ames passed information which led to the unmasking of countless valuable agents. For this reason, whether based at a station abroad or in a headquarters building, all spies must be aware of the activities of their enemies. This is what is known as counter-espionage.

Real spies must constantly be on the alert for enemy officers who will always be trying to trick them into giving away secret information. Three honey traps, controlled by Sandy, close in on Gabriel.

All intelligence organisations have security branches whose job is to monitor all staff for possible compromise and to oversee all active recruitment operations to make sure that they are not traps set by a foreign service. In stations abroad, every officer is expected to be vigilant in watching for signs of enemy intelligence officers and to report any sightings to the security branch so that they can build pictures of enemy intelligence activity. This type of information about an enemy service is known as **orbat** (order of battle).

When the loyalty of a spy is suspected, the security branch may run an operation to test that officer. This was replicated on the course by setting a **honey trap** (an offer too tempting to refuse) for the last four recruits just before they were to be sent abroad on the final mission. The trap was complicated, involving the supposedly accidental release of information to the recruits and the participation of publicist Max Clifford who pretended to be handling publicity for the series. The recruits were separated from each other and led to believe that they had failed the course. Clifford then offered them a tempting amount of money for information about the series. Sadly, it is a test that one of the recruits failed.

The Cambridge spies

Five men who were recruited by the Soviet Union during the 1930s at Cambridge University. There were others recruited at the same time, but these five are the most famous. They represent Russia's greatest espionage success of the Cold War and created a legacy of incompetence and vulnerability which it has taken British intelligence many years to expunge.

Kim Philby: Became a journalist after his recruitment at Cambridge and used his cover as a correspondent to spy for the Communists in Spain during the Spanish Civil War in 1936. He served with the Special Operations Executive (SOE) during World War II and joined MI6 in 1945. He was initially placed in the Iberian section because of his experience in Spain, but soon worked his way into the Soviet section where he could be of most use to his NKVD masters. He betrayed almost all of MI6's anti-Soviet operations and many of those of the CIA with whom he worked closely. Philby rose rapidly through the ranks and was even considered as a possible candidate for 'C', head of MI6. In 1949 he was sent to the MI6 station in Washington as the liaison officer with the Americans. There he worked closely with Guy Burgess to pass much valuable intelligence on nuclear secrets, NATO and western intelligence efforts. Hearing that Burgess was under suspicion and about to be arrested, Philby tipped him off, enabling Burgess and his associate Donald MacLean to flee to Moscow. Philby was suspected of the leak and eventually resigned, famously defending his 'honour' in a televised press conference in 1953 (see *www.britishpathe.com* for an extract). In 1963 conclusive evidence was provided against him by a Soviet defector. Due to MI6 incompetence, Philby was able to flee from his home in Beirut and escape to the Soviet Union. He died there in 1988.

Guy Burgess: Worked for the BBC during World War II and joined the Foreign Office in 1944, eventually becoming

cont'd

personal assistant to the Minister of State where he had access to a great deal of valuable intelligence. In 1949 he was posted to Washington, but his dissolute homosexual lifestyle and drunken behaviour finally caught up with him. Warned by Philby that he and Donald MacLean were about to be arrested, the pair fled to Moscow. Burgess died there, an alcoholic wreck, in 1964.

Donald MacLean: Joined the Foreign Office after Cambridge and despite his barely disguised homosexual behaviour and often violent, drunken outbursts, he served on postings to Cairo and Paris and was even thought of as a future ambassador. He became First Secretary at the British embassy in Washington and it was while he was there that the security net finally began to close in on him. He returned to Britain, but shortly after was warned of his impending arrest by Philby and Burgess and fled to Moscow. He endured a miserable exile and finally died a broken man in 1983.

Sir Anthony Blunt: Blunt joined MI5 in 1940, soon rising to take charge of the Watchers, the specialist surveillance branch. He also acted as personal assistant to the head of the Service and even represented MI5 at meetings of the Joint Intelligence Committee which gave him access to the most sensitive intelligence available. After the war he left MI5 and trained as an art historian becoming one of the pre-eminent experts in his field and Curator of Pictures to the Queen. In 1963 his position as 'the fourth man' was exposed and Blunt confessed, but struck a deal by which he escaped prosecution in return for revealing full details of his involvement. Although the deal was observed by the authorities, suspicion continued to follow him until his role was formally exposed by Prime Minister Thatcher in 1979. Blunt was stripped of his knighthood and lived a life of public disgrace until his death in 1983.

cont'd

John Cairncross: Following his recruitment at Cambridge by Blunt and Burgess, he joined the Foreign Office in 1936. During World War II he worked for the Government Code and Cipher School at Bletchley Park, the forerunner of GCHQ. He passed many vital codes and code-breaking techniques to the Russians. He then moved to MI6. When Burgess fled in 1951, Blunt cleared all incriminating documents from Burgess' London flat, but missed documents implicating Cairncross. Cairncross confessed to a low-level involvement and to avoid a scandal at a time when the Anglo/US intelligence relationship was in danger, he was allowed to resign quietly. His full involvement was revealed by Blunt in 1963 and like Blunt he made a full confession in return for immunity. The authorities agreed because they could not afford another scandal. Cairncross settled in Italy and died there in 1995. He is generally referred to as 'the fifth man' because he was the last of the major Cambridge spies to be publicly revealed.

3 Living a Secret Life: Cover and Legend

He alone is an acute observer who can observe minutely without being observed.

Johann Kaspar Lavater

Obviously a spy cannot succeed if people suspect who he is and all spies must be able to travel and operate without others guessing their real purpose. Spies achieve this by working under **cover:** under the cover of another name, under the cover of another occupation, sometimes even under the cover of another nationality (see False Flag recruitments in Chapter 5). It is not as simple as being given a dossier with your new identity and a few forged documents. Although every service has departments which specialise in creating cover identities for its operatives, none of them can provide the depth of information which a cover role truly requires. Ultimately it is down to the individual officer to research his cover identity, consider all the questions he might get asked and learn to use naturally all those nuances of behaviour and small mannerisms of speech which convince others that they are truly what they claim to be. The only way to master that kind of painstaking detail is through the application of study, imagination and long hours of hard work.

If you want to become a spy, this ability to work under cover is one of the first skills you must master. It does not matter how good you are at other parts of a spy's work, such as recruitment, agent running or surveillance, if you cannot create a cover and live under it as naturally as if you have been doing it all your life then you will never make it as a spy. But even before a spy learns to work under cover, there is another basic technique which must be learned and which has to be mastered if he is to be able to work under cover. That skill is **going grey**.

Going Grey

This refers to the skill of moving amongst other people and blending in with them so effectively that you do not attract attention. It is the first skill of any spy who has to perform surveillance duties and a skill which all spies have to make use of at some stage.

It is not an easy skill to master. We can all blend in to a social environment which we know, we understand the rules of dress and behaviour, many of which we observe unconsciously. But to do this in an unfamiliar setting requires more than simply wearing the right clothing. And even the clothing isn't as easy to get right as you might think: when the British army first began deploying soldiers as undercover operatives in Northern Ireland they drew a lot of criticism from experienced units such as A4, the specialist surveillance section of MI5, because of the undercover 'uniform' they all seemed to wear. It was claimed that you could always spot them because of their identical jeans, white trainers and bomber jackets. Many of them also retained their distinctive British army moustaches. But even after they mastered these simple steps, there were other problems to overcome. A person who has had military training and long hours of drill often stands out from other people by the way they stand or walk and it is not easy to watch others and yet disguise the fact that you are doing so.

These are the points which a spy has to consider when going grey:

Role: When considering going grey in an area, a spy must first understand what she is supposed to be doing there. This is not the same as considering a cover story for an operation because going grey means not even being noticed, let alone challenged. Complete success at going grey is when there is no interaction with anyone else in the area at all because the spy's presence is simply accepted by those around her. So the role adopted must be something which is obvious to the eyes of another observer: for instance, a cleaner is

Robert Nairac

Failing to go grey can be fatal mistake for a spy. Robert Nairac was an officer in 14 Intelligence Company, the British army's undercover surveillance unit in Northern Ireland. A graduate of Oxford University, he was a man of considerable intelligence and he prided himself on his ability to move undetected amongst the local community, including drinking in their bars where he would sing Republican songs. Yet he was also a man who broke rules such as not taking back-up with him when out on one of his undercover excursions.

On Saturday, 14 May 1977, he visited the Three Steps Inn at Drumintree on an intelligence-gathering mission. Against all instructions he was again working alone. This time some aspect of his behaviour aroused the suspicions of local IRA men and he was ambushed as he left the pub. He was kidnapped and tortured before being executed. Undoubtedly a brave man, he earned the admiration of his torturers for his courage in telling them nothing. His great hero was T.E. Lawrence, leader of the revolt against the Turks during World War I. With a little more luck and a second chance he might have emulated his hero, but it wasn't to be. He was awarded a posthumous George Cross for his bravery, but his body was never found. It was reportedly disposed of by the terrorists in a meat processing plant.

identified by their overalls and equipment, a decorator by their paint-spattered clothes and brushes, a security guard by their uniform and general demeanour. All of these roles are ideal for going grey because people take one look, identify and (usually) don't ask any further questions. But whatever role you do adopt, it should not be something which draws attention. On one training exercise, Austin had to spend forty minutes in an exclusive restaurant waiting for the chance to copy a document in a restricted area of the premises. By dressing smartly and adopting a confident attitude he was able to remain undetected. However, he finally decided that the only way to get access to the document was to make an approach to a member of staff. He claimed he was an undercover police officer. This was believable because he was wearing a concealed radio, however such a dramatic cover story immediately drew attention to him. All the staff later agreed that once he had said this they were curious about him and made a point of remembering what he looked like.

Appearance: Having decided on a role, the right clothing is the next step. If the role chosen has a specific purpose such as cleaner or security guard then the choice of clothing is quite simple, although consideration must be given to any security passes which are carried. In many cases however, going grey will mean simply trying to pass as an anonymous member of the local population in which case the spy has to give careful thought to the type of clothing which is usually worn in that locality. But more than this must be considered. Distinctive jewellery or tattoos can't be worn as they attract the eyes of other people. Hair length and even colour may also need to be changed. Men or women who are considered particularly attractive must also tone down the way they look. Amongst the recruits, Nicola, a slim, attractive young woman with light blonde hair, had problems. Although she was very particular about her appearance she had to dye her hair brown, wear spectacles and go without make-up because of her natural beauty.

Equipment: As well as clothes, attention has to be given to any equipment which is carried as part of the role. To gain access to many restricted areas, a physical search area has to be passed through, so the spy has to consider not only those items of equipment which are visible but also those which are carried in pockets etc. The spy must also know how to use the equipment carried – it is no good pretending to be a gardener in a park so that you can monitor a meeting only to find that you don't know how to operate a hedge trimmer!

Technical knowledge: As with equipment, the spy must have at least a rudimentary knowledge of the profession he is pretending to undertake. Consider the example of an officer who pretended to be a telephone engineer conducting routine maintenance. He had carefully picked the right clothes and equipment, but, having gained

Suzi (before)   (after)

Austin (before)   Austin (after)

All the recruits were trained in the basic spy skill of 'going grey': the ability to change appearance to suit the local environment and blend in. Suzi and Austin show how it's done. Suzi in characteristic mode (*before*) and dressed for Mirabelle's (*after*); Austin transformed his look from streetwear (*before*) to smart (*after*).

access to the target room, was unable to open the circuit box he was supposed to be working on. It might seem that it is easier to pretend to be a member of the general population than to have a specific profession. While it is harder to prepare thoroughly for these roles, obviously they are much less likely to invite challenge than someone who is dressed right but is just generally 'hanging about'. The investment of time and effort is usually worth it.

Confidence: The next most important point about going grey is having the confidence to feel comfortable in your chosen role. No matter how good a disguise, other people can generally detect signs of awkwardness and nervousness in others and this can lead to them becoming suspicious. Very often a spy gets little time to prepare before going grey, certainly never as much as she would like, but despite this the spy has to act as though she is perfectly at ease in the environment and this is really just a matter of nerve.

Body language: No matter how confident a spy is feeling, she must guard against the often unconscious signs which show that she is nervous. Lack of eye contact when speaking to people, excessive

---

Confidence and going grey

A good example of holding one's nerve under pressure, or what many people would call 'bottle', was demonstrated when the recruits' skills at going grey were tested during the training course. Simon and Jennie were challenged to gain access to a restricted area of a prestigious theatrical bookshop in London. After considering several possible cover roles, Simon and Jennie concluded that the layout of the shop meant that their best chance was simply to 'go for it' since engaging the shop staff in any form of conversation was more rather than less likely to lead to a challenge.

Their plan was that Simon would distract the counter staff with an enquiry whilst Jennie would simply walk through the shop and go through the unlocked door marked 'No Admittance'. Although the counter staff might

cont'd

---

not be looking, she would still be in full view of any customers in the shop. Worse still, Simon's distraction ploy failed and Jennie still had to carry out the plan. Although she later confessed to being so nervous that she felt physically sick, she held her nerve, walked across the shop and in through the door. Because she acted as though this was perfectly normal no one challenged her.

But once through the door her ordeal was still not over. Behind the first door was a flight of steps leading into the cellar and ending in another door. This led to the restricted area of the premises and she knew that there would be several more staff working there. Knowing from the intelligence that there was no communication between this room and the upper level of the shop, Jennie and Simon had prepared a cover story in which Jennie would claim that she had applied for a job at the shop, that she had just delivered her CV and that the manageress had told her to have a look round. This was fine as a plan back at the training school, but standing there on the stairs the story began to sound awfully thin to Jennie. She knew that if she had delivered her story with anything less than complete confidence it was almost certain to be challenged. But in the event Jennie's demeanour was so calm and assured that she was not asked to explain what she was doing there and the staff even helped her collect a photograph of the document she was sent to get! This is a good example of spies making their own luck.

By contrast Simon's attempt to create a diversion failed because once he approached the counter, his mind went blank and he really couldn't think of anything to say. This lack of an ability to think under pressure was to prove a constant problem for Simon during the training. As the trainers pointed out to him several times, they were not questioning his courage in any way and Simon was certainly prepared to undertake dangerous tasks if he was given enough warning. But 'bottle' is a completely different ability and it is one that any spy must have if they are to operate in the field. Jennie had it.

hand movements and blush responses in the face are all signs that something is not quite right, and a spy must master these. A good example of this was provided on the training course: Gabriel and Nicola were challenged to enter a factory and get a copy of a document which was pinned to the wall on the factory floor. The pair made an initial mistake in that Nicola went with Gabriel on the mission. As an attractive woman she was bound to draw attention on a shop floor consisting entirely of men. Fortunately she had observed the other rules of going grey so well that the damage was minimal. However, even though they collected a copy of the target document successfully, what really gave them away was the speed with which they left the factory. They were so relieved that they had completed the mission that they almost rushed out of the premises and this drew the attention of several of the staff – it made the pair look as if they had been up to something.

Geography: Keeping one's nerve is partly an innate ability and no training can make up for that, but there are other things a spy can do to make things easier. Careful preparation is one, knowledge of the layout of the target area is another. It is always easier for a spy to act confidently if she knows where she is, what the function of each building in the area is and where elements such as exits and security posts are located. Wherever possible a spy should try and get access to the target location before the day of the mission and 'walk the ground' to get a feel for the atmosphere of the place and the salient points around it.

Documentation: If challenged it is always useful to have some piece of documentation to fall back on, whether it is a security pass or letter of introduction. Another factor which spies must pay attention to is '**wallet litter**' – all the pieces of paper, credit cards etc. which they carry on them must be consistent with the cover they have chosen. Security identification is required in many occupations these days, but both criminals and spies have learned that people actually pay very little attention to what is being shown. When a meter reader or council official arrives at someone's door they often have to show an identification card to gain admittance, yet very few people know what such a pass is meant to look like and most don't do more than glance at the photograph on the pass to make sure that it matches the bearer. In areas where security

Use of body language, learning how to read and control the subconscious reactions of others, is an essential skill for a spy. In this exercise, the recruits had to persuade photographers and advertising executives to look at their portfolios, using only body language and with almost no training.

How to do it: Jennie uses an open face, expressive gestures, good eye contact and leans in towards her interviewer. She passed.

How not to do it: Max is turned away from his interviewer, makes no use of his hands and has no eye contact. The interviewer's chin resting on the heel of his hand communicates lack of interest and mistrust. Max failed.

identification has to be worn, even if it is not possible to acquire a pass to counterfeit, it is often possible to copy the general look of the pass and wear that on clothing. Provided one can get access to the area in the first place, experience shows that no one is likely to take a close look.

Speech: Another give away for any spy hoping to go grey is their voice. It is no good pretending to be a builder yet speaking with the rounded vowels of a public schoolboy. Similarly you are unlikely to convince someone that you are a visiting professor if you keep dropping your aitches. Of course, there is more to it than this: every language has regional variations – someone from Kent will stand out if they operate in Liverpool and vice versa. A spy either has to learn to disguise this or to invent a role which convincingly explains what they are doing in the area. No matter how difficult it seems, it should always be possible to create some excuse: In the film version of A.E.W. Mason's adventure story *The Four Feathers*, the hero Harry Feversham wants to disguise himself as a Sudanese native so that he can return the signs of cowardice – the feathers – given to him by a group of British officers. The problem is that he does not speak any of the necessary languages and has no time to learn them. He surmounts this problem by having himself marked with a brand which signifies that he has had his tongue ripped out and cannot speak. While it isn't always necessary to adopt such extreme measures, this shows what a little creativity can achieve.

Backstops: A final step which can help give a spy confidence is to know that if they are challenged they have a 'backstop', someone who can vouch that the spy is who they claim to be. Ideally this would be an agent who works at the target premises and who can be contacted if needed. But often this luxury is not available and it is enough to have a phone number which supposedly belongs to the cleaning company, security force or similar organisation where another officer can provide enough information for the cover to hold.

Living Under Cover

Going grey is largely about appearance and attitude. But once the skills of going grey have been mastered, spies move on to learning how to live under a more detailed cover, one in which they can work closely alongside other people and where they can expect to be quizzed about their background and experience. This requires a whole new level of skill and concentration: not only are the cover stories far more detailed, but an experienced spy will have several covers active at any one time and he must be able to move smoothly between them without forgetting the details or skills he needs to maintain the fiction successfully.

Unless a cover is being adopted with the intention of going grey, it is often better to adopt a role which is lively and interesting. This makes the spy more likely to attract potential agents and has the added advantage of being the opposite of what most people's perceptions of a spy are. Bluff, noisy, larger than life characters are usually the last people to be suspected of spying. A good example is Colin McColl, 'C' of SIS from 1988 to 1993. He wore designer suits and was fond of wearing a distinctive Australian bush hat. As a student at Oxford he had been famous for his lively parties and later, on diplomatic postings, he was known for his enthusiasm for amateur dramatics. According to Mark Urban in his excellent book written in 1997 *UK Eyes Alpha: Inside Story of British Intelligence*, one of his colleagues described McColl as 'the last of the old actor managers'. Hardly a 'grey' figure, yet a very successful spy.

Whether adopting a high-profile lifestyle or not, a spy doesn't simply select any cover. She will have four principles in mind:

- The cover must provide **camouflage**. This is the principal reason for using cover. It allows you to move amongst the enemy without detection. In the most extreme cases it will even cause for the enemy to believe that you are one of them and give you unlimited access to their secrets.
- The cover should provide **opportunity**. Either the opportunity to meet an agent, to recruit a possible intelligence asset or to get your hands on a vital document.
- The cover might also provide **bait**. One of the principal duties of a spy is to recruit new agents who will collect intelligence. To do this the spy needs to be attractive to potential recruits in some way, either because she is a figure with power, influence, money or something else which the potential recruit is looking for. Above all the cover must

present the spy as someone above the recruit in terms of the 'power ladder' (see Chapter 5).

- Finally, the cover must be **supportable**. It would be point-less sending in a spy as a former special forces officer when he is clearly a nine-stone weakling. One of the first things an operational team will do when selecting a cover for an officer is to make a list of her strengths so that they can tailor a suitable cover accordingly.

Living under cover for prolonged periods is draining. The spy has to be alert twenty-four hours a day and the smallest slip can ruin months of work. Even the spy's name will be different and he has to make sure that he uses it or reacts to it every time it is used. This sort of work requires a particular mental stamina and a fine attention to detail.

Types of Cover

Many spies, especially those who are based in their home country and travel abroad frequently on different missions, will have a range of different covers supported by **legends**, or background stories of vary-ing detail and complexity. The different covers available are as follows:

Snap cover. Adopted at a moment's notice, often without any preparation at all, in order to create an opportunity for meeting a target e.g. at a party, in a hotel or at a business conference.

Short-term cover. Good enough to cover a one-off foreign country mission in which hostile attention is very unlikely.

Official cover. Since the sixteenth century, almost every nation has placed spies within its diplomatic missions. Some, though not all, of these spies may be declared to the host country. Undeclared officers will require detailed cover stories about their supposed history in the diplomatic corps. The advantage of official cover is that if any of these spies are caught then they will be able to claim diplomatic immunity and simply be expelled from the country for 'activities incompatible with their status'. This is known in the trade as being made *persona non grata* or 'PNG'ed'. It may be embarrassing for the spy but at least it is not fatal. The disadvantage for spies of living under official cover is that they are fairly easy for security services to spot.

Non-official cover. Any other form of cover story. It is harder to spot, but the penalties are potentially far more serious. Without diplomatic status the spy risks imprisonment, torture or even death. In the CIA these cover stories are referred to collectively as 'Nox'.

Deep cover. A more durable form of cover. It will be intended for use by the spy over many years and because the spy has numerous other operations to deal with, the upkeep of the legend for this cover such as making sure bank accounts show regular activity and that other documentation is kept up to date will be dealt with by a special headquarters department.

Sleepers. Cover so deep that the spy does not attempt any espionage activity at all until 'activated'.

The difference between cover and legend

A **cover** is the role adopted by a spy to disguise her true purpose.

A **legend** is the background story with all its surrounding props and details which makes the spy's cover seem real. This is sometimes misleadingly referred to as the '**cover story**'.

In the 1920s MI6 officers used to have cover in embassies as passport control officers. The duties were light, giving the officers plenty of time for their other work. At the same time, the work gave them a natural access to applications for visas and other useful paperwork. This cover role gradually evolved into other embassy posts in the political and later economic branches. KGB officers used to favour postings in the political branches or at TASS or *Izvestia* correspondents. Cover as journalists was popular because it gave them a natural reason to snoop into all kinds of areas.

Now times have changed again. Embassies are no longer the best places from which to spy. The enemy has changed and the terrorist target must be tackled in a different way, just as the tactics of SOE parachuting men with radios in suitcases into enemy territory was not suitable during the Cold War.

There are some cases where people live very openly as spies, but this is because they are fulfilling a very particular purpose.

Intelligence stations based in embassies are usually led by a 'blown' officer – an officer who is generally recognised to be a spy by most other intelligence services. It is good for everyone to know who the local 'spook' is. Defectors or potential agents know who to go to and the local intelligence services who to liaise with. It provides a useful role for older or more experienced officers who might otherwise be confined to a life as desk officers and helps to draw attention away from any other officers who might be serving on the station.

Covers That are Never Used

In matters of morality remember the golden rule of espionage: an intelligence service will do whatever it believes must be done. That having been said, there are certain rules which intelligence services in Western nations will try to observe at almost any cost. One of these is to *never* use charities or humanitarian organisations as cover. If any spy were caught using such a cover it would not only severely embarrass his government, probably resulting in high-level resignations (including his own), but it would also place every genuine aid worker in danger. Similarly, cover as clergy or as officials of mainstream religious organisations would not be used.

Spies will also do their best to avoid cover as journalists of an accredited news organisation, again to avoid embarrassment to their own governments and to ensure that real journalists are not placed in danger. The golden rule will always apply, but Western intelligence agencies are reluctant to upset or endanger journalists because the media can be valuable allies in publicising certain stories – a relationship which some critics claim can be too close.

Legends

A legend is the support structure for a cover. Thus some covers (snap cover) have almost no legends at all. Some (deep cover) have very detailed legends which need a considerable staff to keep them up to date. In the most extreme cases (sleepers), the legend is something you live and constantly create. It is indistinguishable from your real life. In covers requiring complex support stories the legend will include all sorts of props, back-up preparation and supporting actors which make the cover believable including false addresses and false businesses. These are known as **backstops**. Creating a successful legend for your cover requires thorough research and imagination.

It is not as easy as it sounds. On the training course the recruits' ability to construct an effective legend was tested several times, the first as soon as they were summoned to the course. Each recruit was given an alias and a cover as a pharmaceuticals sales specialist. They were to use this cover during their journey to the school and up to the point they were told the cover had been lifted. Yet none of them did any research about pharmaceuticals such as looking up the names of leading companies or scanning the latest pharmaceuticals stories on the business pages of newspapers. Most of them even had items in their luggage which revealed their real names.

The recruits were then moved into houses and flats with cover stories that they were related to each other in some way: Gabriel and Max were lovers, living at Gabriel's mother's house. Gabriel's mother was being played by Suzi. Nicola and Simon lived together as a married couple whilst Austin and Jennie were related by fostering, with Reena posing as Jennie's best friend. I visited them a few nights after they'd had a chance to work on their legends. It took less than five minutes to break down their stories. They hadn't used their imaginations sufficiently. They hadn't sat back and thought of themselves in their cover roles and decided what were the obvious things they would know about each other if the relationships were real.

Take Jennie, Austin and Reena. Jennie was the linchpin of the group, chosen deliberately by the trainers because she was the most capable. The cover story was that her parents had fostered Austin and that her friend Reena had lived just a few streets away. Yet when the three were asked simple questions such as the colour of Jennie's front door or what her garden was like, all three gave completely different answers. They had often prepared for more complex questions such as what happened at Jennie's eighteenth birthday party, but as with all of the recruits the preparation was patchy. Suzi, who was supposedly Gabriel's mother, couldn't remember the names of any of the schools he had been to.

Each team should have sat down together, closed their eyes and tried to visualise their backgrounds to see the buildings they have in common such as houses or schools. In the case of Jennie, Reena and Austin, Jennie should have taken the lead since she had first hand knowledge of all the main locations. The other two could then have chipped in with questions if there was some part of the scene which they could not visualise. The human mind tends to recall events through the visual cortex and a lie sounds much more convincing when the liar is describing a picture he sees rather than making something up on the spot or reciting by rote. This is why imagination is such a key part in the process. By the end of the training course all of the recruits had become much better at creating legends and all of them were able to spend several days working alongside targets without the targets spotting that their legends were simply lies.

How to Lie Without Getting Caught

Lying is easy – it is simply telling someone something that is not true. *Effective* lying is telling someone something that is not true and having them believe it.

There are a number of steps which can help a lie sound convincing, but the underlying key to effective lying is believing the story yourself. There is a strong connection between living an effective cover role and acting. Some of the most successful spies, like Stella Rimington, former head of MI5, have also been successful at amateur dramatics. Sidney Reilly, a successful British agent just after World War I was a fantasist and con man. You can also see this tendency begin to develop in small children. As they grow up and learn to lie they sometimes also learn to convince themselves that what they are saying is the truth. They develop a great sense of injustice if caught out even though you have caught them red-handed. I have seen the same tendency in interviews with adult criminals.

Picture it in your mind. Tell the story in the picture. It DID happen this way, you are remembering it, not imagining it.

To lie without detection a spy must consider the following points:

- The lie must be **plausible**. Stick as close to the truth as possible. Make sure that what you say is consistent with what the other person knows or is able to find out.
- Keep it **simple**. A complex story is harder to maintain. Many interrogators will keep returning to certain details during questioning in the hope of tripping you up. The more detail you give them the easier this will be especially as you become more fatigued.
- Don't **volunteer** too much explanation – it sounds false. If asked, add one or two details to help your credibility – but don't give up too much of your story too early.
- Master your **voice**. Maintain an even tone, avoid hesitation words such as 'er' and 'um'. Try to picture the lie you are making in your mind and talk about what you see; this will make it easier to talk smoothly about the subject.
- Watch your **body language**. Lean forward towards the questioner, not back, to indicate sincerity. Don't touch mouth or face, don't hide mouth behind hands or fold arms. These are classic signs of lying which all interrogators are aware of. Furthermore, in normal conversation, your body language should match your message. If the subject is important or urgent, sit forward and use hand gestures; if it is a casual matter, sit back and adopt a relaxed posture or smile.
- Control your **eye contact**. Eye and pupil responses are hard to fake – evolution has taught humans to pay a great deal of attention to the language of eye contact, even if only subconsciously. Maintaining eye contact is important. We all know how small children tend to look away when they lie to us. Adults trying to lie often make an attempt to maintain this eye contact, but can end up glancing back and forth at the questioner, a behaviour which humans have learned to regard as equally suspicious. On the other hand, if the look is too long and fixed it immediately appears artificial and begins to seem like a challenge to the questioner. The answer is to use long looks while telling the lie, but with occasional glances away to avoid the challenge response.
- Control your **breathing**. Lying can make those unused to it feel slightly dizzy and they may find it hard to think clearly

when challenged. This is because they are nervous and breathing has become shallow or they may even be subconsciously holding their breath. Deprived of the normal amount of oxygen, the brain responds with dizziness. Remember to breath slowly and deeply.

- **Prepare** thoroughly. Of course this isn't always possible, but try. Prepare backstops, think what the likely questions are. You will then be able to put your story across smoothly without having to pause and think of the next thing to say.

- **Be detached**. Under aggressive questioning don't try too hard to get the questioner to like you. Common courtesy is fine, but don't act as though you have something to prove. What you are saying is the truth and they can either take it or leave it. You don't have to be their friend. Remember that you are an innocent person being falsely accused.

Like any skill, lying can be improved with practice. As an interrogator I often noticed how drug smugglers of fairly low intelligence could lie quite convincingly whilst much more intelligent white collar criminals could be poor liars – their faces often gave them away, particularly through the blush response, that rush of blood to the face we have when we are confronted or embarrassed.

The best use of this approach on the training course came from Max. For personal reasons he had become used to not telling the truth about his work or his past. Even those he shared a house with on the course could not tell when he was telling them the truth and when he was lying. The only problem for Max was that he wasn't consistent. He told so many different lies about himself that the other recruits knew he must be lying about something and simply didn't trust him at all. If he could have mastered this more completely he might have made an excellent spy. His 'practice' certainly served him well on the missions. Even when he had to work alongside other people for a number of days, they did not suspect that he was lying to them.

Lie Detectors

Machines for detecting lies come in several different forms, but they are all based on measuring the physical responses of the body to questioning. Crude machines measure changes in blood pressure, heart rate, respiration etc. More advanced models examine minor nervous responses in the body. Americans place great faith in them; every employee of the CIA, FBI and NSA has to undergo regular lie detector tests.

To beat the machine it is necessary to either blur or fake these responses. Suggestions on how to achieve this have included hyperventilation, deliberately shortening the breathing during questioning, biting the tongue or even curling up the toes and fists tightly to boost blood pressure readings. The problem with this approach is that a failure to relax and let the machine do its work may simply be recorded as a failure by the person who is in charge of the test and this will almost certainly lead to a more detailed investigation.

It is generally agreed that there is only one sure way of beating a lie detector. The important point to remember is that lie detectors cannot actually tell whether you are lying or not – only whether you *think* you are lying. There have been notable cases where well-known con men have been subjected to lie detector tests and, even though it is known for certain that they are lying, they have passed. Analysts believe that this is because good con men have the ability to convince themselves that what they are saying is the truth. Once they have convinced themselves, there is no need to fake unconscious body responses such as eye contact and posture, nor the responses monitored by lie detector machines. It is something good spies are always working at (and most politicians as well . . .).

Finally, even if you fail a lie detector test: **never confess**. Lie detectors only have something like a seventy per cent success rate (to put that into perspective, tossing a coin guarantees fifty per cent success). And the main reason they are used by organisations is because the fear of them either intimidates people into not doing bad things in the first place (such as drug or alcohol abuse) or into confessing what they have done. Remember, you *are* innocent. Even if they tell you that the machine shows you are lying, how do you know they are telling the truth? A lie detector machine is only a tool and they can be mistaken. Take comfort in the fact that the CIA officer Aldrich Ames sold secrets to the KGB for eight years and he passed every lie detector test he ever took. This is also true of many other leading criminals. A lie detector has only really succeeded if you admit you are lying. As long as you protest your innocence there is room for doubt.

Deflecting Difficult Questions

When working undercover the thing all spies fear is being caught red-handed creeping around in a restricted area and being challenged by a security guard. The only answer is to have a reason prepared or as they say in the army PPPPP: 'Proper planning prevents poor performance'.

Most of the time, though, cover stories are not tested so dramatically. Nevertheless there will be questions which you have simply not prepared for. Spies prepare for two different types of situation: social and interview. In a **social** situation you are simply talking to someone and they ask a question quite casually which you aren't ready for. Your first line of defence should be to try to get away with vagueness. If used with humour this is usually enough. If not, you can revert to the strategies listed below. In an **interview** situation the questioner is already curious or even suspicious and in this case vagueness will only cause increased suspicion. You must quickly assess the danger from the questioner. Questioning from a security official is more dangerous than forceful questioning by someone at a party. Questions from those in authority need to be dealt with as straightforwardly as possible because these people will be suspicious of those who talk too much. Try to convince them that you are doing everything you can to cooperate and steer the questioner's attention to areas in which your cover story is better prepared.

Other strategies which can be used are:

Partial answers. For instance: Question: When were you born? Answer: Oh I'm a December baby, I've spent my whole life having Christmas and my birthday practically on top of one another which reminds me did I tell you about . . . (and then lead into an anecdote or change of subject).

Jocular answers. For instance: Question: When were you born? Answer: Old enough to drink and that's what really matters – what are you having?

Answering a question with a question. What do you mean? Why do you ask?

Not answering the question asked. Study politicians when they are answering questions on television. They are all masters of this strategy. They kill time with long answers which sound full but actually say nothing, constantly avoiding the tricky question and coming back to ground they are sure of.

Use anecdotes. They burn up time which the questioner could be using to ask other difficult questions. They also give an opportunity to use humour which can defuse tension. But don't overdo it. Watch the questioner's body language responses to see if they become bored or hostile.

Confrontational answers. Answers such as 'You're a bit nosy aren't you?' These are rather a last resort as they will either scare the questioner off or lead to an increase in hostility and suspicion. I knew a surveillance officer who was sent into a notoriously rough pub to cover a meeting of some local drug dealers. He was disguised as a decorator in suitably paint-spattered overalls. As he was sitting at a table reading a newspaper, one of the gang, a small, weaselly man, walked over and challenged him, 'Who are you?'

'I'm a decorator. What's it to you?'

'What are you doing in here?'

'I'm having a pint and reading the paper, what does it look like?'

'Where are you working then?'

'Number 43.'

The weasel opened his mouth to ask another question at which point the officer said, 'Now that's three f**king questions, are you going to go away or am I going to take you outside and kick your head in?'

The weasel promptly backed off and rejoined the group.

Of course it helped that the surveillance officer was an eighteen-stone ex-boxer. I wouldn't recommend this approach in every situation, but sometimes showing hostility can cause the questioner to decide it's not worth pursuing the matter.

Aldrich Ames (1941–)

Ames Joined the CIA in 1962. His career followed the usual course for a CIA officer including headquarters appointments and overseas postings. He began working for the KGB in June 1985. He originally intended it to be a one-time 'scam' to earn money, but once he was compromised he just kept going. He worked in the CIA's office that handled clandestine operations around the world and was therefore in a position to give highly valuable intelligence. Between 1986 and 1989 he was posted to Rome where he found it easier to communicate with his KGB handlers. By the time he was discovered and arrested in 1994, he had betrayed over one hundred covert operations and more than thirty agents, at least ten of whom were executed. During that time the KGB paid him more than $2.7 million. Astonishingly his extravagant lifestyle hadn't raised any security concerns since he passed his regular lie detector tests! With hindsight it is hard to see how Ames got away with it for so long. As the official inquiry into his case stated: 'He had access to all the compromised cases; his financial resources improved substantially for unestablished reasons; and his laziness and poor performance were rather widely known.'

Ames was finally trapped by garbology (see page 82). A counter-intelligence investigation team which was looking for the agent they believed was betraying CIA agents. Ames was a suspect because of his irregular finances, but there was no proof. Eventually, in 1993, a note was found in his trash from his KGB controller. The team placed Ames under intense surveillance and he was eventually arrested at a dead letter box in February 1994.

When confronted with the evidence, he pleaded guilty to all charges, was convicted and sentenced to life imprisonment without parole. Ames has justified his actions by saying that most of the people he betrayed were in fact double agents. There is no way this can be true. It is a form of self-justification which amounts almost to madness.

Finally, if you get completely caught out and it's clear that you are lying, move to a **back-up story**. Just because your cover story fails it doesn't mean they think you're a spy. You could claim to be a reporter, a private detective, a jealous husband, anything which fits the situation. Just make sure that you have something prepared rather than trying to make it up on the spot.

4 What Is 'Intelligence'?

Generally, in the case of armies you wish to strike, cities you wish to attack and people you wish to assassinate, it is necessary to find out the names of the garrison commander, the aides-de-camp, the ushers, the gatekeepers and the bodyguards. You must instruct your spies to ascertain these matters in minute detail.

The Art of War
Sun Tzu

Once upon a time the difference between information and intelligence was clear: gathering intelligence meant getting access to your enemy's secrets. But in recent years, with the development of the internet and twenty-four-hour news coverage in many parts of the world, it is no longer so clear what intelligence services should provide. New areas have been introduced such as 'open source intelligence' and 'grey intelligence' which many old hands would probably turn their noses up at and declare not to be intelligence at all.

These new categories of intelligence have brought their own problems. It sometimes seems that much intelligence produced today is vague and even misleading. The intelligence which led to the war against Iraq in 2003 is a case in point. It encouraged governments to believe that Iraq possessed weapons of mass destruction and to enter a war on that basis (although willing politicians also had a hand in this). It is now known that these weapons did not exist.

Analysis of the war on Iraq appears to be showing that the intelligence services relied too heavily on expatriate groups and other self-interested parties rather than on well-placed intelligence sources. And the same mistake is being made in the war against terrorism. Agencies which were set up to win the Cold War are just not suited to recruiting the necessary sources to defeat international terrorists. Former CIA director George Tenet said in 2004 that it will be five years before America will 'have the kind of clandestine service our country needs'. Considering the amount of money which the USA spends on its intelligence and security services (more than $26 *billion* per year) this is a shocking admission and much of the problem may be to do with the wide range of information which is currently accepted as 'intelligence'.

But all intelligence services are ultimately answerable to their customers – the government, various government departments and law-enforcement agencies – and this means giving the customers what they want. So a modern spy has to be aware of all the different categories of intelligence, including the new ones, if she is to get the best use out of her station's assets.

Types of Intelligence

There is more jargon surrounding the concept of intelligence than almost any other aspect of espionage. And as the world becomes increasingly interrelated and information-rich, the classifications grow broader and broader until today it is often no longer clear what is intelligence and what isn't. This section aims to help navigate the way through the maze.

Black, White and Grey Intelligence

The starting point for any classification used to be that intelligence is secret. However as more and more analysis of openly available information was produced and circulated as 'intelligence', a division was gradually made between **black intelligence** (from secret sources) and **white intelligence** (from open sources). More recently a new category has appeared: **grey intelligence**. Michael Herman, an academic and formerly a senior official at GCHQ, has defined grey intelligence as, 'information which is not published or widely diffused, but to which access can be gained, provided that one knows it exists and has adequate channels of information.'

In other words it is information which is difficult to find or is protected by very low-level restrictions. Examples of this sort of material are conference reports, trade association reports and un-published doctoral theses.

High-Level and Low-Level Intelligence

It is not that one is important and the other is not. The best way to understand the difference between high and low intelligence is to think of the recipient.

For instance, the layout of a foreign embassy and the location of the code room is intelligence because it is undoubtedly secret, but it's not a government-level intelligence report and is therefore low level. However, it is *important* because it should enable penetration of the code room allowing access to further intelligence. Of that further intelligence there will again be a mixture of high and low level. The planned rotation of certain staff is secret, but low level. Important foreign service documents, e.g. treaties and trade agreements come from the same code room, but are almost certainly high-level intelligence – the reports will be circulated by the service to ministers and other high-ranking intelligence recipients.

The basic rule is: *low-level intelligence should lead to high-level intelligence* – or there's no point in collecting it! (It may be true that all intelligence will prove useful 'one day' but try justifying that to your area controller . . .)

Raw and Finished Intelligence

Raw intelligence is the reports which come back from agents in the field, from satellites in the sky or from telephone-tapping operations. Obviously this material cannot be given to customers just as it is. It needs to be reduced into the briefest possible report without losing any of its accuracy.

Extraneous material needs to be taken out as does any information which might indicate who the source of the intelligence is. Then the report needs to be refined, cross-checked for accuracy with other sources, and evaluated for reliability against the agent's previous reporting. Even imagery (pictures taken by satellites or spy planes) needs to be interpreted by trained personnel who can tell the difference between an ordinary outbuilding and a chemical weapons factory (there's obviously a grave shortage of these at the moment . . .).

After this process is complete the report will be considered finished intelligence and circulated to customers.

Classification of Intelligence

Intelligence reports can either be classified by the type of intelligence collected or by source. These are the types of intelligence which intelligence services will be looking for:

Political Intelligence

This is what most people traditionally understand when they think of intelligence – penetration of the secret workings of another government.

Military Intelligence

This is the next largest type of intelligence, information about the plans and capabilities of another nation's armed forces. Much of this is collected by **sigint** (see page 77).

Economic Intelligence

One of the fastest growing areas of intelligence collection. It is also the area in which the Western intelligence allies most frequently come into conflict with each other. Britain is an island nation which relies on its trade. It is hardly surprising therefore that a great deal of the intelligence which the British intelligence agencies produce is economic intelligence intended to give the country a trading edge. For instance, MI6 used to provide intelligence on the deliberations of the German Bundesbank to try to give the Treasury advance notice of its intentions and help Britain to set more competitive interest rates. And in 1995, France expelled five US intelligence officers for trying to bribe a French official to betray France's plans for the forthcoming negotiations on international trade and tariffs.

Commercial Intelligence

This is company or project specific rather than being concerned with the broader national plans which economic intelligence usually reports. There are two reasons for its growth in recent years: first because the intelligence services of every nation are always under pressure to show that they are giving taxpayers 'value for money'. With political and military intelligence this can be quite difficult to demonstrate, but with commercial intelligence, service chiefs can point to specific areas where their information has gained contracts or helped fend off foreign rivals. The other reason for this development is because a useful source of agents is business people travelling abroad. Intelligence services are always trying to maintain good links with companies both as a way to have access to these travellers as agents and to provide cover for their own officers travelling abroad. Once again it causes a certain amount of strife between the allies. The same US intelligence officers who were expelled from France in 1995 for gathering economic intelligence had also been gathering intelligence on specific export bids and bribing French businessmen to provide company specific intelligence which would be useful to US firms.

Criminal Intelligence

Although Western intelligence services have always provided intelligence about terrorist threats, their entry into the area of criminal intelligence is a very new development caused by the collapse of the Soviet bloc in the late 1980s. It became clear to intelligence chiefs that there would soon be a lot of spies without anything to do. In the UK, MI6 opened a counter-narcotics section as early as 1988. It was not until 1995 that the government announced that MI5 would be joining the fight against organised crime. Police forces were not happy. The intelligence services may have been good at their job, but unlike the police they never had to produce evidence in court. Operating methods have changed to accommodate this, but it is still an uncomfortable alliance with frequent allegations of 'turf wars' between the agencies.

Sources of Intelligence

1. Humint

This is the technical term for all intelligence originating from a human informant. There is a considerable range in secrecy in these sources from the highly placed espionage source guarded by the highest security levels down to interviews with refugees which are rarely considered secret at all.

Just as the level of secrecy varies in humint so does the quality. Humans are subject to deception (just like other sources), they can exaggerate their intelligence to get more money or deliberately mislead. Agent handlers can also exaggerate or subtly change information, and there have been cases where intelligence officers have been found to have made up imaginary agents for their reporting (often because they believed it to be true and just couldn't find anyone to say it). Quality humint, that is, highly placed, discerning and completely reliable sources with access to up-to-date intelligence are the hardest assets for any intelligence service to provide.

Advantages

- Humint sources can be used in other ways e.g. to place bugs, to obtain copies of ciphers (in the old days code books, these days downloaded from computer systems).
- They can help to interpret the intelligence they provide.
- They may be the only assets who can obtain enemy equipment and software.

Disadvantages

- They often need to be trained in secret communication and contact techniques in order to be used effectively.
- They need to be welfared, they get afraid, they get family problems.
- The identification and recruitment of potential agents takes a long time.
- Communications are vulnerable, reporting is slow.

- Agents' observations are subject to human frailties and false interpretations.
- Spies may fabricate or even be double agents.

2. Sigint

Short for 'signals intelligence', sigint makes up the vast bulk of intelligence. It is estimated that eighty to ninety per cent of UK intelligence reports are made up from sigint. The reason it is so popular is because, once you have invested the vast sums necessary in the equipment, it is so easy to collect. Satellite interception is so expensive that Britain does not possess its own spy satellites, but has had to contribute to American programmes in return for part of the take. For nations which cannot afford spy satellites, other forms of signal interception are possible. Not only do all these systems hoover up masses of communication a day (including e-mail), but the US, UK, Canada, Australia and New Zealand all share their sigint with each other to ensure a truly global collection capability.

Sigint is an area of intelligence collection almost as old as humint. As early as the sixteenth century, European states had special departments known as **Black Chambers** for opening enemies diplomatic correspondence. World War I saw the first signals interception specialists following the introduction of radio and by World War II the encryption and decryption of these radio messages had become of paramount importance, alongside the ground-breaking work of the experts at Bletchley Park who used the first computers to break code-making devices such as the Germans' Enigma machines.

Sigint tends to be further subdivided into **comint** and **elint**:

Comint is short for communications interception. This is what most of us think of as sigint – phone interception and radio signal interception.

Elint stands for electronics interception and is more specialised involving analysis of radar signals to determine the location of radar station sites and the quality and sensitivity of the equipment used there.

Specially equipped aircraft are often sent dangerously close to an enemy's airspace to gather elint and this can sometimes lead to an

KAL 007

On 31 August 1983, Korean Airlines Flight 007, a Boeing 747, was on a scheduled flight from New York to Gimpo in South Korea. However, after refuelling at Anchorage it strayed increasingly far off course until it was almost 500 km from where it was supposed to be. This course took it over the Kamchatka Peninsula and dangerously close to several Soviet missile bases and radar installations. The Soviet air force sent fighter aircraft to investigate. Accounts then become confused, but the Soviets claimed that the aircraft was repeatedly challenged yet refused to alter course. Eventually the order was given to attack the aircraft. A Su-15 fighter launched an air to air missile and the airliner was destroyed, killing 269 passengers and crew.

The United States was outraged and President Reagan condemned the attack. The Soviets claimed that they thought the aircraft had been a US RC-135 reconnaissance plane on an act of deliberate provocation. Other allegations were made that the pilot had been paid by the CIA to 'light up' Soviet air defence radars so that elint could be collected by other aircraft and there was certainly an RC-135 in the area at the time. The most likely explanation is that the drift out of the normal air lanes was a tragic accident. Air accident investigators noted that the change of course was consistent with a failure to alter compass heading after leaving Anchorage.

Whatever the truth there have certainly been numerous incidents of civilian airliners becoming entangled with air defence systems. Only five years before, another Korean airliner had been shot at and brought down in a similar area, although again it was claimed that this was a mistake. Elsewhere in the world the Russians themselves used Aeroflot aircraft in order to collect elint and several other nations are believed to have done the same.

international incident. In 1999, India shot down a Pakistani aircraft which was gathering elint along its border and in 2001 Chinese fighter aircraft forced down an American plane which was gathering electronic and signals data. Frequently, civilian airliners have been mistaken for this type of aircraft and there have been allegations that intelligence services occasionally pay pilots to 'drift off course' and test air defences.

3. Imagery

World War I saw the first airborne photography and developments in camouflage to fool it. These methods of collection continued until 1957 when, following the launch of the Russian satellite Sputnik 1, the 1960s saw both the USA and Russia developing satellite surveillance. The reliability of satellite surveillance was slow to develop and the mainstay of imagery collection in the West during the 1960s was the U2 spy plane. Anyone who doubts the power of imagery as an intelligence tool should recall the events of 1962 when photographs showing the preparations being made in Cuba to receive Soviet rockets led to the Cuban missile crisis – imagery almost started World War III!

Interestingly in terms of imagery collection we have gone from planes to satellites and now back to planes. Satellites became increasingly sophisticated and the latest generation of US satellites carry cameras with all-weather, day and night capabilities and resolution of ground objects down to ten centimetres. But now less costly pilotless drones are commonly used to monitor areas and even to deliver missiles. These are remote-controlled planes, are relatively cheap, highly directable and can remain in place over one area far longer than most satellites. By comparison, satellites are hugely expensive. It is estimated that the US 'keyhole' satellites cost $2 billion each and that doesn't include the launch infrastructure and running costs. They were excellent when large troop formations were being monitored during the Cold War, but the 'war on terror' requires monitoring of an entirely different type of enemy. Use of drones is bound to increase.

4. Techint

Technical intelligence refers to intelligence acquired by any technical devices such as sound, video or location bugs or telephone taps (where the device is actually placed somewhere on the phone line rather than satellite interception). Most techint will relate to a specific intelligence service operation rather than being used for general intelligence collection, but during the Cold War it was the fashion to try to infiltrate enemy embassies with as many technical devices as possible. In some notable cases, buildings were so infested with bugging devices that it was cheaper to move out and set up in another building rather than hunt the devices out.

5. Masint

This is one of the more obscure types of intelligence collection. Short for Measurement and Signature Intelligence, it involves the scientific analysis of air, water and other readings to determine activity on the other side of a border. Much of the raw material for this analysis is gathered by satellites. Examples of success for this type of intelligence are the detection of the first Soviet nuclear test from seismic and air-sampling records or the tracking of deep-water nuclear submarines during the Cold War by systems of sonar buoys.

6. Computers

Computers have revolutionised many areas of our lives over the past twenty years and intelligence is no exception. Computers are now used in all intelligence services for the collection and analysis of intelligence data and so computer systems have also become a target. Hacking is now an espionage skill carried out by specialist technicians rather in the way that intelligence services used to employ specialist burglary teams. Even in terms of propaganda there is a constant struggle going on between warring groups: during the Kosovo conflict NATO websites were regularly hacked and defaced by Serbian computer experts and there is a constant cyber war going on between Israeli and Palestinian hackers as they each try to dominate the picture of conflict put out over the internet. In recent years there have also been scandals as British military and intelligence officers have mislaid laptop computers carrying sensitive information. As wireless networks become common in the West, this area of the intelligence war will continue to grow and become more sophisticated.

7. Osint

The term for 'open source' intelligence. This sounds rather like a contradiction in terms, but it is another growth area for spies following the development of the internet. It is even developing its own jargon: making use of all the information available from non-secret sources is called **data mining**; collections of information gathered by companies from customer records or the electronic databases of other institutions are known as **data warehouses**. These data warehouses can have their information searched and manipulated in so many different ways that experts refer to the contents as **N dimensional data cubes** which they can **slice and dice** to produce pretty much any form of intelligence requested. It truly is a whole new world for spies and it is a form of intelligence collection which is going to become increasingly commonplace. US immigration authorities are now gathering fingerprint and biometric data on everyone who visits their country; in the UK and other European countries the use of personal ID cards containing biometric data may well be introduced in the foreseeable future. Add this to CCTV records, bank records and company information and it is clear that the data warehouses will only get bigger. One wonders if Orwell's Big Brother state cannot be far behind.

There is still debate as to whether osint is really intelligence in the true sense of the word or just a form of research. It can lead to confusion about how reliable government 'intelligence claims' are. For instance, before the invasion of Iraq, the UK government published a document based on 'intelligence sources' which was later shown to have included an academic thesis written more than a decade ago.

The problem is that osint is such a powerful tool that agencies which do not lay a claim to exploiting it could find themselves falling behind their rivals. In the 1980s when the US was seeking intelligence about Japanese commercial intentions, it was estimated by academics that ninety per cent of the necessary information could be gleaned from publicly available sources, nine per cent from grey intelligence sources (see above) and less than one per cent was needed from truly secret sources. In 1996 a US Presidential Commission referred to 'the vast universe of information now available from open sources'. At the same time the British Defence Intelligence Staff (BDIS) calculated that there were more than 8,000 relevant databases available worldwide which had barely been touched – and that was almost ten years ago. Imagine how that capacity has grown with the proliferation of internet use.

The recruits made significant use of the internet on all their missions. Jennie was on one occasion asked about a gym where she was supposed to have worked as a receptionist. She made an excuse, rang Gabriel, her back-up officer who was instantly able to access a full description of the building and staff on the internet. In a matter of minutes Jennie had the information she needed.

8. Garbint

Often referred to as **garbology**, this is in fact a rather formal word for searching through people's rubbish. Although people don't normally think of James Bond rooting through dustbins, this has proved to be a surprisingly useful intelligence-gathering tool particularly in gleaning profiling information on individuals since their rubbish can reveal likes and dislikes, bank account details and even whole letters full of personal information which have been thrown away. Even blank paper cannot be discarded casually by a spy. Machines known as ESDA machines can detect the faintest of imprints on blank sheets of paper if the sheet above has been written on. They are so sensitive that they can still produce a readable image even if they were ten or twelve sheets further down in the pad.

Even computers give out electronic 'garbage'. Although a great deal of money is often spent guarding computer systems from hackers it wasn't realised for some time that computer monitors emit radiation which can be picked up outside the building and used to produce a picture of whatever is on the computer screen. When this was discovered in the 1980s, the UK government spent a great deal of money placing radiation foiling cages around all their computers. But today, with wireless computer networks, many individuals and companies have become vulnerable once again.

Garbology can even be used to collect intelligence on embassies and military forces. For instance, the British Military Mission to the Soviet forces in East Germany, known as BRIXMIS, used to sort

Garbology

A spy's life isn't all glamour. Some of the best intelligence turns up in the worst places. *Above*: Sandy demonstrates. *Below*: the recruits take the plunge.

through Soviet army rubbish dumps to try to find documents. Under the terms of treaties dating from the end of World War II they were allowed to travel freely all over the country. The Eastern bloc military forces seemed to have very little discipline about what they threw away and whole cases of sensitive documents would simply be thrown on rubbish heaps whenever there was a clearout. Much could also be gleaned from seemingly innocuous documents such as ration requisition forms which allowed BRIXMIS to estimate troop strengths and movements. The UK's Chief of Defence Intelligence at the time said, 'It was amazing what could be found out.'

In 1979, before the US embassy in Tehran was captured during the Iranian revolution, documents were strip-shredded by CIA officers based there. But through hours of painstaking work, Iranian students were able to reassemble them into complete documents much to the subsequent embarrassment of the US government. Intelligence services have learned their lesson and these days sensitive documents will be at least cross-shredded (into tiny diamond shapes), but more usually they will be burned.

Requirements

Intelligence services don't just gather intelligence on any subject they like. The government gives them a list of **requirements** – areas of concern on which they want intelligence. Outside the intelligence world people don't think much about requirements, but to real spies they are one of the most important factors in all operational decisions. All intelligence services are judged at the end of each year on how well they have met their government's requirements and area controllers and station heads in intelligence services will constantly be assessing whether their assets are directed against their local targets and whether they have filled their quota of reports against each requirement. If they do not meet these requirements, staff can be moved, promotions to more prestigious sections or stations can be missed and heads of services may even be forced to resign. Requirements are the gold standard against which the effectiveness of an intelligence service is judged.

And intelligence services can never rest. Requirements are constantly changing as new concerns come to the fore. So for instance, in the UK illegal drugs became a 'target of opportunity' in the early

1980s (i.e. British intelligence services would pass any intelligence they found but they wouldn't go out of their way to get it), but by the end of the decade the subject had been so upgraded in priority that MI6 opened an entire counter-narcotics section.

As soon as a station is informed of its local requirements by its headquarters section, the officers working on that station will sit down and work out how to direct their existing assets against those requirements and where they need to recruit new agents or redirect old ones.

Eventually a well-run station's organisation should look something like this:

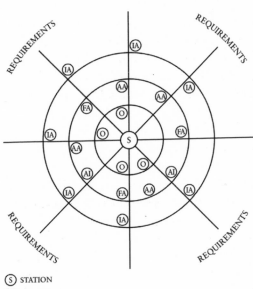

(S) STATION
(O) OFFICER
(AA) ACCESS AGENT
(AI) AGENT OF INFLUENCE
(FA) FACILITIES AGENT
(IA) INTELLIGENCE AGENT

The assets within a station's web must always be moved so that the correct requirements are being attacked.

Assessing and Grading Intelligence

Production of raw intelligence by the stations is not the end of the process. In every intelligence service there will be sections responsible for issuing finished intelligence. With every report from stations which crosses their desks, officers will be asking four questions about the raw report before they decide whether or not to issue it:

- The **truth** or probability of the facts reported.
- Their **importance** if the facts are true.
- Whether or not the report answers a **requirement**.
- Whether it is **timely** (a lot of agents try to sell information which is already old!)

Once they have decided that the intelligence report can be issued, the service must disguise the source – obviously they don't want to reveal what the origin of the information is, but at the same time they want to give customers an idea about how reliable the source is. So all intelligence reports are given a description which disguises the source yet still aims to let the customer know what they are getting. The description at the head of the report will indicate whether the source is believed to be reliable, whether it is a new or established source and how regularly the source reports. Intelligence which comes from allies or sigint sources is described in exactly the same way so as to further confuse the picture if anyone tries to work out how many agents are working on a particular target. In this way there is almost no chance that the identity of an agent will be discovered unless it is betrayed by an officer.

Source descriptions are not set in stone and may change from report to report even though the source is the same. For instance, a source who has been reliable when reporting in one area may not be so reliable if he starts reporting in another (he may just be trying to get more money by reporting on another subject or it may be that he has lost his old access and is trying to cover the fact up). The source description would have to reflect this new development.

Customers will be expected to comment on the value of the intelligence. The headquarters of the service will then collate all this feedback and assess how well they are meeting their customers' requirements. However, there is a tendency to inflate the value of the information. Secrecy gives intelligence a cachet which it does not always deserve (consider the criticisms of the Franks Committee of intelligence on Argentina in Chapter 1).

How Useful Is Intelligence?

The UK spends a third more on spying than it does on diplomacy (more than £1 billion vs. £700 million according to 1999 figures from the Treasury). A question which analysts are always trying to answer is: do we get our money's worth from the intelligence services? It is difficult to answer because the intelligence services are protected from scrutiny by secrecy.

There is no doubt that the right intelligence report at the right moment is invaluable. A report that your enemy is planning to attack or that he has just invented a dangerous new weapon can change the course of history. This is the sort of thing we expect when we think of 'intelligence'. But in the real world this sort of reporting is rarely, if ever, available. Most of it is far more mundane and not all that useful. But governments should be constantly assessing and refining their intelligence picture. This leads to what is known as the intelligence cycle:

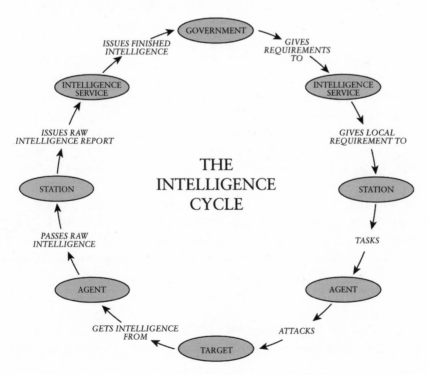

This system works well in theory, but the weak point of the cycle is at the governmental stage. It is here that analysis and collation of intelligence should take place and yet all the evidence available is that this does not happen as well as it should and that mistakes are made as a result: an independent commission in the United States appointed to examine America's intelligence machine in the wake of the 9/11 attacks on the World Trade Centre concluded that vital intelligence which could have led to the foiling of the attacks had not been collated and disseminated. George Tenet, head of the CIA admitted, 'We all understood bin Laden's attempt to strike the homeland. We never translated this knowledge into an effective defence of our country . . .' In this country, leading academic commentators such as Michael Herman have questioned whether enough effort is put into analysing and using intelligence compared with the massive effort devoted to collecting it.

There is also some indication that, in a performance-driven management culture, Western intelligence services have become obsessed with the quantity of intelligence reports rather than their quality. A good example occurred before the First Gulf War: satellite technology enabled Western governments quite clearly to see Iraqi troops and armour moving on the border with Kuwait. The problem was that no one knew what Saddam was going to do. We didn't have any of the key humint sources who could tell us what he was planning and the few scraps we did have led Western analysts to conclude that he *wouldn't* invade Kuwait! Or perhaps this shows that little has changed over the years and that intelligence is rarely as good as we imagine: former British Foreign Secretary David Owen remembers a night in 1968 when Russian tanks were poised outside Prague in Czechoslovakia. Before he went to sleep he read the latest reports from MI6 and GCHQ assuring him that there was absolutely no chance of a conflict. He was woken just a few hours later to be told that the Russian tanks were attacking the city . . .

Even with as momentous an event as the collapse of the Soviet Union, it is now generally accepted that the Western intelligence services completely misunderstood what was happening. Charles Powell, a senior British diplomat and Downing Street adviser has especially strong views on this:

The biggest single failure of intelligence of that era was the failure of almost everybody to foresee the end of Communism.

It caught us completely on the hop. All that intelligence about their war-fighting capabilities was all very well, but it didn't tell us the one thing we needed to know, that it was all about to collapse. It was a colossal failure of the whole Western system of intelligence assessment and political judgement.

The failure to find weapons of mass destruction in Iraq and all the consequences of the momentous decision to invade are only the most recent in a list of intelligence failures. But upon analysis the failure appears to be not just that of the intelligence services but also that of our assessment systems. Perhaps the real problem is not how we collect our intelligence, but what we do with it when we have it.

5 Profiling, Cultivation and Recruitment: How to Get Other People to Work for You

He that complies against his will, is of his own opinion still.

Samuel Butler

Why Use Human Agents?

Profiling, cultivating and recruiting agents is a long and uncertain business. Despite all the effort which will go into a recruitment operation, it is estimated that fewer than one in five of these operations is a success. And even if an agent is successfully recruited, the work has only just begun: running agents is both labour intensive and extremely risky. The agents themselves often require money, gifts and constant welfaring to ensure they keep their nerve. Their intelligence product is uncertain and there is the constant threat that they may be discovered or turn of their own accord to become a devastating weapon in the hands of the enemy intelligence service, entrapping their case officers and exposing operational procedures.

Machines don't lie or invent results, they won't turn traitor and once in place they work twenty-four hours a day, 365 days a year at little risk to serving officers. So with all the modern advantages in satellite technology, remote-controlled drones, communications interception and sophisticated bugging devices, why do intelligence services persist in using human agents?

There are in fact several advantages:

- Although machines can do a great deal, there are certain tasks which are beyond them such as stealing documents or equipment. Without agents in place these are tasks which would have to be carried out by a field officer. Agents **lower the risk** of danger to the intelligence officer by undertaking some of these tasks.
- The best human agents can **investigate**. With other assets such as satellites or bugs you have to know the physical location of the intelligence you want. Even then, satellites and drones can only photograph the outside of buildings, sigint resources can only intercept information which is actually transmitted. Human agents can be told to go and investigate or to find a way to obtain a particular piece of information.
- They are **cheap**. Of course, it sometimes doesn't seem like that when you are faced with a grasping agent who demands another £5,000 before he will give you the next piece of information, but overall the cost of an agent network stands up well against other sources even allowing for the costs of the intelligence service running them. For instance, intelligence-gathering satellites literally cost billions of pounds and once the costs of research and development and support are included this cost multiplies. Sigint networks may require many ground stations and a huge staff to monitor and analyse the product. Pound for pound, compared against other less flexible methods of intelligence gathering, agents should be good value for money.
- They are a **continuing asset**, working on a target long after one field officer has moved on and been replaced by another.
- They are **deniable**. If a spy, as a British citizen (or whichever nation you are working for) is caught, it could be severely embarrassing for the government. If an agent is a national of a third country this becomes much easier and the spy can deny all knowledge of their activities. (John le Carré's *The Looking Glass War* excellently conveys just how brutal this process can be.)
- For many countries which don't have access to advanced technology, they remain the most **widely available** and productive intelligence resource.

Odette Hallowes (1912–1995)

She was born and raised near Amiens in France. Her
father, a soldier, had been killed during the First World
War. In 1931 she married an Englishman, Roy Sansom,
who worked in the hotel industry. They moved to London
and soon had three daughters. After the fall of France she
was determined to do something to help. She joined the
French section of the Special Operations Executive (SOE),
the clandestine organisation, then part of MI6, responsible
for organising resistance behind the lines. At first it was
thought that a mother who was constantly worrying about
her daughters hundreds of miles away could never be a
successful spy, but her native upbringing and determined
personality meant that she could not be turned down.

In October 1942 she was secretly dropped by a small boat
onto the coast of France as a fully-trained operative. Her
mission was to help coordinate resistance activities in the
Burgundy region. She worked closely with Peter Churchill,
another SOE operative in the region, but squabbles between
various members of the Resistance constantly thwarted their
activities. In April 1943, Odette and Churchill were arrested
at a hotel following the infiltration of their network by a
German spy. The two of them claimed to be married and that
Churchill was in fact the nephew of Sir Winston Churchill,
the British Prime Minister. For a while this spared them the
worst of the interrogations, but eventually Odette was sent to
the notorious Fresnes prison in Paris where she suffered the
most appalling tortures including electrocution, near-
drowning and having all her toenails pulled out. She gave
away nothing of importance and her bravery under torture
has since become legendary.

In June 1943 she was sentenced to death and sent to
Ravensbruck concentration camp. (Churchill had been sent
to Sachsenhausen concentration camp). Although they were
nearly killed several times, both survived the war. Eleven
other female operatives in Odette's section were executed,
many of them within earshot of her cell.

cont'd

Odette became a national heroine, the subject of a book and the film *Odette* starring Anna Neagle. In 1946 she was awarded the George Cross, the civilian equivalent of the VC. She always saw the award as something for all the men and women of SOE rather than just for herself. After Roy Sansom's death she married Peter Churchill, but the marriage did not last and she married again, finally finding happiness with Geoffrey Hallowes, a wine merchant. At one stage her George Cross was stolen during a burglary and a public appeal was sent out asking for its return. Such was the affection in which she was held that the medal was returned together with a note of apology from the burglar. She remained active in a wide range of civic and charitable projects right up until her death in 1995.

Profiling

Profiling is the process of selecting a person who will make a good spy. Most intelligence services will have whole teams devoted to this hunt, either receiving reports from field officers and then drawing up detailed plans or conducting their own studies of possible targets in a particular location and then making recommendations for action to the field officer responsible for that location.

There are certain key qualities a profiling team will be looking for in a potential target:

- They must be highly **motivated**. The profiling team must be able to see a reason why the target might wish to work for the service.
- They must be **discreet** whatever their role is, no matter how small – and the station should occasionally test this.
- They should have **nerve**. These are the people running the risks. It is not easy going to undercover meetings, or providing help you shouldn't, without proper training and a large organisation to back you up, such as an intelligence officer has.

- They should be **self-motivating**. You don't want to be holding their hand all the time. The point of an agent network is that it should work for you without having to be constantly directed. There are two ways to provoke this: money (payment by results) and ideology (such as the commitment to the Communist ideal by the Cambridge spy ring).
- They must be **likeable**. This may seem an odd quality and is not an absolute requirement, but it has always been a pretty good rule of thumb for a field officer when considering a potential agent: the two of you are going to be working closely on very sensitive work. If there is some reason that you can't like an agent despite all their faults then you have to ask yourself why. It may highlight some error in your profiling or cultivation, some area you haven't explored which may lead to trouble later.

Of course you would be very lucky indeed to find a target who had all these qualities and it is up to the judgement of the profiling team and the officer on the ground as to whether the target has enough of these qualities to be worth pursuing. The key quality is access. If a target looks recruitable and has access to a high priority intelligence then the service will almost certainly begin an operation against them.

How to Gather Information on the Target

There are several potential sources:

- **Previous case files**: It is extremely likely that your systems already hold information on the target even if he or she has only been mentioned in the margins of a contact report. One of the jobs of field officers is to make file notes of any people they come across in the course of their work who might be of interest in the future. Nowadays computer archives make this process even easier and a basic search will usually yield enough information to open a case file.
- **Existing intelligence agents**: If you have an agent in the local police or security forces they may be able to get hold

of a file on the target. Not only may this give you personal information but it may indicate if this person is already under suspicion by the authorities as a security risk.

- **Access agents**: Either they will already know the target or, more likely, they can be tasked to get alongside the target and gather as much information as possible. This ensures that the field officer's interest does not become clear too early – certainly not before a **cultivation strategy** has been devised by the profiling team.

- **Intelligence allies**: Another service's database may have additional information not available to you or the other service may have already attempted a recruitment which failed and may be prepared to share the reasons with you. The other service might already have an agent working in the same area as your target – your operation might risk compromising theirs and they might be prepared to trade the intelligence with you rather than take the risk of a second operation running in the same area. Of course, revealing that you are interested in a target is technically a breach of security – the more people who know about your interest the less secure the operation is.

- **Garbology**: We have already encountered the skill of 'dustbin emptying' in relation to intelligence gathering in Chapter 4. But, contents of rubbish – bank account details, recent purchases, correspondence – can be even more useful in profiling.

- **Surveillance**: Of course this may be risky for the local station to carry out, but specialist teams can be flown in to follow the target. This is obviously an expensive option and would only be used in cases where you suspect that a target is too good to be true and may be a trap planted by local security forces to lure you out.

- **Tech ops**: Bugging of telephones, workplaces and residences may be used and can provide some of the best possible profiling information.

- **Personal interview**: A cover reason can always be created so that the intelligence service can get an officer alongside the target to make an assessment of their potential.

Elicitation – The Art of Getting People to Talk About Themselves

Any encounter with another person while you are working under cover should be seen as a timeline. Your object during the timeline is to maximise the amount the other person spends talking about themselves and minimise the exposure of your legend. But you can't simply 'pump' people for information especially in the sorts of situations spies operate in. Often they will never have met their target before and people are quite sensitive as to whether or not they are being grilled.

So how do you do it? To some people it seems to come as naturally as breathing, but if you're like me it needs a little bit more work and preparation.

First there is your **mental attitude**. At least in your mind you have to assume control of the conversation. Think of talking to the managing director of a company you work for at a social gathering in the office: she is likely to ask about your work, your family, your future with the company. You are not likely to pose the same questions back to her (it depends how much you've been drinking I suppose!) because she has control. In a conversation with a potential target, control should be easy to assume because you are the spy – you need feel inferior to no one. But be careful – you can really stand out if you take charge of the conversation when it is not appropriate for you to do so (take the company director example above – if you end up grilling her on her home life and employment prospects it could look distinctly odd). So the taking of control must be diplomatic and sensitive. Use this control to steer the conversation towards the information you want. But again, be subtle. 'So tell me all about your family,' just isn't good enough, especially in an environment such as a foreign embassy where people are on the lookout for intelligence officers.

Next you need to see the other person as **interesting**. Conversation dies because you don't feel this interest and they don't feel interested in you. Oddly it works rather like body mirroring – the more interested you are in them and what they have to say, the more they will be interested in you (although you may be working from a fairly low base . . .). As an intelligence officer of course you should have little difficulty in seeing them as interesting because in your eyes they are a potential asset, either an intelligence source or a facilities agent or access agent. Or they may be the opposition . . .

Then there is **active listening**. This is a technique for keeping a conversation going and encouraging a person to say more about themselves than they otherwise would. In any interaction between two people both sides are looking for encouragement and signs of approval from the other. We often talk more expansively in response to praise about the value or importance of our work. Active listening ensures that you give it. Points to remember are:

- Nodding and signs of agreement
- Smiling
- Good eye contact, but don't stare. Use long looks with occasional glances away
- Using supportive phrases such as 'I see' or 'I understand'
- Leaning slightly forward towards the speaker to show interest
- Using silence – sometimes if you leave a gap in the conversation for a moment or so the other person will continue speaking or add some detail to what they were just saying
- Use open-ended questions, ones which your target can't simply answer with 'yes' or 'no'
- Don't be afraid of direct questions. Most of us want to be polite and helpful, so we answer direct questions even from relative strangers

But again you need to be sensitive to the mood and rhythm of the conversation: blurting out 'that sounds really fascinating!' is possibly too much and can just sound insincere. Active listening is a skill like any other and needs to be practised.

Another aspect similar to active listening is **body mirroring** – using similar postures and gestures as the person you are talking to. But don't be too obvious or your behaviour will unconsciously be interpreted as manipulative – there is a balance to be struck and again this requires practice. The recruits on the *Spy* training course spent some time practising these skills before trying them out on the exercises. You will soon learn what works and what doesn't if you watch the reactions of those you are talking to.

Always remember that you are looking for topics of conversation which will produce **information** (this is where the spy skill of noticing small details plays an important part). If you are in the target's office or home you are in the perfect place to get the target to talk about himself. If you are just faced with the target in an unfamiliar setting, there are still possibilities: the club tie they are wearing, the smart suit – where did they get it? Their watch – your wife bought one just like it and she had so much trouble getting it. Use your imagination.

Spies are almost always operating against foreigners and the customs of other cultures can be radically different from European customs. A good spy is always sensitive to these nuances because they can radically affect whether a meeting is successful or not. So be aware of **local custom**: is it appropriate to use first names when initially meeting a stranger? Is body touching allowed? In some societies a polite touch on the arm is seen as friendship affirming, in others it would be considered inappropriate. It is these small signals which can often cause a target to clam up.

Key Information Which a Profiling Team will be Seeking

1) Biodata

Biodata is the term for all the basic personal information relating to a target such as date of birth, address, names of family members, education and so forth. In any profiling file, this is the first information you will find. If you can't answer these basic questions then you are probably missing something.

2) Likes and Dislikes

The purpose of gathering this information is to help the agent who will conduct the cultivation to get close to the target or 'get alongside' as it is known in the trade. Speaking to people who know the target, hacking to analyse computer usage, break-ins to the target's home to examine books, music collections and papers and garbology (see Chapter 4) may all be used to build this picture. A key use of access agents is to run them alongside the target to gather this information.

3) Indication of Motivation

From the two sources above the profiling team will try to assess the likely motivation for the target to spy for their service. Determining this correctly before beginning a cultivation is a luxury which profiling teams don't often get. More often it is the field agent conducting the cultivation who gradually senses what the key factor is which will persuade the target to become a fully-recruited agent.

The following are some of the motivations which a profiling team will be considering:

- **Money**: Possibly the least reliable, yet the most common these days. It has always been said that the American services make most use of this because they have so much money. As one American said, 'It's like going around offering money for sex, you get your face slapped a lot but sooner or later you get lucky!' The European services (including the KGB), on the other hand, are always supposed to have been more creative in their approach to recruitment because they are always strapped for cash. Like most humour it has an element of truth in it.
- **Love**: Some intelligence services will use the prospect of sex to lure a target, but the more sophisticated services will use this loneliness as a way of starting a lasting friendship which is a much more secure basis for a recruitment.
- **Ideology**: Either religious or political. With the demise of the Communist bloc, this motivation is far less common, but there are still regimes around the world which are so oppressive that people will work with outside agencies to bring about change.
- **Guilt**: Those who have taken part in the activities of an oppressive regime may be willing to turn on their former masters as a way of atoning for what has happened. But any target who has regrets about some action or lapse in the past may well be looking for a friend who will support and understand them. This is something which a skilful profiling team can use.
- **Need for help**: This is often a basis for gangplank or crash approaches (see page 116). The need can be for medical, employment or legal help – the list is almost endless. The point is not to use the favour against the target like some sort of debt, but rather not to mention the debt at all and use it as a basis for friendship.

- **Ego**: Some people just want to be important, to play a part in the great affairs of the world. George Blake, the famous British traitor of the 1950s, was at great pains to point out that he did not work for money or ideology but because he made a decision to change the world. Interrogators said that they had rarely met anyone with such a superiority complex. Not all agents will reach these heights, but there will always be some who want to believe how valuable and important they are.
- **Revenge**: There may naturally be a reason why someone wants to hit back at a regime or an organisation which has crossed them. Where a reason doesn't exist, the service can always consider creating one, for instance sometimes Irish terrorists were told that another terrorist was sleeping with their wife. It wasn't always true, but in the paranoid world of terrorism, it was effective.
- **Boredom**: This motive has to be accompanied by a certain lack of moral sense but as with ego, people who see their lives going nowhere reach a point where they want to do something exciting. With a little manipulation this can be turned towards espionage. The great East German spy-master Markus Wolf used to have his operatives target bored middle-aged secretaries in West German ministries for this very reason with considerable success.

Or it may be a mix of any of these reasons. Even if a motive isn't fully developed to the point where someone can be recruited, a good profiling team will devise a plan to develop it to the point where it can. If motivation is sufficient but the target would never work for your service for racial or religious reasons, then a **False Flag operation** may have to be used (see page 115).

Blackmail

There are of course intelligence services which will use blackmail, particularly in terrorist cases where a suspect can be faced with the choice of working for the authorities or facing a long prison term. But intelligence services try to avoid blackmail wherever possible. Someone who is being blackmailed will not work hard for you – like slaves they will do the absolute minimum to get by. As their resentment at their situation grows, they will look for ways to work against you, even to lead your operatives into danger. Contrary to popular belief, neither prostitutes nor blackmail are used except in extreme circumstances (but remember the golden rule of espionage). It is not good agent management and with skilful work a service can turn the situation to their advantage far more profitably.

With someone who has a dark secret, it is far better to work with them than against them. If they have had a drug dependency, help them to find treatment and support. If they are having an affair, use that as a basis for trust between you, let them know that you know, but never threaten to expose them. If they have a large debt, gradually help them to pay it off, without suggesting there is something they must do in return (at least initially). Agents work best when they feel that what they are doing is their own idea rather than your order.

Security

The other major concern which a profiling team must be aware of is the security of the operation and all profiling units will have a security officer attached to the team whose sole purpose will be to consider security issues. Principally she will be considering three things:

- Is the target a honey trap placed there by another intelligence service to expose your officer?
- Has the target panicked and told local security forces or anyone else about the nature of the officer's interest?
- Has the cultivation been conducted in any way which is likely to arouse the suspicion of local security forces? (For instance the most attractive targets are those with access to secrets, but these are exactly the sort of people who might have their phones bugged by local security forces or even be subject to occasional surveillance.)

Once you have decided that your target has access to secrets, is secure and has at least some of the other necessary personal qualities to become an agent, the team can move on to the next stage.

Cultivation

Once a target has been selected by the profiling team, the process of recruiting the target begins. This is known in intelligence circles as **cultivation**. Bringing a target from first contact to fully fledged recruit is an art rather than a science. There are no hard and fast rules and tactics will vary from service to service. Much will also depend on the sensitivity and responses of the field officer on the ground. The KGB had a particularly painstaking approach to agent recruitment and makes a good source for study since most recruitments will follow a similar pattern.

Here is an example of an approach. This one is from Mossad and has an end other than recruitment in mind:

> Mordecai Vanunu was a scientist who became aware of Israel's secret nuclear weapons programme. He decided, rightly or wrongly, to expose the truth. In 1986 Vanunu travelled to the UK where his story was picked up by *The Times*, who put him up in a luxury hotel. Mossad became aware of the leak, probably through a source in London, and they were determined to kidnap him, take him back to Israel and make an example of him. There was one major problem which was that to kidnap him from UK soil was likely to cause a major diplomatic incident.
>
> A Mossad profiling team having examined every piece of information they had about him, it was decided that the approach most likely to be successful was to put a beautiful blonde in the hotel. She was Israeli and a fully trained Mossad agent, but claimed to be a American beautician on holiday. With the aid of a support team, Mossad were soon able to ensure that her path crossed with that of the lonely, insecure Vanunu in Leicester Square in London where a full Mossad surveillance team was watching. She listened to his stories and offered him all the support and compassion which no one else was giving him. She got him to agree to meet her again the following evening for dinner. Because Mossad knew that Vanunu would be wary, the officer made sure that she said things which were critical of Israel. Even when Vanunu's friends tried to warn him, he insisted that she couldn't be an Israeli because of the things she was saying.

Eventually she persuaded him to come with her on the next stage of her holiday to Italy. Vanunu knew the danger he was in yet he agreed to go with her so her powers of persuasion must have been considerable. Mossad knew that the Italian government was too weak to make much of a protest. Once in Italy, the pair travelled to an apartment. No sooner had Vanunu stepped through the door than he was attacked by a group of masked men, tied up and drugged. He was then taken in the boot of a car to a nearby beach from where he was ferried out to a yacht by motorboat. He was then kept chained to a bunk in the yacht for several days while it sailed to Israel. He was found guilty of treason by a secret court and was imprisoned in strict solitary confinement for the next eighteen years in conditions of appalling cruelty. He was released in 2004 into a limited form of freedom under conditions of strict security. The Mossad agent who lured Vanunu into the trap has since been resettled in the United States.

Case Study: A Typical KGB Recruitment

The Target

Andersson was a Swedish naval officer stationed at Stockholm just after the Second World War. He came to the attention of the KGB through an access agent who was a close friend. The access agent provided plenty of biodata and other information about Andersson and his character. The KGB profiling team used this and noticed especially that Andersson was a man with good access to restricted areas of Swedish naval bases. Furthermore, the profiling team considered that he might be recruitable because he was a supporter of Communism and felt undervalued in his current work. The profiling team weren't sure whether his interest in Communism had led to him being identified by Swedish security forces as a possible security risk, but they decided that he was at least worth a further look.

Stage One – The Approach

Andersson was invited to a party held by the access agent. At the party was Konstantin Vinogradov, a KGB officer working under diplomatic cover as First Secretary at the Soviet embassy in Stockholm. The access agent made sure that the two were introduced and Vinogradov worked hard at appearing interested in everything Andersson had to say whilst gently trying to find out what sort of access Andersson had and how he felt about the Soviet Union. When he was happy that the profiling information he had been given was correct, Vinogradov told Andersson that he was holding a dinner party at his residence the following week and asked if Andersson would like to come. Andersson said he would be honoured.

The first contact between a target and the recruiter is crucial. It requires a great deal of planning to make sure it runs smoothly.

- It must appear **natural**. In this case, like all good access agents, the friend was always holding parties to which a range of people were invited. Andersson would not have felt that Vinogradov's presence there was unusual.
- It should establish a **relationship of power** or at least of equality. Another reason the dinner party was a good choice was because Vinogradov will have emphasised his importance and Andersson will have felt quite flattered that he was invited. (For more about the **power ladder** see Chapter 6.)
- It should **interest** the target. There should be a feeling that this is something exciting, someone worth knowing, that life is going to be better for going to the next meeting. The KGB may even have considered placing other officers at the party to make Vinogradov seem more authoritative or humorous than he actually was. Anything to catch Andersson's attention.

Of all the stages of a recruitment, the approach requires the most planning. The approach is also when the profiling team must be at their most creative. This is when you first lead your target into thinking you are someone they want to know. And in this instance it really is a case of 'first impressions count'. If your approach touches a nerve or in some way produces a negative impression then you will probably have to start all over again with a new field agent. A really clumsy approach may even put the target on their guard and in the worst cases lead to the target being turned against you and used as a honey trap by the opposition.

One must avoid the suspicion not just of the target, but of those around at that first meeting or those in whom the target might confide e.g. security, relatives, close friends. In this example the access agent will have made sure not to invite close friends of Andersson who might have taken an interest in the meeting or anyone connected to the security apparatus. Similarly, the access agent will probably have closely monitored Andersson over the next few days to see if he'd felt that anything about the meeting was suspicious. Where an access agent is not available, spies would bug the target's house and/or phone.

It is absolutely crucial that an approach must have built into it a reason why the agent and the target will meet again. It is no good having a great first contact and then not seeing the target for another three months. One former security service officer described the approach stage of a recruitment thus: 'Sometimes the position is created for a man so that MI5 can come along and help him – a bit like breaking a man's leg so that you can offer him a crutch.' Looking back, another officer said: 'Much imagination was expended in thinking of ways to get alongside targets who were mostly well protected inside their embassies. Many a bizarre scheme was dreamt up to strike an acquaintance . . . If I ever see a jogger apparently spraining his ankle or a dog suddenly keel over and look sick, I carefully look at the scene to see if I can make out a likely target there . . .'

All the recruits on the training course were tested in their ability to make an approach. A number of coffee bars were selected across London and within each one an unsuspecting member of the public was targeted. The recruits were to go in, sit alongside the target and get three pieces of information: name, date of birth and the name of their first girl or boyfriend. As if that wasn't difficult enough in the limited time available to them, they also had to get the target to agree to a further meeting. There was no profiling information available, the targets were simply selected because they were in the right place at the right time. We thought the third piece of information would be particularly difficult to get. If they could accomplish this then they could certainly deal with a carefully planned recruitment approach. In fact the exercise is based on

'Perfect Stranger', a real MI6 training exercise as detailed by former officer Richard Tomlinson in his book *The Big Breach*.

We were astonished at the recruits' performances: all except one of them were successful to some extent. Simon succeeded in getting all the information and an agreement to a further meeting from an Eastern European gentleman who barely said a word for the first five minutes. Max actually managed to perform the exercise successfully twice! But the star of the day was Austin. Targeted against a young woman, his approach line was typically Austin and he told the girl he was looking for a rhyme with 'away'. 'Gay?' suggested the woman and in the observation post our hearts sank. But Austin persisted and through his charm, good humour and use of the elicitation skills he had learned at the training school, he managed to complete most of the exercise, even getting her e-mail address. Of course it might just have been his aftershave, but we didn't think so. What the exercise does show is how well these tactics can work when used thoughtfully. It also shows how eager people are for something different to happen in their daily lives, which all spies know how to exploit.

Stage Two – Acquaintance

At the dinner party, Andersson was made to feel the centre of attention. All his jokes were funny, the women found his work fascinating, the men seemed to think his comments on the state of the world insightful. In fact, the KGB team assembled at the dinner party rather overdid things, so that Andersson guessed where all this was leading. And he was ready to say yes whenever they asked him to work for the Soviet Union. Unfortunately the Russians didn't know this. In fact they decided that this was going to have to be a long-term recruitment. Vinogradov stayed in touch with Andersson and they met several times more at dinner parties and receptions.

The rules of the second stage of recruitment are:

- It should be a more substantial meeting than the approach.
- Where time allows there should be several meetings.

Sometimes this stage may be omitted, it all depends how well the approach goes, what sort of motive the target has and how much time is available. In this case the KGB had no urgent need to move quickly so they didn't. To have done so might have been to risk Vinogradov's exposure.

Stage Three – Friendship

The eagerness of the KGB officer to make this relationship succeed became rather too obvious when Andersson failed to turn up at one of Vinogradov's dinner parties. Afraid that the recruitment might be failing, Vinogradov turned up at Andersson's house with New Year gifts and a further invitation. If Vinogradov had been under routine surveillance (as Soviet diplomats often were) this move could have been a fatal mistake – a visit to the home of a serving naval officer would have caused alarm in the security services, but fortunately Vinogradov was not under surveillance that night. The bluntness of this move did have one beneficial effect. Vinogradov was showing that he, a Soviet diplomat, was clearly interested in Andersson and Andersson did not warn Vinogradov to stay away as he should have done. This was a sign to the KGB profiling team that the cultivation was going well and that Andersson was ready for the next stage.

Matters were complicated because Vinogradov's posting was drawing to a close. So one evening when Andersson arrived at the flat for dinner there was only one other guest, the TASS representative Viktor Anissimov. Sure enough, by the end of the evening, Anissimov had invited Andersson to a party at his house and the handover from one case officer to the next was complete.

Establishing a friendship with a recruitment target is where the skill of the individual officer comes into play. On training courses the officer will be taught various stratagems and psychological tricks which will help her to move the relationship on from acquaintance to actual friendship and the profiling team at HQ will always be on hand with advice. The field officer will write detailed reports on each of the meetings which the team will analyse giving advice and ideas for the next meeting. The team will also play a counter-espionage role, looking out for signs that the potential target may be a honey trap.

It is hard to say when the line between stages two and three is crossed. An experienced officer will know. It can take just a few days, but with a reluctant or wary target it could take months. Use of first names, a certain smile when they see you across the street and greet you, shared jokes, get-togethers for no particular reason, all these are signs that the cultivation is progressing well.

Stage Four – The Trust Stage

After a few meetings, Anissimov suggested to Andersson that if it came to the attention of the authorities that he was meeting a Soviet diplomat there might be people who would be suspicious. Naturally, insisted Anissimov, there was nothing to be suspicious about, but even so he suggested that they meet more discreetly and certainly never at the Soviet diplomatic quarters. Instead they should only meet in small towns outside Stockholm and Andersson was to be careful about how he contacted Anissimov. He was never to use the official lines at the embassy.

Stage four is where the potential target crosses the line. It is as important as the approach or the recruitment itself. The target has to show enough confidence in the recruiter to do something he really shouldn't. It doesn't have to be a big thing. It just shows that the target is prepared to bend the rules for the officer. There are any number of ways to bring the target across this invisible line and the particular scenario usually suggests one after a bit of thought.

This KGB's action is a good example of a stage four move. The agent points out to the target that what they are doing, whilst not illegal, is not quite right, but even so the target agrees. A semi-clandestine relationship now began which was excellent preparation for the shift to a fully secret relationship once Andersson was recruited.

Taking a target through this stage of the cultivation process is a crucial skill and one which the recruits had to be tested on. They were split into teams of two. One was to work alongside a target for four days, the other to act as support officer, playing any other roles which were required and taking the lead in planning each of the moves which the operational officer would make. The test was a hard one: not only would the operational officer have to maintain cover for several days whilst in close proximity to the target for up to eight hours at a time, but by the end of the three-day period the target had to be persuaded to undertake an illicit action – something which while not illegal, definitely meant that the target had to show considerable trust. Four days is relatively quick for reaching this stage in a cultivation, but then intelligence officers rarely get the luxury of enough time. The hardest part was that none of the targets knew about the mission. They were all ordinary members of the public who had been chosen for the exercise by their employers and were completely unaware that a trainee spy was to be placed alongside them.

Results were mixed. Stars of the exercise were Max and Simon. Max was placed in a barber's shop as a trainee hairdresser and his target was one of the other barbers. Simon had a cover role as the new boyfriend of Max's ex-partner who was holding on to Max's DVD system. Max panicked several times because he felt that his cover had been blown. The problem with working in a barber's was that there was lots of time to talk and it meant that his cover story came in for close examination. But Max held his nerve and continued to work on his target. Even so, by the end of the second day, Max and Simon felt that they hadn't managed to win their target's trust.

What turned the entire operation for them was a little scenario they had devised. Simon was supposed to come into the barber's as the irate boyfriend demanding that Max give up his key to the girl's flat. This had to be planned very carefully – it had to be aggressive enough to arouse the sympathy of the target, but at the same time they had to remain in control of the situation so that the target did not become involved, possibly leading to a fight. Max and Simon managed this by starting the argument in the staff room so that the others in the shop could hear but not see what was going on. They then took the argument into the street so that once again the others in the shop could not get involved.

That one little staged incident turned the whole operation in their favour. The others working in the shop including the target warmed to Max and deeply resented Simon, so much so that the target volunteered to act as lookout while Max went back to the flat with the key to reclaim his DVD. It was a hard thing to ask since the target was losing money while he was out on the street helping Max, on top of which it was never certain that Max had a right to the DVD in the first place. Initially the target was reluctant, but Max worked on him and got him to agree. It was a perfect illustration of a stage four move.

Not all the teams were as successful. Austin and Nicola were targeted against a young man working in an exclusive boutique. Austin was supposed to be a sales trainee, Nicola a visiting friend who was moving to the area. They had been told that the target had a fanatical interest in two things: classic American cars and women. They frantically researched US cars and it was thought that Nicola's feminine charms would do the rest. But from the first day it was clear that the team had a real struggle on their hands. Although the

Manipulating others

Simon arrives to begin his carefully planned confrontation with Max.

By winning the target's sympathy, Max is able to persuade him to stand guard while Max recovers the DVD player.

target agreed to go out for lunch and Nicola worked desperately hard to get his attention, nothing seemed to work and neither she nor Austin could really make a connection with him. Sure enough, when they tried to get the target to sign a forged rental agreement, he refused.

Austin and Nicola had not researched classic cars deeply enough with the result that, instead of sounding like a fellow enthusiast, Austin came across as simply irritating. Nicola's approach was too pushy and she may have underestimated the target's sensibility. Furthermore, the target had been suspicious of Austin from the outset because he thought that his employer intended to replace him with Austin. When the sting was finally launched he assumed that it was a trap to get him sacked. As for why Nicola failed – sometimes the chemistry just isn't there.

Stage Five – Information

The ease with which Andersson agreed to meet Anissimov 'discreetly' should have tipped off the KGB profiling team that he was ripe for recruitment, but still they delayed. It is possible that they could not believe their luck and that they were suspicious that this was some kind of trap set by the Swedish intelligence service. It is also possible that some other factor in the mountain of profiling information they must have by now collected on Anissimov may have cast doubt on his suitability. Whatever the reason, the KGB continued to move slowly. Over the following year, Andersson was asked to provide more and more information about his work and about his background, but still nothing which could be classed as intelligence.

At one stage it appeared that Anissimov had overdone it. Following their talks about Communism and the Soviet Union, Andersson announced his intention to join the Swedish Communist Party. This would have immediately caused suspicion and he would never have been allowed access to secret information. Anissimov had to work hard to dissuade him from the idea on the grounds that it would only cause him difficulties. He also warned him to stay away from other Communist party members.

Stage five represents the first point of the relationship when the officer tries to get information from the target. This is still not secret intelligence, but the more the target talks about his work and other matters, the easier it will be for him to pass secrets later. At the same time the officer tries to make the meetings more clandestine to prepare the target for more secretive meetings once he is fully recruited.

Stage Six – Intelligence

Finally, after a year of careful testing, Anissimov said that he would be very interested to see Andersson's identity papers and security passes. This was sensitive information and would probably be classed as low-level intelligence. It was completely out of line for someone who was supposedly a Soviet newspaper correspondent to ask for it and Andersson knew it. Yet he readily agreed and even offered to provide more documents. This shows how far down the line Andersson had travelled towards being a fully recruited agent.

There is not a great deal of difference between stages five and six. The key difference is that the type of information being requested is sensitive and some of it may even find its way into a multi-source intelligence report. It is really the last chance to sound out the target before the cultivation team finally decides to put the recruitment question.

Stage Seven – Recruitment

Soon after, Anissimov formally recruited Andersson as a Soviet intelligence agent. In many ways Andersson was relieved that all the cards were finally on the table. The whole cultivation process had taken more than three years.

Anissimov probably had a little speech prepared for this moment, such as: 'Andersson, I work for the KGB. We would like you to supply us with intelligence about your country. We are willing to pay for this information and later, if you so wish, to offer you and your family a place in our country with a generous pension.'

The key point about any recruitment pitch is that it must make clear that this is an intelligence operation and exactly what the target is being asked to do. If the target agrees to this, then that's it, recruitment is complete.

Yet it is never that simple. The recruitment phase is the most doubtful stage of any recruitment process. For many people the formal declaration that they are being asked to become a spy is too much. Many of them prefer to retain some pretence that they are 'merely' a trusted source or that their information is for an elite international think tank rather than another government. This is called the 'fig leaf' and a surprising number of agents require this even though to all intents and purposes they are fully-recruited and conscious agents. Everybody knows what is going on, but nobody actually says so.

And there are some who, faced with the naked reality of what they are doing – even targets who have seemed ideal recruitment material right up to the very last stage, suddenly turn and flee as if this is a last chance to save themselves and they must take it. The spy novelist John le Carré, a former officer himself, summed up the uncertainty of this moment in one of his greatest works, *The Spy Who Came in from the Cold*:

> And finally they would know it was a gamble. They would know that inconsistency in human decision can make nonsense of the best planned espionage approach; that cheats, liars and criminals may resist every blandishment while respectable gentlemen have been moved to appalling treasons by watery cabbage in a departmental canteen.

Even if the recruitment proposal is refused, all is not lost. The key thing is not to pressurise the target. They have made a decision and you abide by it. The last thing you want is an unwilling agent. It has to be a voluntary partnership with shared goals or it is nothing. Although it is disappointing to see months of work come to nothing, the situation can be saved to a certain extent by getting the target to agree that they will keep a card in case they need help in the future or will stay in touch as friends. There is always a chance that one day the target will need that help or that the fact that you didn't apply any pressure shows that you can be trusted.

Other Types of Recruitment

Of course not all agent recruitment operations go through seven neat stages. In fact this is only one way of looking at the process. Some services would say there are more stages, some would say there are less. The key point is that the relationship has to be taken from a first contact through to a recruitment proposal. But there are other ways of doing it than the classic KGB method:

False Flag Recruitments

In the case of a False Flag recruitment, deniability is not even an issue since the agent himself thinks that he is working for another country. In some cases services may even recruit under a False Flag, get the agent to commit an atrocity, then expose the agent to make it look as though some other country is responsible. The other country takes the blame. For instance, suppose Mossad were to recruit a number of Arabs who believed they were in fact working for al Qaeda. If they then committed an atrocity in the USA, the benefits for Israel in terms of increased funding and political support would be considerable.

A False Flag recruitment is used for one of two reasons:

- The target would never agree to work for your country for some national, religious or personal reason.
- You want the agent to believe that they are working for another country so that if they are ever caught, another country will get blamed.

If you can pull it off the rewards can be great. The agent will work for you quite normally, but if he is ever captured, even if he is tortured or given truth drugs, he will swear to his dying day that he is working for someone else. It is not even that difficult to pull off – most people are so surprised to be asked to spy in the first place that it never crosses their mind that the people who are recruiting them aren't who they say they are. With a little careful 'set dressing' to carry off the subterfuge, most agents are easily hooked.

The downside of such an operation is that if you are ever caught doing it the consequences for relations with the other country are likely to be severe, so this sort of operation is unlikely to be undertaken without very high-level government approval and probably only against a country which is already your enemy.

Crash Approaches

They had a low-grade Soviet trade delegation in town, chasing up electrical goods for the Moscow market. One of the delegates was stepping wide in the nightclubs. Name of Boris, Mr Guillam has the details. No previous record. They'd had the tabs on him for five days, and the delegation was booked in for twelve more. Politically it was too hot for the local boys to handle but they reckoned a crash approach might do the trick. The yield didn't look that special but so what? Maybe we'd just buy him for stock, right. Mr Guillam?

Tinker, Tailor, Soldier, Spy
John le Carré

Very often a really good intelligence target is only available for a short space of time. This is particularly true of people who are travelling from a closed society such as scientists on academic visits to Europe from the Soviet Union during the Cold War. The intelligence officer has no choice but to try and make the recruitment pitch at the very first meeting. It's all or nothing. Hence the term 'crash approach'.

There is really only one way to do this, there is no time to muck around. The field officer has to remember that the profiling team wouldn't have selected this target unless they thought there was a chance he would accept, so the officer must simply lay all her cards on the table. She must tell the target where she is from and why she is talking to him. There is always the risk that the target will call his security services so the officer has to be prepared to leave the area quickly and there may well be a team nearby to help her make a quick exit.

She should very quickly get an idea of whether the target is going to listen. If the target agrees to consider the offer then he can be given details of a secret contact number which he can ring. The details can always be sorted out later.

Gangplank Approaches

This is a particular type of crash approach, used when the target will be leaving the country in the next few days or even hours. Usually a gangplank approach is used to secure a defection because the person would not be accessible in their home country. Your leverage is that they are leaving and they want to stay whether for political, economic or health reasons. The only advantage you have over a traditional crash approach is that it occurs in your own country so if the target isn't happy he simply leaves the country.

Walk-ins

A walk-in is someone who offers their services to your intelligence service without any kind of cultivation or recruitment. The most famous British walk-in was MI6 officer George Blake who simply offered his services to the Russians.

There is the concern that they are still working for the enemy. The main thing to do with any walk-in is to try and remove this suspicion and even if their services are accepted, they will be treated as a potential security risk until the relevant security branch considers that they have proved themselves. If a person does walk in to the embassy and offer their services it has to be asked how long it will be before he is missed by his own security people, what proof of his bona fides he can offer and whether there is a risk he will go back. A defector is far less use than an agent in place (see page 119) and they should be discouraged if at all possible. Even with those who want to defect it should be suggested that they will need to work as an agent for a short time before they can be offered that option. Only the most high-value personnel or those in considerable personal danger will be offered the option to defect straight away.

With these questions addressed, the station must form an opinion about the walk-in's emotional state and motivations. Is he stable mentally? He may be prepared to work for you today, but will he have changed his mind tomorrow? Why is he offering to do this? If it's for money, the chances are that he will be working for a higher bidder within a month or he will have stopped working altogether because he has the money he needs. The station will also copy all documentation which he is carrying. All of this must be put into an immediate report for experts at HQ to come to a decision. If necessary he can be granted safe haven at the embassy while a decision is made – he can always be thrown out later.

Double Agents

One of the greatest prizes in spying is to recruit an officer working for a hostile intelligence service – a double agent. Sometimes an officer will volunteer his services (a walk-in), sometimes they are the result of a careful profiling operation, but this kind of agent is also one of the most dangerous to run. You have to be sure that he really is offering to work for you and that this is not some kind of trap and that his nerve won't fail and he returns to working for his own side.

Knowing what the other side doesn't know is very useful. As soon as you start asking questions they will know where your intelligence about them is poor. They can also learn about your operational procedures and agent communications equipment. So before adding a double agent to your stable of assets, you have to be sure of the following:

1) Is He Telling the Truth?

Of course you can never be absolutely sure, but the thing to do is ask him at the first meeting for pieces of highly sensitive intelligence: names of department heads, identities of agents, details of technical operations being run in the area. Some of these should be checkable against intelligence you already hold. If he is reluctant to answer these questions then either he is deceiving you or his mind is not fully made up and he must be handled at arm's length until he changes his mind or proves his loyalty in some other way. Get as much information from him as quickly as possible. This is not as easy as it sounds, he will be cagey because he knows how the game is played and he will try to 'drip feed' you. Limit the exposure of your personnel, only use one or two, preferably blown officers for the interrogation.

2) Will His Nerve Hold?

It may be that he wants to defect, but he must be told that he first has to earn that chance. You then have to assess how long he will be prepared to stay in place in his organisation. If it will only be for a few weeks, then the operational planning team must design your requests during that period for maximum effect. In rare cases, particularly where agents have changed their allegiance for ideological reasons, it may be possible to convince them that they can do most good by staying in place (as was the case with George Blake).

3) What is His Motivation?

This is a key question. He is making the biggest change of his entire life. Why?

4) Does the Other Service Still Trust Him?

This is a difficult decision to make since, if you send him back and he is arrested because his service is suspicious, you will have thrown away a valuable asset for nothing. Therefore the majority of your questions must be directed at determining whether he still has the full confidence of his associates or whether he has decided to come over because he is under suspicion for his beliefs or activities. Often the decision to change sides will be made suddenly and the officer simply appears at your embassy or other cover location. If you are going to put him 'back in play' it is vital that he is missing for the shortest possible period of time. Where possible a counter-surveillance team should be sent to shadow him back to his workplace to see if his service is having him followed.

If the agent is not a 'walk-in' but has approached you whilst maintaining his cover then the job is easier. There will be more time to test him. It also suggests that his nerve is holding up well, although he may just be cautious and there is no substitute for the judgement of the field officer on the ground.

Defectors

Strictly speaking a defector is not an agent. With the exception of sleepers, an agent is an active asset who *remains in place* working against the target. As soon as a defector comes over to you his value starts decreasing as the other service work out what he knows and start taking defensive measures. A defector usually starts life as a walk-in. If you have a defector walk-in your first concern is to get him to go back. So the first question is: *can* they go back? This has to be done very quickly because once they think they have successfully defected even if it has only been a few hours, it is almost impossible to get them to return. The usual procedure is to tell him that before you can accept him as a defector, re-settle him in your country and give him all the advantages he is dreaming of, he must first go back and prove himself.

Sometimes however, you have to admit defeat and allow the defector to leave the country. Even if you can get them to go back, they tend not to make good agents. Some agencies even label them 'defectors-in-place' rather than fully-fledged agents.

But however you recruit your agent and whatever his access, the next stage is to run him without him being discovered.

6 The Psychology of Agent Recruitment: How to Win the Trust of a Stranger

Physical attractiveness is a far better recommendation than any letter of introduction.

Aristotle

To the uninitiated, winning someone's trust can seem like an innate ability – you've either got it or you haven't. But in fact the experience of spies over several hundred years has shown (and modern psychologists have confirmed) that winning trust can be made easier by employing certain tactics. There are quite a number of ruses a professional spy will use when trying to win a target's trust. They include obvious advantages such as common interests, attractiveness and apparent wealth. But there are other more subtle weapons: eye contact, body posture, proxemics (see page 134), humour, vocal tone, content of the message, anecdote. These are the real weapons of a spy because once you have truly won someone's trust you can get him to betray almost anything.

This may sound like psychobabble, but research indicates how influential these lesser signals can be. For instance one body of research compared the influence of the words in the message, the qualities of the voice delivering the message and body language such as facial expression and posture. It was found that body language accounts for almost sixty per cent of the impact of the message, the voice for thirty-five per cent and the actual words of the message as little as five per cent. Even more surprising is that when words conveyed one message but the body language was designed to convey another, test subjects relied on the body language every time. If you are failing to convince people at home or at work, it may be that these lesser signals are giving you away and you need to master them.

The Power Relationship

Both consciously and unconsciously, human beings are constantly comparing themselves with each other on what might be called the **'power ladder'**.

They weigh up the advantages and disadvantages we all have in terms of wealth, status, looks, influence with others, social skills, technical skills, morality and so forth and then compare this with what they see as their own value. Then they place themselves either higher or lower than others on the power ladder. Here is the rule:

No one ever allows themselves to be recruited by someone who they consider to be below them on the power ladder.

The power ladder is not easy to judge. It is not as though we were all born with numbers on our foreheads. The process is much more subtle than that. Part of the problem is that we all attach different values to different qualities – some of us will admire morality more than wealth, some of us warm more easily to those with high social skills, but discount those with high technical skills and so on.

So the rule that you can't be recruited by someone you don't respect isn't a simple one. Someone's position on the power ladder can come about in many ways.

For instance, the highly intelligent, but mild-mannered professor working on a secret chemical weapons project might respect the muscle-bound professional bodyguard who just happens to be passing and rescues him from a gang of vicious muggers. Engineering that situation for an officer might mark the beginnings of a recruitment.

Some of the ways we place people on the ladder may even seem illogical – we would tend to pick someone good-looking over someone who we thought ugly, but if the other person is *too* good looking, 'out of our league' as we might say, then, after the initial shock of meeting them has worn off, we are more likely to be

The best use of sex in agent recruitment

'Boris' was a senior Soviet army officer in his fifties. He liked to drink – a lot. He also liked the company of beautiful young women and was occasionally unfaithful to his rather frumpy middle-aged wife. However, it was clear to the French profiling team who thought they could recruit him that he was unlikely to leave her. He wasn't looking for a way out of the relationship, only a way to add some extra interest to his life. Reports from those who knew him indicated that he also saw himself as a knowledgeable man who felt that he should have more influence than he actually had. A man who was considering at some point in the future leaving the army and entering politics. From these points and a great deal of other information the targeting team came up with a plan: they decided that Boris was looking for a female friend whom he could admire, but not someone he thought he could use sexually as that would lead him to place her lower than him on the power ladder. So the targeting team chose a good-looking female officer under cover of being a senior adviser to a political think-tank. She was well connected and apparently wealthy. To allay his suspicions that this was some kind of honey trap, two things were important: first, although she was a tremendous flirt who didn't hold his occasional infidelities against him, she was happily married and therefore unattainable. The second point was that her area of political interest did not overlap with any of 'Boris's' responsibilities so it seemed unlikely that she was using him to get information.

An approach was engineered and a recruitment began. Although clearly wary, the army officer enjoyed the flirtatious relationship (although he didn't give up his relationships with other women). Gradually the cultivation advanced until the officer began to drop hints as to who she was really. When 'Boris' stayed in contact, the profiling team knew they were going to be successful.

uncomfortable than impressed by their friendship and they will have to work much harder to win our trust.

This brings us to the second rule:

There is unlikely to be trust between an agent and an officer if the agent feels the officer is *too far* above him on the power ladder.

This point was well illustrated in a recent television series in which managing directors of companies returned to the shop floor. Initially they were distrusted by their co-workers. It was only once they had been there for some time and the co-workers had seen that the directors were people like themselves that those barriers of distrust began to break down. The judgement of how to play this power relationship when trying to recruit an agent is the job of the targeting team. They will take all the information they can get about a target and try to work out how to place the field officer higher on the ladder – there could be a range of options: making the officer appear wealthy, giving the officer something which the target needs, making the officer appear generous, statesmanlike, professional – the range of options and combinations is almost endless.

Persuasion Strategies

'Give to Get'

Don't start a friendship by expecting something from the other person. The strongest relationships are all formed the other way round – one of the reasons children have such a strong bond to their parents is their parents' unconditional love for them and the fact that they provide all their food, warmth and clothing. When we start courting, we tend to approach the other person with a gift of some sort hence the old cliché of men turning up with chocolates and flowers. This has to be subtle because any gift from someone provokes the 'give back' response and if that response is provoked to someone outside our circle of friends we immediately question that response and ask ourselves whether it has been done deliberately. So it has to be done naturally and with good humour.

Rather than gifts, information or perhaps an introduction to a helpful contact, (who might well be another intelligence officer working on the operation) would be more subtle. In the series, Simon achieved a high mark in one exercise where he had to get a complete stranger to agree to a further meeting with him. His solution was to engage the man in conversation and, once they had established an acquaintance, to offer him a racing tip. It is part of Simon's skill that he made this sound convincing and worthwhile – it wouldn't work for everyone. But when interviewed later the target agreed that he probably would have met Simon again because he couldn't see what Simon expected to gain out of it, and so the offer had seemed genuinely friendly.

Praise

It is an old cliché: flattery will get you everywhere. The trouble is it's true. I once worked for a year with another officer who was known for his ability to charm almost anyone into working for him. I watched him closely and at first was horrified how nakedly he used this tactic. I thought that people must see through it. But they never did, or if they did they never seemed to mind and he was invariably able to persuade people to do what he wanted.

People like to feel important. Even when they feel that you are not being entirely sincere they often appreciate that you are making the effort. If you are trying to recruit an agent you want them to feel that they are successful and important people who can help to change things in their country. You don't want them to feel that you are talking down to them. But beware – if they have placed you lower on that ladder it can just look like toadying, so use flattery sensitively.

Consistency

Do what you say. Be punctual. Be reliable. Whether builder, diplomat or spy, people admire professionalism. You may be asking this person to risk their lives one day, so they have to know they can count on you absolutely. Paying attention to these points also tells the other person that they are someone you care about. Consistency and timeliness in your actions are two ways of reinforcing this belief.

Eating and Drinking

These are social activities which we tend to share (other than at purely formal occasions) with people we trust. To be able to share a meal with a target is a good sign: if you are eating with someone else then they are usually relaxing and revealing a little of their true self. If alcohol is added to the mix or even if you just get the target out for a drink, then so much the better. We are all well aware of the effect alcohol has on us, the only point to remember is to keep it under control. And this applies to them as well as you. If they become drunk and embarrass themselves that actually sets the relationship back. If they become drunk and don't care then that is also a bad sign because that person is unlikely to make a suitable agent. A spy wants the target to drink enough to lower his natural defences and speak honestly, but not so much that he goes off his head. For a spy, an evening spent with a drunken target is often just wasted time.

The Tools of Persuasion

Eye Contact

This is the one everyone knows. If we want to know the truth from adults we might ask them to 'look us in the eye'. Some people report being suspicious of someone because of their 'shifty eyes'. We often sense if someone is bored because of a vacant look which enters their eyes or because they start to look elsewhere.

Eye contact is one of the major ways in which we make an immediate assessment of another person and our social behaviour is designed to encourage the use of this tool: take the example of someone introducing two other people to each other for the first time. They will initially be face on, with the mediator standing to one side midway between them. He is encouraging them to make eye contact. Then, once he leaves, the two may move closer to hear each other but they will tend to either half turn or otherwise look away so that the incidence of eye contact is reduced.

But if you know how important eye contact can be and then overuse it, it can have the opposite effect and people can become uncomfortable – it begins to seem like a challenge, an attempt to dominate. Hypnotists stare at us to try and dominate our minds, a thug in the street will stare not even blinking as he challenges; 'What you looking at?'.

The general rule which spies adopt is to use plenty of eye contact but in long looks rather than quick, darting glances and to allow themselves moments to drop their gaze so that they do not appear to be trying to dominate or challenge. Some recruits found this a difficult skill to manage. Austin has a strong character and early in the course it was felt that his eye contact was too challenging. However, by trying to tone that down he then made too little and began to look shifty. It took considerable effort before he was able to get it right.

Facial Expression

This is also one of the more obvious ones, but it requires discipline and practice to use effectively. For instance, if a smile or a laugh is forced, people standing close to us can usually sense this – apparently it is a deeply embedded mammalian survival trait. The same is true of expressions of interest or friendship. It seems that when we try to fake these responses we often overdo the expression and the other person senses it. Keep your face mobile, use it expressively. This is interesting to the other person whereas a fixed expression generally communicates deceit or subterfuge. But again you have to be comfortable enough to do this deliberately and yet relax – studies have shown that just as people are very good at detecting overdone facial responses, they can also detect expressions which are fleeting or weak, as if caused by nervousness. So how can this be done? It seems that relaxation is the key. This should allow you to control your facial expressions without overdoing them through tension in the muscles. The good news is that a little alcohol (for both them and you) may actually help!

Use of Hands

Hands are best employed when telling a story or emphasising a point. Gestures make your speech more dramatic and easier to follow. When the other person is talking, keep your hands still and preferably out of sight as this indicates trust. This can also be used to lessen the effect of stature. A shorter person who wishes to emphasise their points generally needs to make greater use of gesture than a much taller person would. Above all try and relax – people who are nervous tend to freeze and not use their hands at all.

Knowing when to use touch also requires fine judgement. Touch should be restricted to a neutral area such as an arm or shoulder. If you want to mark a handshake as especially hearty don't grip more tightly, instead place your other hand on the clasped hand whilst smiling, making eye contact and saying something appropriate. This is generally unusual enough without being threatening for the other person to make a particular note of the gesture. But again don't maintain the clasp for too long or it appears insincere.

Again, touch is strongly affected by differences in culture and gender. Some cultures, such as the Mediterranean, are very tactile, but others, some Asian countries for example, frown upon any sort of uninvited physical contact.

Body Posture

Here are some brief examples of how body language betrays thought:

- Leaning forward indicates interest.
- Hands in pockets can indicate trust or, sometimes, boredom.
- Arms folded indicates defensiveness.
- Hands in front of or touching the face can mean anxiety and can also mean lying.
- Supporting the head on the hand indicates lack of interest in what is being said.
- Tapping or swaying feet indicates boredom or a desire to move on.

There are hundreds of examples and different ways of interpretation. Body language is almost a science in itself, far too long and complex to discuss in a book like this. The point is that whether you buy a book on the subject or just start observing others more carefully, you need to take the time to study this aspect of non-verbal communication if you are going to consistently win the trust of others. And remember it is important not just to use it to influence others, but also to interpret what others are unconsciously telling you. On the course, both Jennie and Max were playing the

Even a small show of trust can be the start of a successful agent recruitment. Reena gets a complete stranger to accept the envelope during the 'Do Me a Favour' exercise.

Dr John Potter explains to the recruits the surprising amount of detail which needs to be both observed and controlled when properly using body language as a recruitment tool.

roles of sports photographers and were quizzed by a genuine professional photographer. Both recruits had the same preparation, but during the interview Jennie stood facing the interviewer with an open expression, frequently leaning forward as she explained various points. This communicated enthusiasm and commitment and she passed the exercise. On the other hand, Max stood at an angle to the interviewer, frequently looking away and maintaining an upright stance. The interviewer wasn't taken in at all. Body language had made all the difference.

Use of Voice

There are a number of principles which can be applied to the use of your voice to ensure that it does not undermine your skills of persuasion. We are not all blessed with the rich tones of Richard Burton, but everyone can improve their delivery. As Prime Minister, Margaret Thatcher famously lowered the tone of her voice to sound more sincere and authoritative.

- **Speed**: Generally agreed to be the most important point about vocal delivery. Speaking too quickly implies that you are uncomfortable, trying to impress or that you lack control of the situation. In any pressure situation, it is the voice which speaks calmly which will draw attention as people will be looking for reassurance and assume that the person with the calm voice can give it. A meeting with a spy is certainly a high-pressure situation. Adjust your voice accordingly.
- **Tone**: In general, lower tones sound more authoritative because as children we learn to obey the deeper voices of adults, particularly fathers. Your voice should be soft, yet forceful enough to be heard clearly. Vary the pitch of your voice at least a little as you are talking to emphasise certain points – it simply makes your voice more interesting to listen to and you are more likely to hold the target's attention.
- **Regional accents**: Far from being a drawback these can work to your advantage. On the training course, one of the strongest recruits in social situations was Simon. The Irish lilt in his voice was very easy on the ear and the same can be true of several other accents such as French or Scottish. Even 'rapid' languages such as Italian can sound musical. So

don't worry if you don't speak received pronunciation English, it might work to your advantage provided the other principles such as speed, tone and clarity are observed.

- **Verbals tics**: Avoid 'um', 'er', 'ya?', 'you know' and all those other little bits of verbal polyfilla which we all casually use. They undermine the sense of control which you are trying to establish. People associate authority with short, clearly phrased sentences. If may seem unimportant, but every small point you can use to establish yourself as a figure of authority means that it is more likely that your recruitment will be successful.

Appearance

Your clothes are part of the unconscious communication of your position on the power ladder although different people will interpret appearance differently. For instance, most upper- and middle-class social groups appreciate a smart, but sober look, whereas other social groups may associate trust and authority with a different look. Consider an MI5 officer trying to recruit someone from a group of eco-warriors or fascists. So the most important point to remember is not that you have to make your dress smart, but that it should be appropriate to the environment and the occasion.

The situation is slightly more complicated for **female officers**. In films, female secret agents often dress to show the maximum amount of cleavage and leg. In reality, research has shown that women whose dress sends clear sexual signals may find it easy to talk to others, but they are unlikely to be trusted by them – men as well as women. Studies also show that men are unlikely to approach women who dress too masculine. The guide would seem to be that dress for women must be feminine, but not so flirty that it provokes the wrong response. All the trainers on the course agreed that Suzi's performance improved markedly when she adopted a smarter appearance. Austin, too, could adopt a variety of looks. When turned out in a smart suit he conveyed far more authority and confidence and it often directly improved his performance.

Colour can also be important. The evidence that is available indicates that bright colours overused in dress undermine trust. A dash of colour such as a tie, or belt can be seen as individualism, but not more than that. Authority and trust seem to be represented by sombre colours such as blacks and grey. Research shows that greens, reds and oranges are the colours least associated with trustworthiness. It goes even further than this: it may be that success is connected with our choice of colours. When it came to choice of car colours, successful people tended to favour darker colours although often in metallic paint finishes such as silver rather than grey. Is there any truth in it? Some psychologists seem to think so and a good spy will use any edge he can get.

What if you weren't born with the looks of Pierce Brosnan or Halle Berry? Is there any hope? Well, while we may have a high regard for physical beauty, experiments by psychologists show that we choose to interact with those who we think are as generally attractive as ourselves. We tend to look down on those less attractive and to be distrustful of those who we regard as more attractive. Trust is really a matter of both parties feeling comfortable in a relationship and that is unlikely to happen if one of you is constantly measuring himself with the other person and feeling inadequate. Of course, part of feeling attractive is how other people make you feel and a good recruiter will always make his agents feel that they are talented, courageous and valuable in various ways. Where the officer is much more attractive than the agent this helps the agent to see themselves as lifted into the same attractiveness bracket. And if you are not naturally blessed with good looks or a fantastic figure then things which are in your control such as cleanliness, smartness in dress, strength of character and humour can make up for it. If the target is someone who rates physical beauty to such an extreme that it becomes a problem, then the chances are they are not agent material anyway.

Hairstyle is another factor which will affect success. As with our general appearance, hair immediately makes a statement about who we are and how we lead our lives. Several of the recruits were asked to change their hairstyles once the course had started and it had a marked effect on reading other people's reactions. The most notable case was Suzi who was given a much more controlled cut and everyone agreed that there was an immediate improvement not only in the first impression she made but also in the authority she seemed to have. So a smart, conservative cut would seem to be the best as it implies control and consistency, but as with all these points you must bear in mind who you are trying to recruit.

Height is yet another factor to consider. Once again it is something derived from childhood, but we tend to associate height with authority. Tall people must take care not to loom over the target as this can seem intimidating and wherever possible they should try to interact with the target in a relaxed, preferably seated environment. Short people have the opposite problem. They must enhance their authority. When talking they should make greater use of hand gestures and facial expression to communicate energy and dynamism. Anything which emphasises wealth may also help – expensive clothes or cars and settings which emphasise their achievements, such as sport, or a cultural setting. Simon was one of the shortest of the recruits yet his lively manner, enthusiasm and expressive use of gestures more than compensated for it. His 'gift of the gab' would have made him an excellent agent runner.

Anecdote and Humour

Consider the impact of these two approaches:

If you tell someone that 40 million children in Africa are dying of AIDS people's reaction tends to be: it's sad, but so what?

But if you tell them that you recently visited an AIDS hospital in Kenya and met John, an eight-year-old boy whose parents had died of the disease and who was responsible for feeding his two younger sisters aged six and four, that they are living in the streets because they have nowhere else to go and you are trying to raise money to help them, you may well get a different response.

Human beings like listening to stories. The story has got to be relevant, it mustn't be too long and it has to be interesting. There is an art to telling them, but it's no good just saying that you aren't any good at it. Start making a note whenever you hear a good story – either someone else's anecdote or something which crops up in the news – once you start looking for them you'll be amazed how many there are. Then start using them in conversation whenever you get the chance. Recounting stories really is one area where practice helps.

The same rules apply to jokes, which are really just short stories although the technique for telling them may be different. Once again start making a note of good jokes you hear and practise telling them. You *will* get better with practice. You just have to be prepared for one or two to fall flat before you discover a timing and delivery which works for you.

However, a spy has to bear in mind that it is notoriously difficult to judge between cultures. What one person finds daring and hilarious another person might find crude and offensive. A spy will always be looking to understand this difference. Gender jokes, jokes about how stupid officials can be and jokes about sport seem to carry over well in most cultures. Just stay off the risqué material until you know your target really well!

Gifts

We all like to receive gifts, especially if it is something we want and we consider the action appropriate. But we are equally sensitive to the inappropriate use of gifts. So although this is a useful tool the timing requires careful consideration. It used to be said that KGB officers were easy to spot if they were trying to recruit you because whereas most Soviet diplomats were strapped for cash and milking their postings for all they were worth, KGB officers under diplomatic cover were only too eager to present you with gifts if they thought you showed any promise at all.

A good example of the appropriate use of a gift was shown by two of the recruits during the course. Gabriel and Jennie had to convince a sports centre receptionist to cover for them whilst they supposedly had an illicit night out (Jennie had told the receptionist that she was married to another, abusive, man). The receptionist accepted Jennie's mobile phone and did cover for her when her 'husband' rang. Afterwards, Gabriel bought her some flowers. This was exactly the right time to buy her a gift. Before would have made it seem as if they were 'paying' the receptionist for covering her. By giving the present afterwards, it makes it clear that the receptionist acted through her own free will but makes her feel part of the conspiracy. Gifts should be used to confirm stages in the friendship, not as a way of reaching them. If a spy finds themselves doing the latter, the chances are that they will end up with an agent whose main interest in the relationship is what they can get out of it.

Proxemics

Physical distance is important in human communication. If someone stands too far away they can seem unfriendly or suspicious. If they stand too close they can seem threatening or insensitive. Of course, eye contact, facial expression, body language and vocal tone are important as well. But sensitivity to distance is an important part of the equation which is often overlooked.

The term 'proxemics' was coined by researcher Edward Hall in the 1960s. Essentially it concerns the use of space and how various differences in our immediate environment affect our behaviour. Proxemics divides space into four zones:

- Intimate (less than one foot).
- Personal (2 to 4 feet).
- Social (4 to 10 feet) – the distance at bus stops.
- Public (12 to 25 feet) – the distance for a speech.

Although these definitions remain broadly constant from society to society, the way they are used can vary. Thus in Japan, business dealings are often held at a distance amounting to social space. In the Middle East, business is conducted in much closer proximity, almost at a distance which invades personal space and which Europeans can find threatening. In fact Semitic, Mediterranean and Latin American are known as 'the contact cultures' because they tend to use touch more frequently and conduct their business at much closer distances than North Europeans. Sexual differences can play a part as well. In European societies men generally prefer women to stand closer to them than they would if the same person were another man. In some Asiatic cultures a female standing closer to a male can still seem inappropriate and can have the opposite effect. A good spy will be sensitive to all these slight but absolutely crucial differences.

Position is as important as distance. For instance if you sit next to someone it is possible to lean that much closer without them feeling threatened because the incidence of eye contact is reduced and they do not feel they are being confronted. Height is also a consideration. A manager delivering a rebuke will frequently stand over the desk of a subordinate echoing the height of a parent over a child. Another frequently cited tactic is placing a subordinate in a chair lower than yours so that subconsciously they will feel intimidated.

Objects also play a part. When we are in an office a desk marks a territorial boundary. If people lean on that desk or come round to the other side of it, we can feel intimidated as this side of the desk is our 'territory'. Wherever possible a spy will choose places without these encumbrances, as any item placed between him and the target makes it harder to break down the target's caution.

Another consideration is the **view** someone has of us. If we are face to face with them then they can see all the signals coming from our posture, our face and our distance. If you know how to manage these elements this can make your message more convincing. If you sit alongside someone, they will hear your voice, but only occasionally glance at your face and you have no control over distance. This allows the listener to hear your message without seeing any other signals. The chances are that they are less likely to be convinced by what you are saying. Consider this from the point of view of sitting in a small circle of people. The person you are likely to have most interaction with is the person sitting opposite you because you can see all of them all the time, allowing your brain subconsciously to note these body signals.

Once you start to examine this subject it can seem vast. There are not only differences between cultures, but also between racial groups within those cultures. For a spy this is a lifelong study.

Conclusion

When the methods of winning trust are broken down into their constituent parts like this, it can seem deceptively simple. Like explaining a magic trick, once you know how it is done, it seems so easy that it is almost a disappointment. But knowing how it is done and being able to perform it smoothly are two completely different things.

There are many academic books on the subject which go into far more detail than this on all these aspects of unconscious communication and winning trust – you'll find some of them listed at the back of this book. This is just a general introduction to the field to give an idea of the sort of factors which a spy thinks of when dealing with other people. It can all seem bewildering at first – there are so many elements to remember that it is hard to believe that anyone can observe all these different points and still appear relaxed and natural. But, as with any of the skills of a spy, it really is a matter of practice. These points need to be used again and again, until you apply them almost without thinking. Start simply: when you meet other people, act as you would normally, but try adding one or two of these elements to see if they have any effect. Another time try some different elements. You will soon find the moves which are right for you.

7 Agent Running

*He who is not sage and wise, humane and just, cannot use spies.
And he who is not delicate and subtle cannot get the truth out of
them.*

The Art of War
Sun Tzu

The Next Stage

Once you have recruited your agent, the next problem is how to
direct and control him.

At HQ, the agent's file will be passed from the profiling department
to the department responsible for that area. Just as the profiling team
comprised specialists so will the team responsible for running agents in
the area. This is a high-level job often staffed by long-serving officers
with a wealth of experience who are now too 'hot' to be of much use in
the field. As soon as the agent is passed to their control they will consider
how the agent is to be run and will ask themselves two questions:

1. Should the agent be run by the local station or by an HQ department?

The first consideration is, who recruited the agent? If the recruitment was by someone from the local station then it is better to
maintain that relationship. If it was by a visiting officer (such as in a
crash approach), then the options are wider.

2. What kind of contact should there be with the agent?

Wherever possible, a face to face meeting with another human
being is the ideal. But in the hardest of operating environments or
where agents are working in the highly sensitive posts (such as a

scientist working on secret weapons projects), such a meeting may be out of the question. In those cases the agent must be run remotely through secret communications.

Depending on the country, there are a range of factors to consider, but a good intelligence service will keep sight of one important point: **the agent is doing a very courageous thing. They need every bit of support, protection and training the service can give them. Their security is paramount**.

However the agent is run, the arrangement chosen will be selected to achieve this.

Sir Francis Walsingham (1532–1590)

Walsingham is generally regarded as the first identifiable chief of a British intelligence service. England was under threat from the Armada and the Catholic powers who wished to overturn the Reformation. To counter this Walsingham had to run spy networks both at home and overseas.

He was trained in law at King's College, Cambridge and travelled to Italy to complete his studies where he became an accomplished linguist. He remained abroad as an exile during the reign of the Catholic Queen Mary. He worked as a diplomat, acting as ambassador to France and helping to negotiate the Treaty of Blois in 1572. In 1573 he became the Secretary of State succeeding his mentor Lord Burghley. It was from this position that he controlled England's intelligence efforts. We know the size of his intelligence network from documents which survive to this day. At one stage it comprised fifty-three 'agents at foreign Courts' plus eighteen special operatives whose function is unclear. It was said of Walsingham that he had 'spies in every Court and in half the mercantile communities of Europe'.

His agents uncovered the Babington Plot in 1586 in which coded messages smuggled in wine casks were intercepted. These implicated Mary Queen of Scots, the leading Catholic contender for the English throne, in a plot to murder Elizabeth and led to her execution in 1587. His intelligence network was so effective that in 1587 he

cont'd

---

obtained precise details of all the men, ships and supplies in the Spanish navy which led him to conclude that the Armada would not sail until the following year. This allowed valuable time to build up the English navy and told them exactly what they would be facing. In the same year his spies obtained intelligence on the disposition of Spanish defences at Cadiz allowing Drake to carry out his famous naval attack which 'singed the King of Spain's beard'.

Walsingham used a range of resources which modern spies would recognise today:

Sigint: Operatives such as Thomas Phelippes. He was Walsingham's leading codebreaker and broke the cipher which revealed the Babington Plot. His team could forge signatures and letters, break ciphers and open and re-seal diplomatic correspondence without detection.

Double agents: Agents such as Charles Paget, supposedly secretary to the Scottish ambassador to France, in fact working for Walsingham. A number of people involved in the Babington Plot were also double agents.

Field agents: Such as Antony Standen. He was an Englishman based in Italy but operating under the alias Pompeo Pellegrini. He provided much of Walsingham's naval intelligence and was paid £100 a year, a considerable sum. Christopher Marlowe may have been another of Walsingham's agents.

Black Ops: There is some evidence that Mary Queen of Scots was framed and that the Babington Plot was not all that it seemed. It certainly led to her execution, which was very convenient.

Walsingham was a model spymaster. He helped to avert a threat to England which was as great as that posed by the Nazis in 1940. He was never ostentatious in either his habits or his dress and after a lifetime of faithful service he died without a penny to his name.

Agent Meetings

Meeting Rules

Agent meetings can be private or public, fast or slow. But wherever the meeting is held there is a certain order which should be followed:

- **Arrange the next meeting.** You never know if this meeting will have to be suddenly broken off for some reason. So you must arrange the time and place of the next meeting first.
- **Take a few moments to assess the agent's state of mind.** Is he confident, fearful, happy, sad? You should never forget that this is a frightening thing the agent is doing. A few moments of reassurance, to establish human contact, is always valuable and may give you important clues about how the agent is reacting.
- **Debrief the agent.** The intelligence is, above all, what you have come for.
- **Task the agent.** Give the agent his next mission.

Security

Wherever possible the agent and his handler should have contact of some sort before the meeting even if it is only to pass in the street. This will allow the agent to give a pre-arranged emergency signal which would indicate that something is wrong and that the meeting should be called off.

In hard operating areas there should be some sort of lookout who can give an alarm if the meeting place is approached by security forces.

Emergency Drills and Fallbacks

Despite your best efforts you might not be able to make it to the meeting on time. This doesn't look good as it affects your image of reliability, but it will happen sooner or later. Rather than have to set up a completely new meeting, spies try to arrange a **fallback**, whereby if the officer isn't on time for the meeting the agent simply goes away and returns, for instance, half an hour later. This second meeting should preferably be at a different location because returning to the same place might make others suspicious.

An **emergency drill** is a procedure which an agent will follow if he is compromised and has a chance to escape. It will normally consist of a way of signalling to the service that he is in trouble (such as a telephone call to a certain address) together with the address of a safe place where he can wait until he is picked up. Neither of these steps should involve other agents as he may already be working for, or being monitored by, the enemy.

Agent Morale and Welfare

Books and films often give the impression that intelligence officers look down on their agents and simply use them. Nothing could be further from the truth. The agent is doing a very dangerous and difficult thing, and no one appreciates that more than the intelligence officer because she knows what it feels like to do that work. The relationship between an officer and her agent is like a close friendship, but one in which she knows that one day she may have to send the other person into danger. She is able to live with that thought because she would only do it if the possible outcome was worth the risk, such as the saving of many lives or the capture of a major terrorist. At the end of the day the field officer is the person on the spot – she decides whether or not to send the agent on the mission, regardless of what her HQ may order. After all, she can simply say that the agent refused or that there was a technical problem and no one can disprove it.

At every meeting the officer will be closely monitoring the agent to see how he is feeling, what he needs and whether he is having any doubts about the work.

Rewarding Agents

There are five principal ways of rewarding an agent:

- **Mutual interest**. For political, religious or personal reasons the agent may share the desire to see a particular enemy or regime defeated. This is the best motivation of all because it is cheap and yet highly reliable. Reward in this case consists of keeping the agent closely apprised of the contribution his work is making and possibly even presenting a letter of thanks from a senior political figure (although obviously the agent would not be allowed to retain this).

- **Money**. The most difficult one to handle. Agents always think their information is worth more than it actually is and with many of them, meetings can turn into a series of frustrating bargaining encounters. It takes a good officer to handle this side of the relationship and yet stay on good personal terms with the agent.
- **Information**. Sometimes the agent is given information or even low-level intelligence which will assist his business, personal or political interests. This has to be handled delicately so that every piece is 'deniable' if the agent suddenly turns on you.
- **Resettlement**. Some agents are effectively 'working their passage'. Rather than being paid large sums of money they are working for a chance to leave their country and be resettled abroad with a house and income. Many intelligence services prefer this to a straight money relationship as the agent has to perform before he gets the reward.
- **Sex**. Everyone always assumes that prostitutes and other sexual favours are used far more than they actually are. It is really just another form of greed rather like paying the agent money and the agent being rewarded will almost never prove reliable. Most Western services avoid it.

Danger Signs

Every agent meeting has a security element. Although there will be a security officer at HQ whose job is to review the case, the first indication of any trouble should be detected by the field officer. These are the most common signs of trouble:

- **An agent who suddenly has access to a new area of intelligence**. This could indicate that he has been turned and the enemy are using him to pass false information.
- **The agent experiences a sudden increase or decrease in confidence**.

- **Changes in the agent's physical behaviour.** Change in the use of eye contact, sweating, fidgeting with his hands – anything which is out of the ordinary for that particular agent.
- **He starts asking lots of questions about you or other officers.** An officer should be friendly, but always guarded. If anything he will give the agent false information rather than sharing confidences with him because any agent could be turned at any time.
- **He wants to take you to meet another possible agent or some new location.** The new friend could be an enemy officer and the new location might be a trap or be bugged.

What if the Agent Won't Do what He's Told?

Rather like using sex as a reward, people assume that spies are much more ruthless with their agents than they actually are. Obviously each officer decides how to handle his agents and develops a style he feels comfortable with, but all officers know that browbeating an agent is only likely to produce a negative response. All agents are bound to experience failures of nerve at some stage. If you've tried all reasonable means of persuasion and he still won't take the mission then he won't. A good officer will go away and find another way to get the job done (or send the problem back to HQ for someone else to solve!). Then he will work on restoring the agent's commitment or confidence, whatever the weakness is, before returning him to active duty. As far as Western services are concerned, tales of blackmail or the threat of exposure to the authorities are the stuff of bad spy novels.

Secret Communication

Secret communication with the agent is vital. Even if you have face to face meetings there will still be a need for communications in case of an emergency such as the agent being discovered and going on the run. There are now a variety of electronic devices available to intelligence services. Just as the computer chip has revolutionised work in the office, it has completely changed agent communications. An agent can type a report into what appears to be an ordinary laptop, press a button and the report will be encrypted, compressed and then beamed across town to a receiving station in a matter of seconds.

But many intelligence services do not have either the funds or the technology for this level of equipment. This is also true of the various terrorist groups operating around the world. They resort to the old tried and trusted methods that Western services were using at the height of the Cold War. One of the reasons the West finds it so hard to combat these groups is their lack of practice in these old methods, which is why these were the methods taught on the *Spy* training course. They work, they are still in use and if we are to beat the terrorists among us perhaps we need to be reminded of them.

The following are the arrangements for the meeting of a Swedish naval spy who was working for the KGB and whose recruitment we examined in Chapter 5:

All meetings were to be at 8 p.m. The day would be signalled in apparently innocuous graffiti on a particular wall – T would mean Monday, W Tuesday etc. If a meeting ever failed it would be held again exactly two weeks later at a particular place near Karolinska Hospital. In case the usual KGB handler could not attend and a substitute had to be sent, Andersson had to make sure he was recognisable by carrying a briefcase, lock side out in his right hand with a roll of paper sticking up out of it. For mutual recognition there were four key words, two for each side, which had to be included in the opening lines of the conversation. If Andersson had his left hand in his pocket, that was a danger signal that the meeting should not go ahead for some reason.

The point to remember with all secret methods of agent communication is that he will require **training**.

Brush Contacts

A brush contact is: **a momentary meeting between the intelligence officer and his agent, usually in public, but so brief that to all but the most careful observers it will go unnoticed.**

Usually a small package or envelope will be passed from hand to hand and, in rare instances such as where there is equipment, an identical holdall or briefcase may be exchanged. However this is risky since most surveillance teams will become alerted once a target starts carrying items around – especially if that is not their usual practice.

There are several advantages of a brush contact as a way of meeting the agent:

- **Security**. There is very little connection between you and the agent.
- **Directness**. You give the briefing material or equipment directly to the agent. There is no question of it being intercepted.
- **Exchange**. It allows the spy and the agent to exchange material at one quick meeting.

However there are also many disadvantages:

- **Stress** on the agent. This can be extreme. The agent will be nervous enough as it is. For a brush contact he must meet a foreign agent, exactly on time and openly pass or receive material in a public place. This will strain the nerves of even the toughest of agents and it is a rare bird indeed that will stand this sort of stress for long. Whenever possible you must get access to the agent for longer meetings (such as when he travels abroad) so that you can welfare, reward and praise the agent to restore their morale.
- **Contact**. It brings you and the agent into close proximity. If one of you is under surveillance then the very presence of the two of you in the same area could lead to compromise by a sharp surveillance team.
- **Material**. If you are challenged, one or both of you is likely to have incriminating material on you. There is no getting away with it. Wherever possible briefing material will be conveyed by secret or encoded writing hidden on something innocuous, but this is not always possible.

These are the requirements of a good brush contact:

- **Timing**. This is vital. Since you and the agent will meet only for a few seconds, the place you choose and the routes to it must allow the meeting to be timed *to the second*.
- **Anti-surveillance**. Brush contacts are usually performed under the toughest of operating conditions. Either one or both of you is likely to be under surveillance and even if surveillance is not expected, it is safest to assume that it is there – one day you will be right! The handover must be done in such a way that even though the surveillance team may know exactly where you are, the actual handover is not seen or even suspected.
- **Route**. Ideally both you and the agent should approach and leave the brush contact point by different routes, so that the amount of time you are both in the same area is reduced to the minimum.
- **Counter-surveillance**. The field officer will be taking counter-surveillance measures as a matter of course, but wherever possible back-up should be provided for the agent. Ideally he will be given a counter-surveillance route to follow which will allow the support team to 'clear his coat tails'.
- **Recognition signals**. It is easiest if the agent has met the handler before and recognises him by sight. But this is rarely the case and there may be a reason why the regular handler can't attend. So the brush contact has to be set up so that handler and agent make visual communication first and that it is acknowledged in a non-verbal way. Sometimes a danger signal may be included (e.g. hand in pocket means I think I am under surveillance so the contact is cancelled) but for many agents this usually just confuses matters.

Sounds pretty impossible, but it can be done. Take this example from the movie *Ronin*, starring Robert de Niro:

An agent and a handler have a brush contact in a crowded underground station. The agent arrives by train. Her handler is waiting at the exit from the platform. He is holding a large street map of the city unfolded in front of him as recognition signal. The agent passes the handler and proceeds up the stairs. The handler then follows her up the staircase and makes his way through the crowd until he is walking alongside her. A few words and a small package are exchanged. Then the handler continues to make his way through the crowd leaving the agent behind. The contact lasts only seventeen seconds.

Consider why this is so effective:

- There is good **cover** for the exchange – a crowded tube station making the exchange public yet very unlikely to be seen.
- **Time** – recognition is made and the agent proceeds up the stairs. The handler has control and can then time the exact moment to overtake the agent as they proceed up the stairs. The agent has to do as little as possible.
- There is a **good reason** for both the agent and the handler to be in the location – travel between two places. These two people might easily be going to completely different areas and it is very unlikely that their momentary proximity would be noticed.
- **Usability** – you could probably use this meeting again and again with a little care (although you might vary which underground station is used). This is good because the agent's confidence will grow the more the contact is repeated.

All the recruits carried out brush contacts; few were successful. Reena arrived on time for her meeting but headed straight for the ticket machine where the brush was to take place. The agent was a few minutes late. Reena was left standing suspiciously by the machine and this was enough for a surveillance team to spot her. Jennie, on the other hand, was a few minutes too late. In fact her contact was still there, but Jennie was so flustered that she didn't spot the recognition signal and missed the contact. That's how difficult a brush contact is.

Brush contacts are very popular for use in films and spy novels. They are in fact hardly ever used by Western intelligence services these days. With the arrival of modern miniaturised communications and computers it is now possible to provide the agent with a small electronic device about the size of a packet of cigarettes. The agent types up his report on a computer and downloads it to the box.

147

The handler will have a similar device. All the agent needs to do is to be at a certain location at a certain time, hit a button on the box and in less than a second the entire document is transmitted to the handler.

However **terrorists** and other intelligence services will make use of brush contacts and Western surveillance teams have to be trained to detect them.

Dead Letter Box

A **dead letter box** or DLB is: **a concealed space or container where items can be left for collection by an agent or where an agent can leave material for an officer to collect.**

They are also referred to as **Dead Drops**, a CIA term. They are beloved of spy filmmakers everywhere and, unlike brush contacts, are still used by all intelligence services today.

Requirements of a good DLB are:

- **Concealment.** This doesn't necessarily mean it has to be out of sight, it just mustn't arouse suspicion.
- **Accessibility.** This means more than it just not being ten feet off the ground. There must be a natural reason why the agent would pass in close proximity to the location of the DLB otherwise a surveillance team will know something is up.
- **Disturbance.** It must be disguised in such a way that it isn't going to arouse the curiosity of adults, children or animals. So no sweet boxes or discarded video tapes and if tin cans are being used they need to be thoroughly cleaned out to discourage dogs, foxes, drug-crazed squirrels etc.
- **Size.** They need to be at least the size of an empty tin can and the bigger the better, since equipment or a large bundle of documents may need to be passed at some stage.
- **Empty and fill signals.** It is not enough just to pick the site of the DLB. You must also select a site where a signal can be left for the agent to let him know that there is something to collect. The most common way is some piece of innocuous graffiti at some place he can observe on his usual route. The

The empty and fill signals are an essential part of the DLB (dead letter box) process. This chalk signal on the back of a telephone junction box left by the agent lets his handler know that there is material at the DLB site awaiting collection.

An ideal DLB should be capable of being emptied and filled without attracting attention. This female agent was able to collect her instructions, which were taped beneath the table, without watching recruits managing to spot what had happened.

empty signal lets the handler know that the material was successfully collected without the handler having to return to the DLB site. Ideally the empty/fill signals should be separate and nowhere near the DLB site. In some scenarios, ready to fill/ready to empty signals are also used to ensure that material is not left in the DLB for too long thereby risking compromise.

Advantages and Disadvantages of a DLB:

DLBs have the advantage of the handler and agent never meeting, giving extra security. It is also less stressful for the agent than a brush contact, as they can go in their own time, satisfied they are not under surveillance. On the other hand, it is possible for the DLB to be found and intercepted. More worryingly, it is difficult to provide counter-surveillance back-up for the agent. Several agents, such as CIA traitor Aldrich Ames, have been arrested at DLB sites in recent years.

The key to selecting a good DLB is **observing your surroundings** and then **using your imagination**. Try not to copy ideas that have been used before if you can help it – professional surveillance teams make a point of knowing as many types of DLB as possible.

Woodland is good. It's hard to keep people constantly under observation during a walk in the woods and it is easier to spot or foil surveillance especially if (for instance) you regularly take the dog for a walk there or go jogging. The woods are full of rubbish and empty tin cans are useful as they have distinctive labels. An apparently discarded beer can securely wedged in a fairly concealed place will do.

On the other hand, urban areas with their twisting alleyways, crowded shopping streets with odd niches in forgotten parts of buildings are also fertile ground as DLB sites. On the course the recruits were given only a few hours to find a site near their flats in London. All but Simon managed to find somewhere. None of them were excellent (for a truly excellent site see the Gordievsky example below), but they give a good idea of the sort of places which can be used:

Max: A hole at ground level in a wooden fence next to a wall.

Gabriel: The space between a wall and a telephone box in an alleyway which was not overlooked.

Austin: The space behind some loose metal sheeting and the wall to which it was fixed.

Jennie: Inside an old seat cushion at the back of a pile of refuse behind a block of flats.

Nicola: Under some bushes at the end of a blind alley.

Reena: Just beneath the surface of the soil at the base of a particular tree.

Descriptions of a DLB must be exact and because they have to be almost undetectable this can be quite a complicated operation in itself. The following is a description of a DLB at a certain address written by a famous spy, Oleg Penkovsky, for his handlers:

In the entrance foyer of the building, to the left upon entering, is a telephone booth, number 28. Opposite the booth is a radiator, painted dark green in colour. The radiator is supported by a single metal bracket fastening it to the wall. If one stands facing the radiator, then the metal bracket will be slightly to the right at about the height of a man's hand hanging from the arm. Between the wall and the radiator is a small gap of about two or three centimetres. The dead letter box will use this gap with the package being hung from the bracket between the wall and the radiator.

Ultimately Penkovsky's great care didn't save him. He was caught, tortured and shot.

Because of the risk of discovery or, even worse, interception, it is important to reduce the amount of **time** that the DLB remains filled as much as possible. One way to do this would be to have the agent check the filled signal site at a particular time each week. Knowing this the officer will fill the DLB as little as a few minutes before the agent sees the signal. She could then immediately go to the site and empty it. But the agent mustn't feel there is so much pressure on her to move quickly that she neglects her usual checks for surveillance.

Historical examples of dead letter boxes

1) Dead letter boxes have been used almost since the spying game began. In the 1580s Mary Queen of Scots was being held prisoner at Fotheringhay Castle and needed a way to send messages to conspirators hoping to free her and start a rebellion. The messages were passed by wrapping them in a waterproof covering and then placing them inside barrels of beer which were taken to and from the castle once a week. The appropriate barrel would be marked with chalk and was opened by the conspirators when they arrived back at the brewers. The system would have worked had not Sir Francis Walsingham managed to turn one of Mary's agents. From then on the messages were intercepted by Walsingham's men whilst the barrels were awaiting collection, copied and decoded. This case also illustrates one of the great weaknesses of DLBs – Mary never realised that her messages were being read and the evidence gathered by Walsingham was enough to have her executed.

2) This is a DLB attributed to the famous spy Oleg Gordievsky, a KGB officer based in London who was in fact spying for MI6 during the 1970s and '80s. As head of the KGB in the UK, he was kept under constant check by A4, the specialist surveillance department of MI5. They had a feeling that there was something suspicious about an alleyway he often used as a shortcut. It had a slight right left turn in it where it went around an old plane tree which meant that – for just a few seconds – he was out of sight of surveillance officers from both the front and the back. There were houses overlooking the alleyway and A4 established a static observation post (OP) in one of these to monitor Gordievsky. However, the OP reported that Gordievsky didn't even break stride as he passed by.

Later, after Gordievsky had defected, he was able to tell the surveillance experts what had really been happening: he had been filling a DLB. At the base of the tree was a large amount of builders' rubble, mainly broken bricks left

cont'd

over from when the surrounding houses had been constructed. The DLB was a specially designed broken brick which was in fact hollow. It was marked so that the person emptying it could spot it easily from the others at the base of the tree. All Gordievsky had to do was drop the brick on the pile as he walked past. The OP couldn't see this because the fence along the side of the alleyway was shoulder high whilst surveillance officers in front and behind were also unsighted. It was an example of perfect anti-surveillance – the team could see him all the time, but didn't have a clue what he was up to. The agent would come along days later (long after surveillance teams would have left the area) and simply pick up the brick, an operation taking only a few seconds.

3) Another DLB from the 1980s was in a waste-paper recycling skip at the edge of a park. The agent lived in a flat near the park and every week he would bring his old newspapers and stuff them through the slot in the side of the skip. The skip was sealed with a metal roof to prevent all the paper inside getting wet. The agent pushed the newspapers right inside. As he did so he reached up and to the left where the DLB was a small magnetised box attached to the side of the metal skip. The skip was regularly emptied, but these dates were known so there was no risk of losing anything. Similarly, the inside of the skip was completely dark and the slot for paper was only wide enough to admit an arm. The box was highly unlikely to be touched or dislodged unless one reached all the way and knew exactly where to aim for. It was easy to conceal the box in the rolled up carrier bags in which he had brought his newspapers. The beauty of the site was that the skip was visible all the way across the park – both he and anyone filling the DLB could do so whilst under observation by a surveillance team without them knowing what was happening. The fill signal was a chalk mark on a wall near the end of a bench on his route to the park. The empty signal was to remove a particular potted plant from his window ledge 'for watering'.

Recognition Phrases

Whenever a spy meets an agent for the first time there has to be a way to ensure that he is talking to the right person and that the agent has not been compromised. A **recognition phrase** is used. The phrase must be innocuous so that it does not sound suspicious to anyone overhearing it, yet worded so that it could not be accidentally said by someone other than the agent. For instance:

Officer: 'Excuse me do you have a light?'
Agent: 'I'm sorry, I lost my lighter somewhere yesterday.'

If the agent doesn't use the correct phrase the meeting will not go ahead.

Sometimes a **recognition signal** will be used. The main use for this is as an emergency signal. For instance, if an agent wants to say that he is under surveillance and the meeting should not go ahead, he carries a certain easily identifiable item such as a shopping bag marked with a particular brand name. The item must be something which it would not be unusual for the agent to carry, but distinctive enough for the officer to spot from a distance. The advantage of a recognition signal rather than a phrase is that there is no contact between the officer and the agent at all making him almost impossible for the hostile agency to spot.

> Oleg Gordievsky once again provides us with a good example of a recognition signal. He had been arrested as a suspected spy and needed to escape. To signal this, he dropped a particular chocolate bar wrapper at a certain point on his regular jogging route where he knew an MI6 officer would be watching. Although there was a surveillance team watching him they never realised what was happening.

Secret Writing

Almost every schoolchild knows how to make invisible ink from lemon juice. The message is written using the lemon juice and then can be read by simply running a warm iron over the paper, turning the dried liquid brown. There are a range of similar liquids which can be used and imprisoned secret agents have used vinegar or even urine. This use of invisible inks is known to spies as **SW** (secret writing). But, like lemon juice, almost all these invisible inks are susceptible to exposure by heat (if not by the smell), so intelligence services have always had to rely on other methods to disguise their messages as well as the inks.

Of course encryption is one answer, but it does not always help because if the coded message is written in invisible ink and it is discovered, the security forces know that something is happening, they have the courier and can probably work out who was going to receive the message. Ideally you do not want the security forces to even know that a message is being passed, so intelligence services in every age have concentrated on concealing the codes.

Even the ancient Greeks followed this practice: couriers would be dispatched with wax tablets carrying innocuous information such as a list of trade goods, but if the wax was melted off the secret message could be found written on the wood underneath. It is said that they even used methods such as shaving the courier's head, writing the message in indelible ink on his scalp and then allowing the hair to grow back. In this age of instant communications it's hard to believe that a method which would take so many weeks to prepare would be any use, but this was an age when travel could take months. In the Elizabethan age messages were written on the shells of hard-boiled eggs in a particular ink which was then absorbed by the shell. The egg would appear entirely normal, but when shelled the message could be read on the surface.

In the (early) twentieth century this practice continued. Messages had to be more carefully hidden because new ways of discovering them had been invented such as VSC and ESDA machines:

- **VSC** – Visual Spectral Comparator. This allows a suspect document to be examined under a variety of different lights such as ultraviolet, infrared and blue. Invisible inks often show up under these lights.
- **ESDA** – Electrostatic Detection Device. This covers the suspect document in an imaging film. The film and message are then put in a vacuum chamber which seals the film to the paper. A corona wand is then passed over the

document. This electric device imparts a charge to the film, but a difference in charge wherever there is the slightest indentation on the paper. Extremely fine carbon granules are then scattered over the film and are attracted to the areas with a difference in charge, producing an image that looks a bit like a photographic negative. The image can then be sealed under a sheet of plastic and the film/plastic sandwich complete with the now visible secret message can then be removed, producing what is known as 'an ESDA lift'.

These machines allowed the secret message to be intercepted without harming the original at all, so the agent would receive it without realising that the security services were following his every move. To defeat these machines new ideas were developed such as writing the message in invisible ink on the inside of envelopes so that when the letter was opened and read it would not be discovered. Another practice was to hide the message beneath the stamp.

The other problem was disguising the inks. If an agent was suspected and his house was searched it was important that the inks he was using for communication weren't discovered. The usual practice was to disguise them in perfume bottles or canisters of cleaning fluid, but with time other methods were invented such as tablets which looked like aspirin but which became invisible ink when added to water or cloths which were impregnated with the necessary chemicals.

Today Western intelligence services prefer to use electronic message systems to communicate with their agents as they are faster and their encryption is usually more secure. But these are beyond the reach of terrorist groups and the intelligence services of minor states who are often the enemy today. These enemies are resorting to these age-old techniques which modern sigint collection agencies are ill-equipped to catch because of lack of familiarity. Add to this the fact that all the intelligence agencies are short of trained Arabic speakers, making document analysis a very lengthy business, and it becomes clear why terrorists often escape detection.

Microdots

Supposedly invented by the Germans and apparently used by the French as early as 1870. Again these belong more in spy films than reality and they have long been surpassed by the sophisticated technical equipment available to most services. However, there are some accounts of their use in the 1950s and '60s. For instance, in the 1960s the CIA is reported to have used a black line which was part of an advertisement on the back page of a copy of the *National Geographic*. The CIA technicians had used a laser to print a tiny message on the line which was undetectable except under a powerful magnifying lens used by their agent.

Part of the problem is that producing microdots requires specialised equipment (one microdot device used by the German secret service was six feet long and weighed over 4,000 pounds!), so they were only really useful for communications from the service to its agents in the field. Few agents were able to send messages back this way and instead had to rely on old-fashioned SW techniques. However, the equipment did become smaller and some agents used microdots with notable success.

The Microdot Masters

Peter and Helen Kroger were an elderly couple who lived quietly in a bungalow in Ruislip, north-west London. In 1961 their neighbours were astonished when they were suddenly arrested as spies working for the KGB. A long surveillance operation by MI5 had revealed that they were running a network of agents passing British naval secrets to Russia.

The Krogers had arrived in Britain from America in 1954 with Mr Kroger posing as a dealer in rare secondhand books. He sent these books all over the world and they were used as cover for the microdots which contained secret intelligence gained by the agent network. The pair sent and received hundreds of pages of intelligence by microdot in this way. When the bungalow

cont'd

was searched it took a while to find the incriminating equipment. The chemicals for developing the negatives were found in false bottoms of talcum powder and other containers. Special photographic film needed to produce the microdots was found hidden as pages of paper in a Bible. The lenses required for the cameras were found buried under a pile of rubbish in the cellar and it was also found that the bathroom had been laid out so that it could be quickly turned into a darkroom for producing the microdots. They had also used a radio set to transmit some reports.

The microdot scheme had worked perfectly. The Krogers had been given away when one of their agents had been betrayed by a Polish defector. He had in turn been followed to meetings with the Krogers' contact, a KGB officer called Kono Molody, who was living as an illegal in Britain under cover as a Canadian businessman called Gordon Lonsdale. He had been followed on regular visits to their house, and when they denied knowing him it was obvious that something was wrong. The search of the house told the rest. Molody was sentenced to twenty-five years' imprisonment but was traded for a British agent in 1964. The Krogers (whose real names tuned out to be Morris and Lona Cohen) were actually spies who had previously been working in the United States. They were sentenced to twenty years; imprisonment each, but were traded in 1969 for a British citizen who had been arrested behind the Iron Curtain.

Evading Phone Taps

An officer must always be aware that his agent may be under suspicion and that there could be a surveillance team watching or that there might be a tap on his phone. For this reason, the officer will try and avoid calls to the agent's home. But emergencies may occur when this cannot be avoided and the call must be disguised. Usually the officer will arrange with the agent that if he receives a call from a particular person including a particular recognition phrase then he should immediately go to a designated meeting place. This is best done by a facilities agent such as a shopkeeper or garage owner so that the call can be made under cover.

Jonathon Jay Pollard was an American of Jewish descent who spied on the United States for Israel in the 1980s. His Israeli handler gave Pollard a list of pay phones near his apartment and assigned a Hebrew letter to each one. The handler would ring up, simply say the letter and Pollard would go to that pay phone making it impossible for the call to be tapped since there was no time for US security forces to set the necessary technical devices.

'Oh my God, there's a hole in it!' One of the targets in the static observation exercise discovers the hidden camera planted by Simon and Austin.

8 Surveillance: The Art of Watching and Following People Without Detection

Nothing would more contribute to make a man wise than to always have an enemy in his view.

Lord Halifax

Surveillance is a key skill for any spy. Almost every major counter-terrorist or intelligence operation has included a surveillance element because there is no better way of tracing an individual or testing his story than the evidence of the eyes of trained observers. And the need for this expertise is growing all the time. Intelligence agencies such as MI5, the police and Customs have always used surveillance teams, but now even agencies such as the DHSS use teams to catch out people fraudulently claiming benefits and private telecommunications companies have surveillance teams to monitor those suspected of being fraudsters and vandals. Then there are the private security agencies staffed by former military and intelligence officers who, for a considerable fee, will follow anyone you like. Private companies use them to monitor employees who are claiming to be on sick leave or to see where they really go on business trips. Even journalists are employing surveillance teams. If you can master this skill you need never be short of work.

The main users of surveillance teams in the UK are MI5 who employ a specialist surveillance department, designated A4, known colloquially as 'the Watchers'. But it isn't just those on the security side who have to be able to use surveillance. Even MI6 and similar foreign agencies whose job is to recruit agents and gather intelligence abroad have to have the capacity to mount surveillance operations in case, for instance, a station wants to check out if a potential agent is a honey trap or to check whether an existing agent is under enemy surveillance. Often these agencies have specialist teams who can travel and operate abroad under a natural cover, but in the real world this isn't always possible and intelligence officers must be trained to act as a surveillance unit if necessary. And there is another reason officers who will be based abroad practise this skill: the best way to learn how to spot surveillance is to spend a couple of weeks with a surveillance team learning how it is done.

Types of Surveillance

There are four types of surveillance: **mobile**, **progressive**, **static** and **technical**. The person under observation is usually called the **target**. Most operations will be a combination of all these types.

Mobile

This is what most people think of when they hear the word surveillance. A team of people follows the target 24/7 whether he is in on foot or in a vehicle.

Progressive

This is surveillance in stages. The target is followed for a certain part of a regular route and then surveillance is stopped. On the next occasion the target is picked up at or near the point where he was last under surveillance and is followed on the next part of the route and then dropped. This process continues until the target's destination is discovered. This type of surveillance is harder to detect than normal mobile surveillance. However it has severe limitations in that the team have to know exactly when the target will use this route again and that the subject will take the same route. It is most often used to 'house' surveillance-conscious suspects (see page 172).

Static

This is the use of a premises or remote camera to watch a particular area. It is mostly used for premises surveillance such as if you know a particular yard or warehouse is going to be used for a criminal operation but you don't yet know the identities of the people involved. The premises used to watch the activity is known as an OP (observation point). Often the team are not lucky enough to have a nice warm building to work from and must improvise by camouflaging an officer and concealing him in bushes or some other natural cover close to the target. This is known as close surveillance. It can be extremely dangerous. In 1985 the M25 road-rage murderer Kenny Noye was being kept under close surveillance by Detective Constable Mick Fordham. When he found him in his garden, Noye stabbed the detective to death.

Technical

This is the use of a device to track the target's movements. It is usually against vehicles where the target is highly surveillance conscious. A range of devices are available both to intelligence services and private security companies. Some of these can be quite sophisticated, allowing a team to monitor the vehicle's progress from a laptop computer and displaying the vehicle's movements on a map or aerial photograph overlay. Other devices will also record any activity in the vehicle on both audio and video. Some will only activate when the vehicle is in motion and will even send a message to the officer's mobile phone to alert him. Using these devices, it is possible to follow the movements of a target without even leaving the office. This is known as **armchair surveillance**.

But although impressive, these devices have several drawbacks. For a start, all technical devices are prone to failure when they are most needed – it is an unwritten rule of espionage and no professional team will ever rely on a technical device alone. Every technical device which we used on the training course caused problems at some stage. Furthermore, a vehicle device does not tell you what happens when a target gets out of the vehicle, such as which building in the area he went to and who he met, so there is still a need for a full surveillance team to be available. So most surveillance teams use technical support only as a back-up to the main surveillance effort: it allows them to hang further back out of sight most of the time and acts as a safety net if there is a 'loss'.

A Typical Surveillance Team

The optimum size for a surveillance team is twelve to fourteen officers in six or seven vehicles. There should be a good mix of appearances and wherever possible racial backgrounds. It is as a surveillance officer that going grey comes into its own. All the rules of going grey will be observed by the team whenever possible. All members of the team will be in communication with each other via concealed personal radios and almost undetectable earpieces as well as concealed radio sets in the vehicles. Vehicles used by the team need to look like ordinary saloons and hatchbacks, but must have extremely good acceleration. The team may also have access to motor bikes, commercial vehicles and even aircraft.

The Reconnaissance

Before deciding which form of surveillance to use, the team will conduct a reconnaissance (**recce**) of the area. The only way to do this effectively is on foot. It gives a better feel for the atmosphere of an area than riding around in a vehicle and allows a greater level of detail to be observed. The recce will take more than one visit wherever possible and may take several weeks depending on security awareness in the area. These are the points the recce team will be looking for:

- Other vehicles in the street. It may be useful to know if they are local or someone new. They could be visiting the target.
- All exits from the target building, particularly where the target could leave on foot if he was trying to avoid the surveillance team.
- Where the target normally parks his own vehicle.
- Possible trigger positions and boxing positions (see page 171).
- Local threats of compromise e.g. police stations, neighbour-hood-watch schemes, residents parking restrictions (in some areas taking someone's parking bay can be tantamount to declaring war and will definitely get the vehicle noticed by local residents).
- Where the target works, what the logical routes away from his home are.

These points will form basis for an operational **bible** which will also include a list of targets, target vehicles and premises. Each of these will be identified by a call-sign e.g. the main target will be Tango One, next associate Tango Two and so forth. Vehicles and premises will have separate identifying letters e.g. vehicles will be Victor 1,2,3,4 etc. and premises Papa 1,2,3,4 etc. The operational bible is a highly classified document and is never taken out of the office but is used to brief any new officers brought into the team.

Static Surveillance

Static surveillance is the term applied to any surveillance operation conducted from a fixed point. The target is not followed at all, simply observed. Almost all observations on a static surveillance will be recorded from some form of OP or observation point – a static position from which the activities of the target are observed.

Types of OPs

There are several different types. Which is used depends on the location and the nature of the operation:

1. A **hide** – usually a hole in the earth covered by a combination of camouflage netting, turf and other debris. Typically used in rural areas.
2. A **room** in a building overlooking the target.
3. A **concealment** – a hidden area within the fabric of a building such as a roofspace or ventilation duct. Some concealments have even been achieved by building false walls into rooms. This method is only used against the hardest targets such as in an area controlled by terrorists, for example by Israeli security forces in the West Bank and Gaza.
4. A **vehicle** usually constructed to look like an innocent vehicle such as a builder's van but which actually contains a fully-equipped observation unit.
5. In extreme cases an OP can even be a designated site out **in the open**, for example on top of a high structure.
6. A **remote camera** can be fixed overlooking the target premises

or concealed in a vehicle. Pictures from the remote are then transmitted to the OP which can be in a building a considerable distance away.

Selecting an OP

Regardless of the type of OP there are several guidelines which should be borne in mind:

1) **Possibility of compromise** – not necessarily by the target. You must also consider who else might have access to the area where the OP is sited such as cleaners or maintenance staff. Animals such as dogs which might live in the vicinity must also be considered in case they are able to sense people in the OP and draw attention to it.

2) **Height** – wherever possible get height. It is far easier to observe movements within the target premises and the surrounding area from a high vantage point.

3) **Comfort** – all other factors being equal choose a site which will provide the adequate comfort for the OP team. This is not a matter of being soft. Uncomfortable, cold or tired personnel will make mistakes and possibly miss crucial movements by the target. It should be possible for the non-watching member of the team to rest in reasonable comfort so that she is refreshed when it is turn for her shift. During one exercise, three of the recruits – Max, Gabriel and Jennie – spent seventy-two hours crammed into an OP in the back of a van. They actually performed better than the other OP team who were in a house. However, they all agreed they could not have kept surveillance up for much longer and Jennie's comments about the toilet facilities consisting of nothing more than a plastic bottle are unprintable!

4) **Sightlines** – it may not be a matter of just covering the target adequately. Sometimes it can be useful to have a view in other directions to observe others arriving or departing. Thus a room on a corner of a building would be preferable to a room only giving one view of a street.

5) **Escape** – it is always useful if there is a second exit to the OP so that, if the operation is compromised, the team can grab any equipment and make a quick exit.

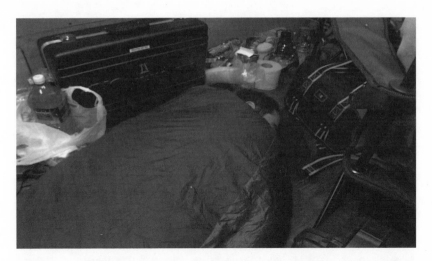

OPs are rarely luxurious. Every spy must be prepared to spend time in cramped and uncomfortable conditions in order to gather intelligence from surveillance. The recruits spent three days and nights in the back of this van.

Gabriel got himself into a good position in the car park but then, with the engine off but the ignition still on, kept the heater on and his foot on the car's brakes which led to all-round disaster: he not only drew attention to his vehicle (brake lights glowing red) but after two hours had run the battery down and he had to be rescued by the AA.

6) **Power** – a lot of modern surveillance equipment requires electric power. Choosing a site with accessible power points may save having to use and change battery packs in the OP.

7) **Ownership** – when using a room such as in a domestic residence it may be necessary to seek the permission of the owner. The owner must be checked carefully, not only because they may know the target, but also because of the danger of them gossiping about their 'unusual visitors'. Where possible a cover story should be used.

8) **Availability** – a site which is suitable for an OP on the day of the recce may not be suitable on other days because of some local factor.

9) **Communications** – an OP site should always be tested for communications before use. There may be unknown factors such as nearby telecom masts or electrical equipment which interfere with radio transmissions. An OP which cannot communicate with the rest of the surveillance team is next to useless.

Someone who allows a room in their premises to be used as an OP is known as an **OP keeper**. This role may involve a certain amount of risk whether the operation is directed against a foreign government or a criminal selling drugs on a housing estate. The team will always make every effort to protect the identity of the OP keeper and comply with his requests.

OP Rules

When leaving the OP for the last time the OP commander is responsible for ensuring that it is left clean – this means without any trace that a surveillance team was ever there. On the course, Austin's team left technical equipment and even compromising notes in their OP after the team had to pull out. On a real operation this could have been enough to have the OP keeper and his family tortured or even killed – imagine a Palestinian who has allowed his home to be used by Mossad, an opponent of Robert Mugabe's regime in Zimbabwe who has allowed his house to be used by foreigners or even a pensioner who has allowed his house to be used to watch a gang of drug dealers on a dangerous housing estate. The consequences could be truly terrible. This is why OP discipline must be followed *at all times*. A team which gets into bad habits will not suddenly be able to change.

Mobile Surveillance (1) General

Whoever has sight of the target, whether in an OP, in a car or on foot is known as the **eyeball**. This is the key position in any surveillance and the eyeball has control of the operation. If he asks a particular officer or vehicle to move they move (unless overruled by the commander) and the radio traffic must be kept down to allow the eyeball to commentate on what he is seeing.

Phases of a Surveillance Operation

There are five phases to a surveillance operation: **static**, **lift**, **mobile**, **box**, **house**.

1) Static

In the first stage of surveillance, a **trigger position** will keep the target premises under observation waiting for the target to move and alerting the rest of the team. There are four ways of doing this: from an OP, from a vehicle, with a remote camera or with a surveillance officer on foot.

When placing the trigger, it is important to remember to cover all rear and side entrances to the property, including ones that might not be obvious e.g. over a garden wall or through a neighbouring property, as the target might be trying to get away unnoticed.

Other vehicles are deployed to cover major intersections leading away from the target premises. This is known as 'boxing' the target (see page 171).

2) The Lift

The key to a successful lift is the **preparation**. If there has been an effective reconnaissance and good planning then even a mediocre team will be able to take the target away. All officers other than those in the 'trigger position' (usually the OP watching the house) will form a 'box' around the target. Forming a **surveillance box** means controlling all points of exit from an area. Officers at each point will be able to either commit or control a particular point:

The lift is the moment when the surveillance team first begins to follow the target and a smooth lift is the key to any successful surveillance operation. Here, Jennie sits unobtrusively in the 'trigger position' ready to call her team into action.

The recruits put the ABC system into operation. Jennie takes up the A position, while Austin and Simon take up the B and C positions off camera.

- **Commit** means that the officer can see the exit but cannot follow the target if he uses it. The team commander must ensure that another officer or vehicle is assigned to follow if this happens.
- **Control** means the officer can both see and follow the target.

The OP officer in a trigger position must note any movement in the property and keep the team informed. There is nothing worse than having no idea what is happening. If something happens which looks as if a departure may be imminent the call will go out, 'Standby, standby,' that is the signal for the mobile crews to wake up, switch on engines, grab map books, throw half-eaten meals into the gutter etc.

3) Mobile

This is the stage of the surveillance where the target is followed as he travels, whether on foot or in a vehicle. If on foot he may be heading towards public transport. If this is a target who has been followed for some time, the team will have developed a number of set plans to cover different routes such as the local railway station once it becomes clear that this is where he is heading. For more details of how this stage of surveillance is handled see the sections on foot and vehicle surveillance below.

4) Box

This is the procedure followed whenever a target stops his vehicle for any length of time or when he enters a building. The commander will deploy footmen to cover the target. Meanwhile, he will dispatch the mobiles to box the target by covering all the important junctions and exits in the area just as the team would do at a lift (stage two). In a professional team, the crews will anticipate this and start moving to cover these points of their own accord. The crew will radio something like, 'Moving to commit Green 47'. This speeds the whole process up and saves the commander a lot of unnecessary radio calls. If he feels they are in the wrong place he can always get them to move.

The vehicles don't just sit at the junctions where they can be seen. They sit out of sight from where they can move forward to cover the junction when the target returns to his vehicle. They will do this on a stand-by warning from the command vehicle or in the case of a loss by the foot team which could mean that the target has returned to his vehicle and is leaving the area.

5) House

When the target has returned to his final address for the day (usually back home) he is said to be housed. When he is certain that the activity is over the surveillance commander will call a stand down and the team will leave the area for a debrief on the day's activities. For targets under serious surveillance there will be separate teams on day-and-night shift and the OP will be manned twenty-four hours a day so that the target can be followed whenever he moves.

Mobile Surveillance (2) On Foot

The A,B,C Method

In surveillance jargon foot surveillance is usually referred to as going **'foxtrot'**. For many years the basis of all foot surveillance has been the 'A,B,C method'. At more serious levels this procedure becomes more and more complicated allowing for extra officers, parallel routes, following from ahead etc. But the A,B,C method is the basis and the technique which all trainee surveillance operatives have to manage first.

The Basic Follow

A is the 'eyeball'. She follows directly behind the target.

B is the 'back-up'. He follows further back than A so that he is effectively out of sight of the target.

C is the 'third man'. She generally follows on the other side of the street, although still behind the target.

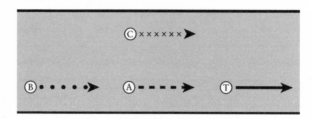

The basic follow.

Target Turns a Corner Away from C

A continues across the road and then turns, effectively becoming C.

B closes the distance and continues to follow the target, effectively becoming A.

C crosses the road and becomes B.

For this to work the team need to close up on the target slightly as he approaches a junction, without being obvious.

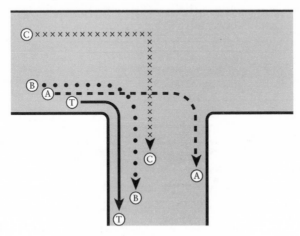

Turning a corner away from C.

Target Turns a Corner Towards C

A continues across the road and then turns, effectively becoming C.

B crosses the road, effectively remaining in the B position.

C turns the corner and becomes A.

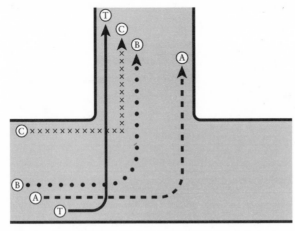

Turning a corner towards C.

Target Enters a Shop or Building

Whether or not the team stays with the target depends on a number of factors. If this is an intelligence surveillance where a brush contact or DLB may be likely the team has to stay with the target at all times and will go with him. However, if surveillance is being conducted by another agency who perhaps are tracking the target to a particular destination (e.g. the Benefits Agency to see if the target is actually working whilst claiming benefits) then they will simply make sure they have all the exits from the building covered and let the target move around freely inside, thus avoiding the risk of showing out. Also, if it is a small shop and the target can be observed from outside there is no need to follow him in. The officer at position C can observe from across the street whilst A and B cover the exit of the target to either left or right. If the team does have to go in to a large shop such as a department store, then there are two possible ways of tackling the problem. Either:

A goes past, then crosses the road to find the best possible OP. If B cannot get access to the building. A now has control and is responsible for calling when the target leaves the building.

B follows the target into the shop or building if possible (B1). If not, B continues and then finds a spot to wait, out of sight (B2), further down the road (e.g. another shop).

C crosses the road to find a place to wait on the other side of the building from B.

Both B and C are responsible for determining if there is a rear or side entrance to the building. If there are mobiles in support, one of these may move to cover any of these exits (they will have maps and be more aware of possible dangers). The plot commander will also deploy more footmen if necessary.

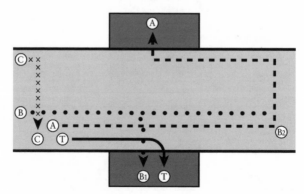

Target enters a shop or building (1).

Or:

A will go past to check for any other exits.

B will go into the store to follow the target.

C will hold position across the street to monitor the front entrance.

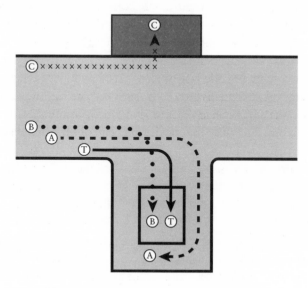

Target enters a shop or building (2).

Target Makes a U-Turn

It is difficult to be precise about this since there are so many possible variables: the width of the road, the distance from the target to B, the alertness of the target etc. Quality of the footmen will often mean the difference between success and failure. However, the general pattern is:

A continues and either enters a shop and re-emerges when given the all clear by C or tries to find a way through neighbouring side roads to rejoin the surveillance.

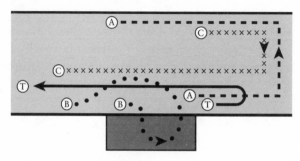

Target makes a U-turn.

B, if out of sight of target, finds a place to wait for the target to pass and then rejoins the surveillance as A. If the target can see B, B continues forwards past target then, like A, either waits or finds a way to rejoin the surveillance using an alternative route.

C becomes the eyeball. This can be a difficult moment since both A and B may be temporarily unavailable as they regain a surveillance position. He should be able to control the right moment for A (and possibly B) to re-enter the surveillance.

This move can be very disruptive. However, if a target makes repeated use of this manoeuvre, it is clear that he or she is up to something and the team will deploy extra footmen to cope.

Always consider what the target is doing: why are they taking this route, why are they going into this shop? It might provide advance warning of a surveillance trap (see Chapter 9). Also ask this question of yourself: why am I standing on this street corner? Why am I in this multi-storey car park? etc. This will help you to give a purpose to your actions so that they can look natural and also have a reason if challenged by security forces or a nosy member of the public.

What follows are factors to bear in mind when on surveillance:

Eye Contact

The cardinal rule when on foot surveillance is avoid eye contact. Ancient Japanese ninja assassins used to be trained not to stare at their targets even when directly behind them because it was believed that some deep-rooted sixth sense warned the victim that they were being watched. It is a basic rule that targets tend to remember people who meet their gaze if only for a moment.

Appearance

Obey the rules of going grey. This might seem the most obvious point, but there are no hard and fast rules. Above all, dress must be appropriate to environment. There's no point wearing a posh suit in an East End pub, no point wearing torn jeans and trainers in a West End hotel. On the other hand, you can go quite a lot of places looking smart; looking scruffy is more likely to be suspicious.

Black is not a good surveillance colour. Reena has made a bad choice for the day's surveillance by wearing nothing but black, as this actually stands out. Greys and greens are far more effective.

Nicola realises the importance of constantly changing her outline so that the target won't spot her. In the early part of the exercise, Nicola had her hair down, but once the target was onto the bridge and Nicola needed to get close again, she put on glasses and tucked her blonde hair away under a hat. She was the only person on her team not to be spotted by the target.

Movement

There are two things that should be avoided at all costs:

- **'Ballooning'.** The tendency of inexperienced operatives to drift around a street with no apparent purpose. They are more intent on maintaining their observation of the target than remaining unobserved. If there is any kind of counter-surveillance they will be spotted immediately and even a single person using counter-surveillance has a good chance of spotting this odd behaviour. An experienced operative will always be moving as though he has a purpose, apparently unaware of the target's existence.
- **Sudden movement.** Many counter-surveillance moves rely on sudden moves to catch the surveillance team out. For instance the unexpected U-turn. The hope is that footmen will suddenly dive into a neighbouring shop, make eye contact or stop dead in their tracks. A surveillance officer should never make hasty or unnatural movements. As with ballooning, the officer should always have in his mind a cover reason for his movement so that he doesn't respond to the target's movements unnecessarily. It is better to lose sight of the target for a moment than to risk blowing the whole operation. On surveillance exercises all the recruits who showed out failed because they reacted suddenly if the target made a quick change of direction.

Proxemics

People who think they are being followed tend to look for the follower at a certain distance – about ten to twenty metres away. Oddly enough this tends to be the distance at which people follow who do not want to be seen. It is as if there is a certain comfort zone in which the observer feels he is invisible and the suspect instinctively knows this and scans his area. It takes a while for newly trained surveillance officers to get used to this. The best officers are not afraid of being very close to the target. As long as their behaviour is natural and they have a good cover reason for their actions they are perfectly safe.

Physical Behaviour

Beware of small movements, or 'tics', which might give you away. Counter-surveillance officers are trained to watch for movements such as touching the ear (to adjust an earpiece when reception is poor or there is a lot of surrounding noise) or adjustment of radio harnesses (which are worn underneath clothing). Another thing to watch for is turning away whenever the target turns towards you. This was the second most common factor which made recruits stand out during our training. It is a natural thing to want to do, but it is very noticeable. It is far better to continue doing whatever you were doing without betraying any awareness of the target's movements.

Mobile Surveillance (3) Vehicles

Mobile surveillance is without doubt the hardest form of surveillance, because of the number of constraints on the team:

- You can't afford to lose contact. Once the target has got away it can be impossible to regain contact.
- Your freedom of movement is controlled by so many other factors: traffic lights, lack of through roads, the behaviour of other road users.
- In order to truly control and anticipate the target you have to drive faster then he does (either to make up ground after you have turned off or to get ahead of him). Worse still, the roads down which you are forced to drive to get into good positions are often narrow side streets with the danger of pedestrians, obstructions etc.

Choice of vehicles is important. Avoid bright colours or obvious markings. Avoid distinctive number plates. You usually need four doors as quite often you will be picking up or dropping off extra footmen. But a big team will probably include some two door hatchbacks for variety. The usual choice is the most powerful available model of a fairly common saloon. But there are no rules. When necessary I have conducted surveillance from a transit van and even, on one occasion, a refrigerated lorry. Aerials for surveillance radios should be concealed.

To give the other vehicles in the team as accurate an idea as possible of the target vehicle's position, the eyeball vehicle gives **commentary**. This is a particular skill which can take months to learn properly. The team need to know factors such as speed, position in lanes, upcoming road hazards (including badly parked vehicles, roadworks and especially police cars!) as well as landmarks so that other crews can estimate how far they are behind.

If there is a loss of the target the commander can do one of two things. He can try to work out the most **logical route** or destination for the target and direct the team to search in that direction. The team must move quickly but have to be aware that the target may have stopped – at a shop or garage, for instance. Alternatively, the commander can order a **starburst** – from the point at which the target was last seen each vehicle takes a different direction and drives as quickly as possible in the hope of catching it up.

Map Spotting

There is need for absolute precision in commentating on a target's movements, but at the same time radio traffic needs to be kept to a minimum. To achieve this a military system called '**map spotting**' is used by most surveillance teams. It is a system which makes navigation simple without crews having to learn thousands of road names every time they arrive in a new area.

Each crew uses a map book with detailed maps of all the roads in the area. The map pages are usually coated in a plastic film so that they can be written on with erasable markers to assist the navigator in plotting moves. On the map every junction is given a small coloured sticker. The colours really don't matter as long as they are used consistently: one colour for motorway junctions, one for major roads, one for minor roads and one for small tracks is usually sufficient. Each sticker is given a number. So to say that the target's vehicle is at a particular junction, the call is simply, 'Tango One Blue One Nine,' or similar. Obviously there are thousands of junctions so it might seem that the numbers would soon get ridiculous. To avoid this, if there is a change of page in the map book, the page number is called first: e.g. 'Tango One now heading Page two Red three seven.' All the recruits on the training course were taught to spot maps and it was the first thing they did whenever they were sent to a new operational area.

How Mobile Surveillance Works

Obviously you can't use the A, B, C system on mobile surveillance – oncoming traffic may become alarmed if C uses the other carriage-way!

A is still the eyeball position and B is still the back-up and should be quite close behind. The rest of the team will try to be as creative as possible looking for parallels and alternate routes. This is where the mad driving will take place!

Standard Manoeuvres

Target stops by the side of the road

A overshoots and finds a place to pull over out of sight of the main road. He will drop off a footman as soon as he is out of sight of the target. That footman will try to regain a view of the target as quickly as possible. B and the rest of the team will hold short. B will also deploy a footman to help A cover the target.

Target enters a car park

A continues past and becomes plot commander, putting out a footman to find out how many exits there are. B will follow the target into the car park. If it's a small car park with good sightlines it may not be necessary for anyone to follow the target in. If it's a multi-storey car park B will aim for the floor above the target if possible, but in any case putting out a footman to get eyeball on the target vehicle as it parks. Other vehicles will take up positions boxing the car park area and putting out enough footmen for a follow.

Roundabouts

A follows round until the last exit. If the target is going around again (either because he is lost or trying to detect surveillance) A will come off at that exit and plot up far enough down the road to be out of sight. B will have held at the threshold of the roundabout if possible. However, if the natural flow of traffic has meant that he has been forced on to the roundabout before the target comes round he will leave the exit before A and plot up in a similarly out of the way position. Meanwhile, C will have moved up to the threshold and will take over as eyeball as the target goes past. C will peel off the exit before B peeled off, if the target keeps going, on the grounds that

that exit is already covered. D will soon be on to the roundabout and will either take up the eyeball or act as back-up to B depending on how the luck goes.

Of course that is the basic theory. In practice the team will make judgements about the exits based on the target's previous behaviour, traffic conditions and the target's likely destination.

How to Remain Unobserved

You never know who's going to get a look at the car, especially when you are in your initial box positions awaiting a lift. You know the movements of your target, but you don't know everyone who is going to visit him. So you always have to assume that someone working for the opposition will get a look at the car and therefore it must not look like a surveillance car. This risk is even greater if you are in hostile territory when ordinary members of the public may be suspicious and call the authorities.

- Radios, maps, kit bags should be kept tucked away out of sight.
- Keep earpieces in your ear furthest away from the side window.
- Watch the profile of the vehicle. Use child seats, shopping bags, anything to make it not look like a surveillance vehicle. Try to avoid two men in the car at same time – a man and a woman is better.
- Get off the main road wherever possible. Even a drive-way will do if you can take the risk and have asked permission.
- Don't get too close to the target once you are moving.
- Hanging back – it looks suspicious if the target is held at a junction or roundabout but the car immediately behind is very slow to close the gap.

Don't make the mistake Gabriel made. He remained in one of the surveillance vehicles for some time to watch for a possible agent meeting. His position in a car park was good. Unfortunately, he kept the heater on and his foot on the brake the whole time he was in the car, meaning the brake lights were always on and the car could be spotted from miles away. Worse still, it drained the battery so that when the team needed to move the engine wouldn't start and the AA had to be called!

Mobile Surveillance (4) Public Transport

Although it sounds complicated, when following a target on public transport many of the same rules apply and there are many of the same problems. There are one or two additional points to watch:

- Try to get several footmen on to the vehicle in case the target makes another change during the journey.
- The footmen on the vehicle should try to get an idea of where the target is going by standing behind the target in the queue and listening in. Some mobiles will then be dispatched to the destination (but not all in case he is lying).
- Underground trains can be a problem if the target makes several changes in quick succession because most of the surveillance team will be trying to fight their way through the traffic in the streets above. But any target who does this is acting suspiciously so the team will either deploy a larger team on another day or arrest the suspect there and then.

Giving Descriptions

The following is an alphabetical checklist which can be useful to make sure every aspect of a target has been covered:

A Age
B Build (including height and weight)
C Clothes
D Distinguishing marks (such as tattoos, scars, blemishes)
E Ethnic origin
F Face (facial hair, tan)
G Glasses, gait
H Hair
I Items (anything carried, such as a briefcase or rucksack)

Boredom

Much surveillance work involves long periods of boredom either in the early part of the day when you are waiting for the target to get up and do something or in the early stages of an operation when trying to establish movement patterns, spending time following the target to the local supermarket, for example. It is easy to remain interested in an operation in the first few days, but unless something exciting happens, one can quickly grow disillusioned and believe that it is a waste of time. This is when most mistakes are made and is the greatest threat to the security of the surveillance team. Good officers stay focused.

Technical Operations

Known in the trade as 'tech ops', technical operations are an essential tool in many espionage operations including surveillance. They include audio, video and tracking devices.

While the range of equipment available to government intelligence agencies is impressive, it is the skill with which it is used which really matters.

The spy must consider whether deployment of specialist equipment is really necessary. For instance, if a spy is found with a miniaturised video camera, it is fairly incriminating. It might be more appropriate for the spy to use a normal digital video camera and, if spotted, simply claim to be a tourist filming in the wrong place.

Complicated equipment may require a specialist technical team to enter the target premises and secretly install monitoring equipment. This will have both cost and security implications. If a break-in is required to place the device it risks the operation. In the programme, one team of recruits had to call off an entire operation because they were compromised when placing a technical device. This sort of risk must always be carefully assessed.

Almost all technical devices require electrical power. Most will work happily on a small battery pack for a few hours, but many operations will last a great deal longer than that. Wherever possible, the technical team will want the spy to select a position where it will be possible to connect the technical device to mains power so that batteries can be recharged or even dispensed with altogether.

All devices have a limited transmission range, which the base

Learning how to deploy technical devices is a key part of any spy's training. Harry demonstrates a range of different listening and video surveillance devices in the classroom, many of which are disguised in ordinary items including cigarette packets and even fountain pens.

A remote monitoring device for recording conversations picked up by a concealed microphone.

station must be within range of. In rural areas the signal will usually carry quite a distance, but in urban areas, transmission ranges of equipment can be dramatically reduced. The technical team will want to see that the spy requesting their assistance has considered this issue and, wherever possible, conducted a test with a similar device.

The final point to remember about technical devices is that no matter how impressive they seem there is always the chance that they will go wrong. I have known technical devices which were operating perfectly only to pack in just when they were needed. Even on the course they gave problems: one team were relying on a bugging device on a car to let them know when the owners of a house were returning, but when they couldn't get a signal from it were forced to rely on human lookouts.

Tech ops are a tool which can assist human surveillance teams, but they will never replace them.

The Drawbacks of Surveillance

An intelligence service will only use surveillance for the most important operations. To become a surveillance officer takes years of training and there are a limited number of personnel who can carry it off well. Although it can be done with just one or two people, to be done effectively surveillance needs a decent-sized team. It is expensive and time intensive, often requiring personnel twenty-four hours a day. There is a considerable risk that the target will become aware of the surveillance and cease operations, perhaps even alerting other possible suspects in his organisation. Recruiting an agent who can tell you what the organisation is up to is always preferable.

9 Counter-Surveillance

Qui custodiet ipsos custodes?
(Who watches the watchmen?)

Roman proverb

Every spy needs to be able to check whether they are under hostile surveillance whether they have just arrived in a strange country or they are just about to go to a meeting with a top agent. Counter-surveillance is the art of spotting a surveillance team which may be watching you and it is a skill every spy must master. It can either be performed solo or with a counter-surveillance team to assist, but there is one point to remember above all – there are no firm rules for counter-surveillance. All of what follows is known by surveillance teams who will always try to work around them because they know they are weaknesses. Your best hope in spotting a surveillance team is to think of some completely new move which will catch them out.

The second important point to remember is to **never underestimate your enemy.** It is not necessarily the case that the best surveillance officers work for the intelligence agencies or the police. Three factors influence the performance of a team: quality of training, how often they work and the level of equipment available. Thus the intelligence services start off with an advantage: they will have the best training, almost unlimited vehicles and manpower (including in some cases air support) and the highest levels of equipment including covert communications, video and tracking devices and night-vision capabilities. Yet some of the smaller teams in the business, by the very fact that they are forced to be creative through lack of equipment, break the rules and if they work regularly enough can be very effective indeed. So **don't** assume that just because the sort of opposition you face is low level that they will not be very good.

The third important point is not to reveal that you are using counter-surveillance tactics. If a team realises that you are using these moves to spot them they will know that you are a spy. They will follow you for the rest of your time in the country with so many resources that either they will catch you or you won't be able to complete your mission. Spies are at their most successful when they are no longer under suspicion (known as **'putting your enemy to sleep'**). If anything, get others at your place of work to act that way and then they are likely to be followed. This will at least use up the surveillance team's resources and help to draw attention away from you. This is known as **'using stooges'**.

What Will the Surveillance Team Look Like?

When faced with a busy street or shopping area it can be dispiriting to think that you have to pick a surveillance team out of all these possible suspects. But don't worry. Even though we don't know who they are, we can narrow down the possible suspects we must examine because the surveillance team is likely to follow certain rules of appearance:

- **Loose clothing**. They have to hide radio sets and the various other bits of equipment a surveillance officer needs. Some of the radios can be quite small these days, but if they are carrying hats and glasses etc. to change their appearance together with binoculars, spare batteries for the radio, note-books, street maps etc., it all adds up. Men will have a tendency to wear jackets even on hot days or several layers of clothing so that they can change profile. Women will very often carry all this equipment in a handbag so noting a type of handbag can help for later identification. The handbag is more likely to be a large shoulder bag than a tiny fashion accessory.
- **Colours.** They are likely to be wearing blacks, greys, browns, dark blues or greens. Anyone with a highly coloured item of clothing can be initially disregarded.

- **Distinctive jewellery.** Of course it can be easily changed, but it will still be avoided as jewellery is designed to draw the eye to the wearer. Rings are a possible exception to this rule as people are less aware of this and they can be difficult to remove – though of course you have to be up close to see this sort of thing. It also catches the light at night. Numerous piercings of the ear or piercings of the nose or eyebrows are highly noticeable. These could be faked, but are so likely to draw attention that this is improbable. I did know one officer who experimented with a false nasal piercing that was in fact only held on by a small magnet inserted in a nostril, but even though this could be removed quickly, it still tended to attract attention to his face and unless there is a heavy disguise (which takes time) it doesn't really work.
- **Ears.** Some surveillance officers have a tendency to touch their ear. Some earpieces have a tiny volume control. Or they just irritate the ear and there is a tendency to notice this sort of thing when under pressure. Keep an eye open for ear-pieces, it may just be a hearing aid, but the wearer is definitely someone to take note of until you can discount him.
- **Eye contact.** They will do all they can to avoid eye contact.
- **Personal attractiveness.** Female officers will avoid lots of make-up, or displays of legs or cleavage. Hair is likely to be short and easy to keep tidy with no complicated braiding or coloured streaks. Showy hair such as heavily permed hair-styles are unlikely. But remember these are only guidelines. Wigs could be used.
- **Shoes.** As a surveillance officer you spend a lot of time on your feet day after day. Even if they aren't watching you tomorrow, they are bound to be on duty watching someone. They may also have to drive at a moment's notice. So women are very unlikely to be wearing high heels and male officers will tend to favour soft shoes like trainers or casual shoes rather than highly polished lace-up shoes which will quickly show scuffs. But be aware that if you have gone into a location which requires smart dress, whoever follows will have changed their clothes accordingly, so this point is of less use in that environment.
- **Age.** Very old or very young can usually be discounted.

- **Umbrellas.** These are distinctive and cumbersome. They are very unlikely to be carried.
- **People with children.** The presence of children with an adult almost certainly rules them out. Terrorists or criminals may use them, intelligence services don't.
- **Sunglasses.** Unless enough people are wearing them for it to be common, surveillance teams will avoid them and will certainly avoid unusually shaped sunglasses.

But beware, a surveillance team will raise its game to match yours and if they know that you are experienced in counter-surveillance they will try to break the established rules to catch you out so these are only the first line of defence.

Tactics When on Foot

Put Them to Sleep

People don't realise that an important part of counter-surveillance is actually doing nothing.

When a surveillance team first follows you they are very alert. You are a new target and they will have been told to follow because of an intelligence tip-off. As the hours and days go by, if nothing suspicious happens, doubt begins to enter the mind of the team. Perhaps the intelligence was wrong, perhaps the deal or meeting has already happened and they missed it. Eventually they will get bored and start to wish they were doing something better against a more interesting target. That's when they will get sloppy and start to make mistakes. So take your time. They have to start working the moment you leave your home base, whereas you can go shopping or go for a drink and take hours before you start making your counter-surveillance moves and by that time they will probably be exhausted.

If you really do manage to put them to sleep, you may be able to get rid of them altogether. Surveillance teams are a highly-expensive resource. If the team follows you for several weeks and nothing happens, their masters will soon think of another target the team would be better directed against.

And once you *are* working, all your counter- and anti-surveillance moves must appear **natural**. The moment that they spot an action or trick which marks you out as an intelligence officer you've had it.

They will be on you 24/7 and will if necessary double or even triple team you. It doesn't mean you can't operate, but it will make your job one hundred per cent harder.

The Sudden U-Turn

This is a very powerful manoeuvre. For much of the time that you are under surveillance the team will want to be behind you because this is the one area you can't observe. If you suddenly turn, all that area behind you suddenly comes into play. You might be lucky. On a poor team there might be an officer who suddenly moves into a shop doorway or makes eye contact because he is surprised at this sudden move. You might see someone clearly talking into their lapel mike or adjusting a radio – it does happen, teams get sloppy. However, a good team will continue as if nothing has happened, not because of your manoeuvre, but because a well-disciplined team will be concerned that there may be a static OP overlooking them at any time.

Make the move look natural. There are plenty of excuses for executing this move: you suddenly remember a shop you meant to go to or a shop window a few yards back has caught your eye and you go back for another look. You are lost and go back to look at a street name before consulting your map. You want to throw away some litter into a bin. You can probably think of many more, but remember they must make sense to the watching team, not just to you.

But the U-turn move is like an ace in a game of cards. Use it wisely because you can only really do it once or twice. Remember the point of perfect counter-surveillance is to detect them without them even realising that you are a spy. Keep doing it and they will be alerted.

Crossing the Road

The good thing about this move is that, like the U-turn, it allows you to see all the activity taking place behind you. This chance to look to your left (or right depending on the country you are in) is known as the 'long look back'. Like the U-turn this can be very useful providing certain rules are followed:

Max is well over 6 foot tall, and he tried various disguises but could not disguise his height. MI5 won't use surveillance officers over 5'11″ for this reason.

Max and Gabriel are 'burned' when their target unexpectedly makes a U-turn and sits down alongside them.

- DON'T use a **pedestrian crossing** – the surveillance team will have prepared for the possibility you are going to cross the road.
- The move must be **sudden** so you will need a cover reason for this sudden change of direction.
- You want your long look back to last as long as possible. It is no good if you are able to cross straight away. So only use busy roads and **use your ears** – listen for the traffic coming up behind you so that you know you will have an extra few seconds to take in the scene. Nicola was the best counter-surveillance officer on the course and she made particularly good use of this manoeuvre. By pretending to be shopping she was able to get several long looks back and she was the only recruit accurately to identify both members of the team following her.

Use the Box

The weakest point of a surveillance operation can be the box – when they are sitting waiting for you to move in the morning from your house. If you know how a surveillance team works you can guess the sort of places where they will be waiting. Obviously if you go out to try to spot them they will move. However, someone else walking the area especially if they are a 'clean-skin', someone not previously known to associate with you, will be much more likely to see them. This scouting by a previously unknown person is one of a team's biggest worries.

Draw them in

If you are suspected of being a spy the surveillance team must stay very close to you in case you have a brush contact with an agent or fill a DLB. So use this fact against them. Many small shops can't be observed from the street. Spend enough time there and someone will have to check on you. (But beware CCTV cameras – the first thing the team will do is speak to the manager to see if they can make use of them.) Department stores are less use because there are so many people that there is good cover for the surveillance team.

Cafés can also be useful. Vary your behaviour, sometimes go to the back, out of the way. They won't like that because, since they need to know if you make contact with anyone, a member of the team will also have to go in. But at other times sit where you can get a view out of the window. A good team will monitor you without being in sight, but one of the team may pass by and confirm a sighting you have had earlier. Teams do make mistakes.

Reduce Their Cover

Surveillance teams love crowds because it makes it much harder for you to pick them out. You might think that it would make it easier for them to lose you and this is true to an extent, but there is only one of you and probably about a dozen or more of them so the odds are in their favour.

Don't help them out. Take them to areas that are less well populated such as parks or woodland.

Get Height

Whenever you go into a building with several floors, use the stairs and take a moment to look out of the windows now and again as you go up. Any time you get a high vantage point it makes life that little bit more difficult for the surveillance team because they can never be quite sure how much you can or can't see. You may get lucky and spot some activity or even a figure you have seen earlier in the day.

At the same time be aware that height can be used against you. In large cities, government surveillance teams often have rooms rented specifically to help them cover certain areas such as public squares or major intersections. And even if they don't have one, if a place is part of your regular counter-surveillance route and they are suspicious of you, they will probably rent one. You are unlikely to spot them. Officers are trained to stay back from windows and to use dark sheets to close off the background of a room to prevent them being seen, so always have in your mind that just because you are clear on the ground doesn't mean you aren't being watched from a building. Choose your meeting sites accordingly.

You may think that you are in a new area and that the team wouldn't have time to set up an elevated OP, but this can be done surprisingly quickly. I was once part of a team waiting for two drug dealers to have an important meeting. They chose a marina with good views across surrounding public squares and they also had gang members out on foot looking for anything suspicious. There had been no time for the team to prepare for this as the dealers called the meeting at short notice specifically to throw off any surveillance. Realising that one office block overlooked the area where they were, another officer and I quickly entered the building, went to the top floor and barged into the office which we calculated would have the best view. It was some sort of boardroom and there was a meeting in progress. We quickly identified who we were and explained what we were doing. We asked if we could use their window (I was already by the window and commentating as we were doing this). The chairman of the meeting was so stunned that he quickly agreed and not only were we able to watch the entire twenty minute meeting, but also got good photographs of the people present.

Use a Team

By far the best way to spot surveillance is to use a counter-surveillance team. These officers are best used by placing them at certain key points on your route (height is useful so that they can get a good picture of the activity behind you but they must be able to spot the detail of suspects). The watcher needs to stay out of sight because a good team will have an eye out for anyone who appears to take an interest in them. The watcher at each point should note anyone acting suspiciously and pass the details to the watchers at the other points. If the descriptions are good enough then those people will be spotted again. You will then need to arrange a final point on your route at which the counter-surveillance team can display a sign which lets you know whether you are clear or not. For instance, one of the team might be waiting at a bus stop towards the end of your route. Remember, a sign such as carrying a particular carrier bag means you are being watched and the meeting is off.

Public Transport

Buy roamer or season tickets to ensure the team can't tell where you are going by listening in when you buy your ticket.

Bus stops which serve multiple routes are useful. If they put someone in the queue with you, you can wait for another bus on a different route. Whoever is in the queue will have to get on or risk showing out. Of course they can watch the stop from a distance, but then someone has got to get on at the last minute so make a note. (One way round this problem would be to load an officer on at the previous stop for every bus – this takes a lot of people and co-ordination and if they are capable of this you are in trouble anyway!)

Trains are useful in that you can walk the length of the carriage as you go to the toilet. Somewhere amongst the other people will be surveillance officers. You might see one you have spotted before. But don't expect to see them again as a new team will probably be waiting at your destination.

Tactics When Driving

Just as surveillance is difficult in cars, so too is counter-surveillance. You have so many things to deal with in modern traffic that it is hard to give the necessary attention to spotting the signs of a surveillance team. Try not to make excessive use of the rear-view mirror, it looks quite obvious to anyone watching your car. Use the wing mirrors whenever you can. And don't rely too much on number plates – over the short term they can be useful but teams can change them quite easily. Try to spot details of the driver as confirmation.

Three Sides of a Square

Make three turns to the left or right on a route where it would make more sense to go from A to B, so that anyone who comes with you is suspicious. A good team will cover it so that car 1 goes straight on at C, but you may have a chance of spotting the back-up take over. Of course car 3 will probably be going A–B anyway but you may catch them out.

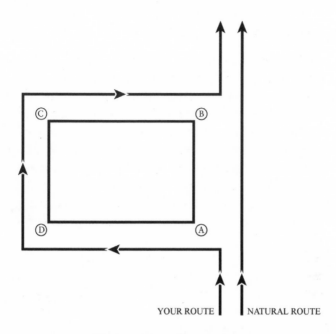

YOUR ROUTE | | NATURAL ROUTE

Three sides of a square.

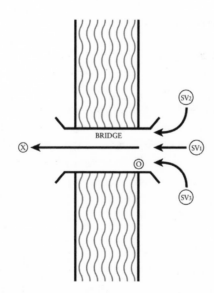

Ⓧ YOUR VEHICLE   Ⓞ COUNTER SURVEILLANCE OBSERVER

SV₁ EYEBALL VEHICLE   SV₂ SV₃ BACKUPS ON PARALLEL ROUTES

Choke points.

Choke Points

If you have other officers to help, you can establish choke points. These are places on your route which following cars must go through. Bridges, particular roads or overpasses are all suitable provided the only way to avoid that place is to take a long impractical detour. Surveillance teams get lazy and will almost certainly follow you through (once they think you are out of sight) rather than have to endure a dangerous high speed drive to catch up. The officers at each choke point should note down registration numbers. If any are the same (provided the choke points are far enough apart or on an illogical route) you have almost certainly spotted a surveillance vehicle.

Drive Slowly

If you do this the traffic behind will have to close up, including the surveillance team and you will be able to get a proper look at them. A good place to do this is a housing estate or similar area. If you pretend you are lost or looking for a particular address, the team will have to keep overtaking you and sending in fresh vehicles or risk a loss.

Hold at Traffic Lights

Makers of spy films seem to like this one but unless you are being followed by a single vehicle, it doesn't work in reality. The surveillance team will have vehicles on a parallel course who will take up the eyeball position at the next junction.

It could work if you picked an area where parallels weren't possible but it is rather obvious and the surveillance team will only work harder on you in future. It is far better to use more subtle methods.

Speed and Illegal Driving Manoeuvres

This includes driving the wrong way up one-way streets or going through red traffic lights. It is favourite of criminals who don't much bother about the law anyway and think that anyone who follows them after manoeuvres like that must be surveillance. But it is not as much use as you might think. If you do it regularly the surveillance team will allow for it, making greater use of motor-cycles, air support, bugging devices etc. If you don't and suddenly start using it they get suspicious. It is also dangerous. It is far better to use more subtle possibilities. If you have been stuck for a while in heavy urban traffic but you are coming to a clearer area, that is the time to really put your foot down since much of the surveillance team will still be stuck in the traffic. At the very least it will break the team up. But in general avoid excessive speed – they are probably better drivers than you and there are more of them.

Night-Time

Disable a car's interior lights so they don't show if you are getting in or out of the car. But don't assume darkness means cover. A good team will use night-vision devices. These are heavy and bulky for footmen to carry and so will usually be deployed in cars, but this sort of equipment is becoming lighter and smaller all the time. Often the surveillance team will be able to see more than you (for bugging devices on cars see Chapter 10).

Anti-Surveillance

Many people get confused about the difference between counter-surveillance and anti-surveillance. Whilst counter-surveillance means to detect and/or monitor a surveillance team, anti-surveil-lance means to take measures which prevent the surveillance team from detecting what you are doing. There are two kinds of anti-surveillance: subtle and coarse.

Obviously the easiest way to lose a surveillance team is to do something sudden and unexpected. For instance, getting on to a tube train and jumping off again at the last minute just before the doors close. In a car one can drive very slowly to see who stays with you and then drive very fast in the hope of catching the team out. Other tactics such as driving through red lights or going the wrong way up one-way streets can also help to lose a surveillance team (if you live long enough!)

This is **coarse anti-surveillance** and would only be employed by a professional spy in the most extreme circumstances. The problem is that whilst these dramatic manoeuvres may well lose a surveillance team, this odd behaviour marks you out as someone who clearly has something to hide. Pull many of these stunts while you are under surveillance and the authorities will almost certainly mark you down as a probable intelligence officer and will devote all the more resources to catching you out. Not just surveillance, but tracking bugs and telephone taps will all be used. In fact, your anti-surveillance will have had exactly the opposite to the intended effect. If you were planning to operate in an area for more than a few days you are finished.

The second type of anti-surveillance is far more difficult to detect and therefore to combat. Once a spy has realised that she is under observation by using counter-surveillance, she has two choices: either cease operations for a few days until the team gets bored, assume she is innocent and move on to a new target or take measures which allow the surveillance team to think they have her under observation and that she is doing nothing suspicious when in fact she is still working. A great exponent of this was the KGB spy Oleg Gordievsky. In Chapter 7 in the section on dead letter boxes we saw how he was able to fill a DLB at the base of a tree even though he was under surveillance from an OP overlooking the alleyway and whilst a surveillance team was following him. He was able to do this because the route of the alleyway and the surrounding fence hid his movements from the shoulders down so that his dropping of the hollowed brick was not seen. This is **subtle anti-surveillance** of the highest order and the mark of a truly professional spy.

Finally

Remember – they will make mistakes. It is easy to imagine that the team following you is perfect and that you will never spot them. Nothing you can do seems good enough. This is can lead to depression and paranoia if you let it get to you. But surveillance teams do make mistakes. There can be misunderstandings between team members, communications systems can break down, suspicious police or members of the public can disrupt operations, or the team can grow lazy because you've put them to sleep.

Try and keep your sense of paranoia under control. On her

counter-surveillance exercise, Jennie reported a long list of people as possible surveillance based on the fact that she had seen them all several times. But she forgot that these sightings were all in one shopping area – none were surveillance, they were just passing shoppers.

Above all, be patient and keep watching.

Harry tears the recruits off a strip for their sloppy work in the static observation exercise and for compromising their OP keeper.

Austin and Simon face the music.

10 Playing Defence

The superior man, when resting in security, does not forget that danger may come.

Confucius

We live in an age of the increasing power of the state. You cannot leave your house without being watched by dozens of CCTV systems. You cannot travel between countries without having your fingerprints and photograph checked and logged on a hundred different databases. Every e-mail and internet search you ever complete is logged and held on record for years. The Big Brother argument of 'if you have done nothing wrong why should you worry if we watch you?' is being used as never before. Only for good reasons of course . . .

We should all take an interest in our own security. Advice on self-defence and physical security is beyond the scope of this book and easily available elsewhere, but we can all learn from the experience of generations of spies and remember to think about who might be watching us – and why. All of the recruits were constantly tested on these skills. They knew that they could be followed or find themselves in the middle of an exercise at any time. The person who stopped them in the street to ask for directions might be an innocent member of the public or might be someone we had sent, the person next to them on the tube might be employed by us to plant a tracking device on them. They knew that their flats might be broken into and covertly searched and they also knew that any incriminating items, such as notes or equipment left lying around, could be taken at any time and used against them. These are some of the skills they were trained in:

Spotting Intelligence Officers

We all think that we will never be targeted by a real intelligence officer. After all, what do we know that could be of any use to an intelligence service? But it is far more common than you think. Even if you don't travel abroad the chances are that you will encounter spies in your own country no matter how lowly your job. For instance, in America, college librarians were approached by their security agencies to become agents and report on the reading habits of students. Even someone with a job as a cleaner might be approached to place a bugging device in the boardroom of an office which they clean. Homeland security is the new concern of all Western security services and the possibilities are endless. To enable them to provide security they are looking to recruit agents and contacts in all walks of life: language schools, university campuses, post and telecommunications industries, your local mosque, almost any area you can think of.

And then there are foreign intelligence services and terrorist groups. All of them are looking for potential agents. If you have ever been to certain fringe political meetings, even if it was only out of curiosity, then there is a good chance that there is a report on you somewhere in an intelligence service system. So what are the signs that an intelligence officer is talking to you?

- **Biodata**. An interest in your personal details such as name, date of birth, members of your family could be a sign of a foreign service. The intelligence service from your own country won't need this sort of information since at the touch of a button they can call up records including your credit history, your phone records and just about anything else. But a foreign service or terrorist group has to start from scratch, so don't give these things away easily (see 'Deflecting Difficult Questions' in Chapter 3) and see how hard the other person works to get them from you.
- **Likes and dislikes**. To a certain extent, a domestic service will be able to start making guesses about these from your credit-card records, garbology and so on. But there is no substitute for a personal interview by a trained officer. The more they can find out about your preferences in politics,

literature and culture, the easier it will be for them to tailor a recruitment approach.

- **Political views**. A friend might be interested in your likes and dislikes, but an interest in your political views, especially if it is early in the relationship, is a very suspicious sign. Try to keep your views on political subjects very close to your chest, especially with strangers. The harder they have to work to get these from you, the easier it will be to spot that this is an intelligence officer.

Intelligence officers are very hard to spot (if they are skilful) because they approach you just as anyone would who was willing to be your friend. They will ask many of the same questions and act in an open and supportive way. None of the targets in our exercise on agent recruitment suspected that the recruits who had come to work with them were training to be spies and that is the spy's greatest strength – ordinary people just don't expect it to happen to them. Your best defence is in **being aware**. The signs are slight so your best hope is to improve your chances of spotting them.

It's an old adage in chess that 'the best defence is offence'. So if you're suspicious of someone, don't let them have it all their own way. **Ask them questions, test their cover.** See how they react to your questions – do they try to avoid giving you a direct answer? Are they consistent in the answers they give? Watch how they interact with other people. What sort of questions are they asking? If necessary make notes after you have spoken to them so you can compare it with the answers to the same questions in a month's time. You have to be careful because people quite innocently give slightly different answers to the same question depending on the situation or the impression they are trying to give. People also lie about their past for all sorts of reasons, not just because they are intelligence officers. So don't become paranoid about this approach, but use it as a tool because intelligence officers are particularly careful about giving things away. It was interesting watching the trainers on the show, even though we had all been in the same line of work none of us would give personal information to the others whilst at the same time trying different tricks to get as much information as possible. In the end it became a sort of game. I won't tell you who won . . .

Protecting Your Home

The greatest threat to you from an intelligence service is that they will break into your home to search or bug it. In many areas you can get a community police officer or private security company to come to your home and advise about domestic security. They will make useful suggestions about window locks, CCTV cameras, boundary security and so forth, but for a spy this doesn't really help because they must assume that their enemy will always get in. If you have a highly complicated alarm system protecting your house it might deter burglars, but an intelligence service will simply call in a large team of experts to deal with it.

The first step in any defence plan is to know your enemy. Every intelligence or security service around the world has specialist departments whose job is to work out how to break into premises. Like little workshops full of mad inventors, these departments are packed with arcane equipment with security systems and locks disassembled all over the place, rather like Q's laboratory in a James Bond film. They have to be able to equip spies to break into any premises including extremely well-defended secret military research bases, so anything you are likely to get from your local private security company is going to be about as much use as an

Simon probes a lamp for signs of a concealed bug or camera.

igloo against a blowtorch. You are never going to keep people like this out. In fact, a very high level of security is only likely to convince them that you are worthy of their attention.

As a spy, your home security needs to be of a different type. Think layers of security. First you need the usual home security. The next layer is for those who get past that, who are likely to be the enemy. These people will want to hide the fact that they have been in your house, whereas you want to detect this because half the battle in defeating an intelligence operation is knowing that it is happening. Your best tactic, as with a surveillance team, is to put them to sleep, make them think that you are an easy target. That way they are more likely to fall foul of the real security measures you take:

- Keep the place untidy and get to know your untidiness. What appears to be chaos to a casual observer should be a carefully noted system to you.
- Use **tells**. These are small signs which when disturbed tell you that someone has been there. In films and books secret agents often use tiny slips of paper jammed into the cracks of doors. The problem with this is that they are too easily seen and can be replaced. Better is a crisp placed under the doormat. If the crisp is broken it is a sign that someone has entered the house. Even if they lift the doormat and spot it, they will just assume your housework is poor – it doesn't look like a security measure. If you are really suspicious place another under the carpet by windows (they won't always come through the doors).
- Place a delicately balanced ornament on top of filing cabinets. It should be small and ordinary so as not to attract attention – perhaps a toy out of a Christmas cracker. If it falls they may forget to stand it up again.
- Black thread can be strung across passageways. Don't do this near the front or rear entrances as the team will be looking for security measures here. Rather use it further into the house where they may be less careful.
- Small security cameras can be bought for very reasonable sums. Place one in an innocuous object such as an ornament. It should be something they can see but would find of no interest.

- Overall, your best weapon is your imagination – imagine them breaking in to your property, think how you would do it and set the traps accordingly. Set deliberate weak points to guide them into your trap.
- Get a dog. Statistics show that it is the defence measure most intruders fear. A dog is also useful for counter-surveillance as it gives you a good excuse to go out regularly using different routes, to stop and turn round and to go to remote wooded places.
- Place books at an angle on top of piles of other books, shelves, desks etc. But this is an old trick so don't make the alignment too obvious (for instance make the alignment of the book towards a point two feet away from the opposite corner of the room rather than directly to it).
- Spies may make their entry look like a burglary, especially if they are short of time. So if you are broken into and something is taken don't assume that is the whole story.
- If you are using a secret hiding place, build another one behind it. They are so pleased at finding the first concealment they rarely look in the same place for another.
- Security markers can be bought from hardware shops. They leave a mark which only shows up under ultraviolet light and are usually used for putting postcodes on objects which might be stolen. Use them to draw outlines around the bases of objects on shelves, cupboards etc. so that you can tell if they have been moved.

How to Check a Room for Bugs

If you detect that your house has been covertly entered, your next concern will be that intruders have left a technical device to record your activities. The next stage is to conduct a search for the device. Professional companies will provide personnel who will 'sweep' for these devices, though this is expensive and lets your enemy know that you are on to them. Even if the device is found, your enemy will simply attempt to plant another device. The best approach is to try and find it so that you can tailor your activities accordingly. Hopefully you can convince your enemy that they have got the wrong person and that you are not a spy at all. You will know when you have succeeded because they will remove the device.

- Be covert. If the device has a video capability they may be able to see you searching, so think of a cover for your activity (such as spring cleaning), play loud music to cover the sounds of your activity and, if necessary, break the search into separate periods over several days.
- Be methodical. Start at one point in the room and work consistently around it. Treat floors and ceilings as separate parts of the search.
- Consider all items, even those you have had for some time. One tactic is to replace an item in the room with an exact copy containing a technical device. Electrical items are favourite for this approach because the device can use the existing power supply to recharge its batteries.
- Be aware that some mobile phones and telephones can be activated remotely to act as microphones. These should always be disconnected in areas where covert activity is being carried out.
- Watch for signs of redecoration or repainting where devices might have been hidden in walls or skirting panels. Examine these areas under artificial as well as natural light and from all angles especially oblique angles which might reveal inconsistencies in the surface. If available, examination with ultraviolet light is particularly effective.
- Don't forget to check exterior as well as interior walls for signs of disturbance.
- Check doors carefully, particularly those which are hollow or have large door locks.
- Check soft furnishings for sign of re-stitching.
- Lift all carpets.

Protecting Your Correspondence: How to Check if Your Mail is Being Opened

Opening and undetectably resealing correspondence has been a basic espionage skill since at least the days of the Elizabethans. All intelligence services have large technical departments who spend a great deal of time and taxpayers' money working out how to open a range of different envelopes and packages. They experiment to find which chemicals can be used to soften the glues that seal envelopes and adhesive tapes. As a spy you should always assume that someone will get access to your correspondence. So if it is necessary for it to contain information then it must be disguised or encoded. There are certain things you can do to check or reduce your risk:

- Always make a note of how long it normally takes post to arrive from different destinations. Any unusual delay might just be because of problems with the delivery service, but it should at least make you mildly suspicious, especially if this is the letter or package containing sensitive information.
- When packages are sealed, lining up tape with agreed places on the parcel may help. But try not to be obvious. When opening mail the first thing the technicians will do is photograph the package (sometimes under different lights), partly to look for clues or coded messages, partly so they can reassemble the package exactly as it was. So don't line the tape up with the corners. For instance, agree with your contact that the line will be exactly two centimetres from the corner. It is just possible that if your mail is being opened the technicians will make a mistake.
- Always assume that anything you send by mail will be opened. If you must send information by this route, use some level of encryption (see page 212).
- E-mails will probably make up the bulk of your correspondence. Always remember that vast numbers of e-mails are collected and routinely read by intelligence agencies. They are also stored for up to five years by service providers. Never send information by e-mail unless you are going to encrypt it or disguise it in some way. There are several excellent encryption programmes available on the internet.

Professor Fred Piper of Royal Holloway, University of London explains the basic principles of encryption using a Caesar wheel.

A good spy always checks every new location for bugging devices. Gabriel examines the smoke alarm in one of the recruits' safe houses.

Encryption

Encryption helps when communicating with agents, but a spy must remember that there is no such thing as an unbreakable code. Even when a code seems unbreakable there are always code books or microchips which can be stolen or copied, allowing the code to be decrypted. The Germans and the Japanese learned this costly lesson during World War II. Any code will only buy you a short-term advantage and should never be trusted completely.

As soon as it becomes clear that you are using a code your enemy will know that something is happening and do everything possible to break it. The best code is one they don't realise you are using, like drug traffickers talking about books, cars or some other agreed item when arranging deals by phone. So it is far better to use a personal code which only you and the correspondent understand. For instance, a system by which the use of the word 'emerald' at some point in a letter means 'go to meeting place number three'.

You can make your enemy's job harder by breaking the information into parts so that a letter contains part of the information, but an e-mail contains the other part and neither makes sense unless the code is understood and both parts of the message are held. One of the reasons that al Qaeda terrorists such as Osama bin Laden are proving so difficult to trace is that couriers are being used to pass messages, but no single courier has access to the complete message.

Finally, codes should be changed regularly. One of the biggest difficulties for the Allies during the Second World War was codes being changed. At the very least it would mean a delay as the new system was decoded. This is unpopular because it means hard work as everyone in the network gets used to the new system, but it is essential if communications security is to be maintained.

Protecting Your Vehicle

How to Check a Car for Bugs

Of course professional spies have access to departments full of technical experts who can sweep the vehicle for electronic bugs. But they are not always available (for instance, if you are working abroad) and many devices are either passive or are activated remotely so they are almost impossible to detect using sweepers. So modern

During the OP exercise Max demonstrates how easily
and quickly a bugging device can be placed on a car.

Once the device has been attached to the vehicle, its
progress can be monitored remotely on a laptop computer.
Max is able to sit in the OP and monitor every movement
of the vehicle superimposed on a street map of London.

spies are usually forced to rely on their own resources – the little tricks which spies all over the world have been using for thousands of years.

The key to protecting your vehicle is to remember that you may not be able to detect the bugging device, but you have a good chance of detecting whether someone has had covert access to your vehicle. If you detect that there has been intrusion then you can begin to look for it or just simply cease operations using that vehicle. Devices implanted in the bodywork of the car are very hard to detect. Devices attached by magnets to the car's underside are much easier to find.

The first thing to do is to consider the security of the vehicle.

A garage offers the best defensive option. A garage which is connected to your house is even better because any covert entry team will be worried that you may investigate and disturb them during the operation. These are the steps you should take to determine whether there has been a covert attack on your vehicle:

- Keep the car dirty. It is easy to wipe handprints from a clean car, but almost impossible to replace dirt in the same configuration once it has been disturbed.
- Make random visits to the garage at night, but try to have a cover reason for doing this such as having your fridge in the garage or storing books or paperwork there. Remember, always live your cover as an innocent person.
- Leave CDs on the seat in a particular layout. The cases of CDs slide very easily even if the disturbance is outside the car and you can use the cover designs to arrange them in a configuration only you will remember.
- Place scrap paper such as sweet wrappers on the floor of the car or under the edge of carpet in a particular layout.
- Place a damp leaf on the gap between the bonnet and the body of the car.
- Arrange detritus such as small pieces of plastic wrapping or ends of wire on the floor of the garage and note their positions so that you will know if they have been disturbed.
- Check the underside of the vehicle regularly.
- Remember that if your home security is good they will try to attack your vehicle during the day. If you park it while you are shopping or on business try to do it in a place that is

public or where you can get a view of it from the building you are in.

- For particularly sensitive operations borrow a fresh vehicle from a friend or colleague. Make sure you have a cover reason for doing this. Preferably take your vehicle to their house and let them borrow yours in exchange. There is a chance that the enemy is only using a tracking device and will assume that your friend's movements are yours.

How to Check a Car for Bombs

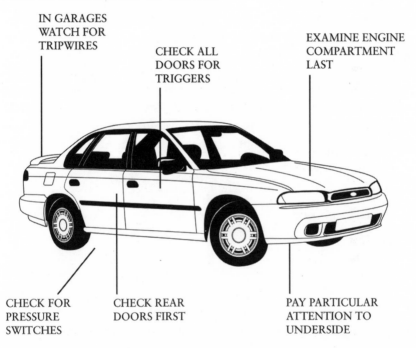

IN GARAGES
WATCH FOR
TRIPWIRES

CHECK ALL
DOORS FOR
TRIGGERS

EXAMINE ENGINE
COMPARTMENT
LAST

CHECK FOR
PRESSURE
SWITCHES

CHECK REAR
DOORS FIRST

PAY PARTICULAR
ATTENTION TO
UNDERSIDE

A bomb is a terrorist's preferred weapon. Any spy working in a declared station or against a terrorist group must be able to take defensive measures. Most of the detection rules which apply to bugs also apply to bombs. A key difference is that, even though some explosive devices can be surprisingly small, they will always be larger than a tracking device. The first thing to do is to consider the type of device you might be facing and how it will be activated. There are eight main possibilities:

1) Tripwire
2) Tagging
3) Pressure switch
4) Trigger wire or magnetic trigger
5) Electrical circuit
6) Timer
7) Trembler
8) Remote detonation

Stage One

In any bomb disposal situation, the first step is to consider the area around the device before even approaching it. Assuming that you have checked the door into the garage for booby traps and have entered safely, slowly circle the vehicle once looking for anything unusual. Have any of your tells been disturbed? This is the point at which you might encounter a **tripwire**. They aren't used often, but some devices such as Claymore mines are very easy to rig in this way and many of these are available to terrorists in the Third World. If it is known that you conduct regular anti-bomb checks on your vehicle then a tripwire attached around the vehicle or to one of the vehicle's doors may be placed there to catch you out.

Visual inspection may also give an indication that your vehicle has been **tagged**. This means marking the vehicle in some way, usually on the roof, so that it can be acquired by weapons targeting systems. This has been used by the Israeli air force to kill terrorists driving cars in Palestine.

Stage Two

Check the wheels thoroughly. A very quick way to place a bomb is to attach it to the underside of the vehicle and place a **pressure switch** in front of one of the wheels so that as the vehicle rolls forward the pressure switch is crushed, the connection in the electrical circuit is completed and the bomb detonates. Such devices are most commonly used in the street or other open areas where there is no time to gain access to the interior of the vehicle or engine compartment.

Examine gently around the rear of the wheel for wires and also check brake cables for damage. Cutting the brake lines, like in the movies, is rarely encountered in reality, but it doesn't hurt to check.

Jennie and Nicola in Tangiers.

Gabriel in Tangiers.

Stage Three

Next, the underside of the vehicle should be examined.

Two areas to pay particular attention to are the floor pan beneath the driver's seat and the area to the rear around the fuel tank.

Stage Four

When you have checked these areas you can move on to the vehicle itself. Use the vehicle windows to check if any of your tells inside the vehicle have been moved. Examine the door frames for signs of **trigger wires** or other tampering. A trigger wire is designed like a very small tripwire, so that when it is pulled or broken the explosive device is activated.

If you are satisfied you may open the doors. Begin with either a rear or passenger side door as these are least likely to be booby-trapped. Then check the interior before opening any other doors. Check your tells and the interior surfaces of remaining doors.

When satisfied with the rest of the interior you may open the driver's door and examine the cockpit area. Pay special attention to the steering column which may have been tampered with to insert an **electrical circuit** trigger (such as one which would activate when the ignition is turned on). Then examine the pedals and levers looking for trigger wires or pressure switches. Remember: *look* carefully first, *then* examine with your fingertips.

Stage Five

You can now examine the engine compartment and boot. Examine the bonnet and boot carefully for signs of trigger wires or magnetic switches. Examine the engine thoroughly. Familiarity with the normal layout of the engine compartment is vital.

These five stages should detect all but the most sophisticated devices. You can never be absolutely sure that you are safe, but at least you can improve your chances.

Tremblers are a type of switch which activate as the vehicles move. Some use a mercury bubble which moves and because mercury is a metal it completes a circuit. Some use delicately balanced components which tip or move and complete the circuit. Tremblers are unlikely to be used as they are very difficult to place successfully, but if they are used they will probably be 'coarse' i.e. they will not be affected by very gentle movements so there is a reasonable chance of finding them during a careful search.

Remote detonators are usually radio controlled and you should be looking for a fine piece of wire for receiving the signal. This will usually be visible. This is another reason why it is good to have the vehicle in a garage attached to your house – the enemy will not know when you are conducting your checks. If they see you enter the garage that is when they might remote detonate the device.

Timers can be mechanical, chemical or electrical. The disadvantage of timers is that they are indiscriminate – they will simply detonate regardless of whether the car is in use at the time or not. Your best defence is to find the device on a routine search.

Resistance to Interrogation

Of course no one can imagine the sheer horror of being in the hands of your enemies and the prospect that they are going to do anything they can to get information from you. No one knows how they will react, what will be the torture that breaks them. None of us really knows whether we would last thirty seconds or thirty hours. During World War II there were cases of strong men who were broken in minutes and of frail women who resisted every kind of torture imaginable.

But a spy can at least consider this nightmare scenario and try to prepare for it. Who knows – it might help and certainly every training course for spies in the world will contain an element of this preparation.

In this context 'interrogation' does not mean being picked up by suspicious local police, it means being caught red-handed and given over to security forces for a no-holds barred grilling. You are in the hands of your enemies and they can do anything they want to get information from you.

Interrogation by real security forces

Jennie is subjected to a physical
search before the questioning begins.

Nicola is confronted with incriminating
documents in an attempt to break her cover story.

Interrogation by Western Security Forces

At one time this wasn't so bad. There were rules and those had to be observed. All you really had to do was sit tight and wait for your lawyer. You might be uncomfortable. You might get slapped around a bit. But you did not face the prospect of torture and execution.

However, the rules are changing. Although the CIA has denied using torture in its facilities, some officers have admitted that suspects are taken abroad and handed over to local security forces to do with as they wish. The security forces get the information any way they like and the CIA do not ask questions later. Prisoners are being held at Guantanamo Bay detention facility without charge or access to family or lawyers. Since the US believes these men to be beyond the reach of international law whilst in this facility it is hard to believe that torture and/or drugs are not being used. Evidence from prison camps in Iraq would suggest that it certainly is.

But make no mistake, even if the 'rules' are followed, you could be in for a bad time. Standard Western interrogation techniques include drugs, sleep deprivation, starvation, subjection to cold (being hosed down naked with cold water and left in a freezing room), constant exposure to white noise, hooding and use of stress positions. The West has not abandoned the use of old forms of torture because it is inhuman, it is because they have found something more effective. Strangely, Western services do not consider this kind of treatment as 'torture'.

Interrogation by Security Forces Elsewhere in the World

This is far more serious because there are no rules, no human rights. These guys love to improvise, particularly with electricity. The only thing which might offer a glimmer of hope is that they are representatives of a government and you are a citizen of a particular country. There might be repercussions so it is possible you will not be treated as badly as one of their own countrymen. Your government might be able to apply pressure for your release.

Interrogation by a Terrorist Group

This is as bad as things can get. These people are animals who represent no one and obey no form of rules. All you can do is hang on as long as possible and pray.

General Tactics

Think of your resistance in terms of layers. The interrogators are trying to burn through those layers. Hold each stage for as long as you can:

1) Stick to your cover story. It's also a way of finding how much they know.

2) Just because cover story is broken, it doesn't mean you're a spy. You could be a criminal or a womaniser or even an agent for *their* government, so confess to something less.

3) Play dumb – yes, you are a spy, but you are a very low-level one, you effectively know nothing. You were just asked to go on this one mission.

4) Give them something to keep them happy, negotiate, confuse, buy time.

5) Silence.

6) Death – if you can kill yourself or get them to kill you without giving them anything then you've 'won'.

It is not good enough simply to clam up straight away. All of the recruits were interrogated as part of the course and Simon tried this. The interrogators, who were professionals, said that they would simply have worked on him much harder because he was so suspicious. They were much more impressed by Jennie and Nicola who stuck to their cover stories despite hours of being roughed up and held in uncomfortable stress positions. There are also some things you can try which might help. Even if one of these steps helps you to hold out for an hour longer it is a kind of victory.

The first step is to get a grip on your **mental attitude**. You are captured. You are almost certainly going to die. Understand that these people are going to hurt you, that if you leave with any toes, fingers, teeth or other parts intact it will be a miracle. Find your anger. The only thing you have left in this world is not to tell these people anything.

Of course this is easy to say, but this spirit of resistance is based on sound research. During the Korean War, an analysis was made of the resistance to interrogation of UN troops captured by the Chinese. It was found that the troops best at resisting were the Turks. Upon closer examination it was believed that this was because British, US and Commonwealth troops were trained to hold out as long as possible and then it was all right to break since 'everybody breaks at

Max under interrogation.

Interrogators will try to terrify you into talking at first with hoodings, beatings and fear. This is the stage when most people crack because of the shock of capture and the horror of what will be done to them. Those that hang on through this usually last much longer. They will try and convince you that no one will rescue you. They may be right, but you have to fight for that chance. In Beirut in the 1980s there was a story about two KGB officers who were picked up by a militia group. They seemed beyond help because no one would admit to holding them. Everyone thought they were as good as dead. Apparently the KGB sent out a message to the heads of the leading militia groups asking for help. Attached to the request was a list of the wives and families of the leaders of each group. There was no direct threat. The two men were released a day later.

some point'. The Turks on the other hand were simply trained to believe that you told your enemy nothing – and it worked. Even the officers who were told that they would be shot if they did not cooperate, simply replied that their subordinates would take over. Of course, some Turks cracked but their success rate was far higher than others and their mental attitude to capture was part of their success. Studies of Resistance prisoners during the Second World War also bore this out. The human body can withstand incredible torture, but only if the mind is right.

The next thing to remember is that you are playing for **time**. As a spy there will almost certainly be a reporting system and your loss will be noted. As soon as your organisation realises you have been taken security officers will be working to minimise the damage – closing down technical operations, moving agents to safe houses. At the same time the organisation will also be taking other steps to find you and secure your release. Every minute you buy with your life buys them time to save another of your agents. You may not escape with your life, but at least you defeat the people who have captured you by holding out long enough to make the information as good as useless.

Pretend to be more **scared** than you are (this might be difficult!) Pretend that you have cracked and that you are willing to talk. Give them rubbish, make up operations, give them the name of 'moles' in their own organisation, anything. The point is that as long as you are talking they are not torturing you.

Pretend to be more **hurt** then you actually are. After they have given you a good hiding a couple of times they have no idea how badly you are hurt. Become incoherent, they *might* lay off you for a while to give you a chance to recover before the next session of questioning.

An officer of a Western intelligence service was sent to a foreign country on a single mission. He completed the mission successfully and was waiting for a few days before leaving the country. He did some sightseeing and practised some counter-surveillance drills just to keep his hand in. On the day before he was due to leave the country, he was

cont'd

---

walking down a street in a rural village when two jeeps in military markings pulled up next to him. He was clubbed to the ground, hooded, handcuffed and thrown into the back of one of them.

When the hood was removed he was in some sort of military interrogation centre. The men holding him never told him what he was charged with. His (genuine) passport was torn up in front of his eyes and denounced as a cheap fake. His belongings were shredded as they looked for clues. He says that he was close to panic and confessing everything. He couldn't work out where he had gone wrong or how much these people knew. He had practised resistance to interrogation, but what caught him out in this case was that the whole thing was so unexpected. The only resistance to interrogation rule he could remember was to play for time. He decided to hang on for just a few more minutes.

He was beaten several times and the interrogation looked like turning very nasty as certain items including an electric drill were produced. But, knowing nothing else about why he was being held, he simply stuck to his cover story. He was held for two days during which he was interrogated six times. On the third day his cell was opened and he was led through the building to the office of a senior officer. He had decided that he couldn't make it through another session and he was sure that this was the time when he was going to crack. The officer poured him a large drink, apologised for the 'slight mistake' and said that he was being released.

It transpired that as he was wandering through the streets taking photographs just as any tourist might, he had taken a photograph of a building which was in fact the headquarters of the local secret police. This action had been enough for someone to denounce him as a spy working for anti-government guerrillas and he had been picked up. He had come within moments of confessing the whole operation when in fact the incident had just been a ghastly mistake.

Pretend to be **less important** than you actually are: they've got the wrong person, you're only involved in a low-level capacity. You're just a driver or a messenger. Anything which prevents them from realising who you actually are.

Finally, **trust no one**, especially other prisoners, doctors, Red Cross workers or interrogators who pretend to be your friend. Beware of tricks – even if the Red Cross worker is genuine they may be bugging the cell to hear what you say. Remember the trick we played on the recruits on the very first day of training when they were allowed to mix unsupervised in the training school and many of them broke their cover straight away.

Mike Baker in Tangiers.

11 Joining the Real Spies

The person who has nothing for which he is willing to fight, nothing which is more important than his own personal safety, is a miserable creature and has no chance of being free unless made and kept so by the exertions of better men than himself.

John Stuart Mill

This book has been about real spies and the skills they use. As you have seen it is far away from the world of glamour, fast cars and money portrayed in the movies. But neither is it quite the world of double crossings and betrayals portrayed in many spy novels. Spies have a much closer bond with their agents than people imagine. It is not a relationship of master and servant, but more of colleagues and sometimes even friends. Much of the work is boring and repetitive, requiring constant thought and discipline. It is often lonely work in which your hard-won triumphs will attract barely any public attention. And like any large organisation, intelligence agencies are rife with as many power struggles, petty turf wars and morons in positions of authority as any other.

If you do still want to be a real spy then there are a final few issues you should consider before taking the step:

Morality

We looked at this issue briefly in Chapter 1, but there are other issues to consider. Remember the golden rule of espionage: an intelligence service will do whatever needs to be done. **Assassination** is one of those tasks. Many leading intelligence services use this. The old Eastern bloc services used it, even assassinating one enemy with a

British Conscience Spies

In recent years there have been a number of British spies
who have broken cover in order to denounce the activities
of their parent organisations and claiming that there is no
adequate recourse for those who have doubts about the
illegal activities which British intelligence agencies indulge
in. Each British intelligence organisation has suffered from
this and while their motives have been questioned, the
conscience spies indicate a serious lack of an ombudsman
for these agencies to which disaffected officers can
appeal. The lack of such an officer may one day have
much more serious consequences for national security.

David Shayler: Shayler joined MI5 in 1991 and worked
there for six years in departments such as G Branch,
dealing with international terrorism, C Branch, where
government officials' backgrounds are checked and T
Branch, targeting terrorism in Northern Ireland.
Disillusioned with the mundane nature and ineffectiveness
of the work, which was far from the challenging and
exciting career he had expected, he resigned in 1997. In
August of that year he provided information for a series of
articles which appeared in the *Mail on Sunday* newspaper
alleging illegal activities by the organisation including
bugging leading political figures. Shayler and his partner
Annie Machon who had also been an MI5 officer, fled to
the Continent and in 1998 Shayler made further allegations
including that British intelligence had plotted the
assassination of Libyan leader Colonel Gadaffi. In 1998 he
was arrested in France, but subsequently released.
Newspapers in the UK were gagged to prevent further
revelations. Finally he returned to the UK and in 2002 was
imprisoned for six months for breaching the Official Secrets
Act (he only served six weeks). The trial was widely
criticised on human rights grounds since Shayler was forced
to disclose his entire case to the prosecution in advance,
practically guaranteeing that he would be convicted.

cont'd

Shayler is seen by some intelligence officers as a self-interested poseur rather than a conscience spy, but his existence does indicate a problem.

Richard Tomlinson: Tomlinson joined MI6 in September 1991. After training he was posted to the section dealing with operations in the Balkans. In April 1995 he was summarily dismissed. The shock of this together with the recent death from cancer of his long-term partner appears to have hit Tomlinson very hard. He claimed that he had been unfairly sacked and demanded an industrial tribunal. MI6 refused. Determined to press his side of the case, Tomlinson wrote a book detailing alleged illegal activities by the organisation including the proposed assassination of President Milosevic of Serbia. MI6 then hounded Tomlinson around the world as he tried to find a publisher for his book, even having him arrested in Australia. Attempts by them to reach a truce with Tomlinson and find him gainful employment were rebuffed. In 1997 Tomlinson was finally tried and imprisoned for one year for breaching the Official Secrets Act. Even after his release in 1998, MI6 continue to hound him, fearful that he might make more revelations. He eventually found a publisher for his book *The Big Breach*. *The Sunday Times* published extracts in 2001 and it is now widely available around the world.

Katharine Gun: Gun worked as a translator at GCHQ. In January 2003 she leaked a copy of an e-mail to the *Observer* newspaper revealing details about illegal NSA bugging operations against the United Nations in order to secure favourable votes on Iraq. This was in clear violation of the Vienna Conventions. GCHQ conducted an investigation to discover the source of the leak and Gun confessed. But even though she openly admitted the offence, in February 2004, the Attorney General declined to prosecute her for breaching the Official Secrets Act. Clare Short, the former Cabinet Minister who backed up Gun's claims, also escaped prosecution. It was widely felt that this was done to prevent embarrassment to the government. Gun has subsequently enrolled on a postgraduate course at Birmingham University studying global ethics.

poisoned ball-bearing fired from an air rifle disguised as an umbrella. There are claims that the Russians still use assassination against Chechen enemies. The Israelis use it frequently to remove their Palestinian enemies and there are still question marks as to whether in 1987 they assassinated the scientist who designed the Iraqi 'Super-gun'. The Americans use it: they have taken out al Qaeda operatives with remote-controlled drones firing hellfire missiles and they tried to assassinate Saddam Hussein on numerous occasions. The French intelligence service killed when it bombed the *Rainbow Warrior*, the flagship of Greenpeace. They may not have meant to kill, but the act of placing a bomb aboard a protest vessel is reprehensible.

Even if your service does not assassinate its enemies the chances are that you will end up working alongside one that does. Many people will have no problem with that – they are terrorists, they deserve it. But sooner or later someone will be hit who did not deserve it, either by mistake or design. Will you still be able to live with it? Under the rules of secrecy you must.

Kidnapping is another tool the Israelis use which other intelligence services avoid, but before any of us claim the moral high ground, remember the golden rule. Rightly or wrongly Israel believes she has her back to the wall and is fighting for survival. In the 'war on terror' it may not be long before other governments start using the same argument. As a spy, you must be prepared to take part in that. **Torture** is used by both the Americans and the Israelis. Much of the product of those interrogations is passed to and used by other Western services. Are you prepared to participate in that process?

Psy ops or **black propaganda** are another element of espionage which is being used to an increasing extent and not always abroad. These operations involve (amongst other things) trying to manip-ulate public opinion. There is certainly plenty of evidence that intelligence services from all nations have used their contacts with the media to place stories which are favourable to them and very often there is no oversight of this. It can be claimed that politicians give spies their orders, but then who briefs the politicians? The spies do and it would take a very brave politician to refuse a request from his intelligence services if they have told him the security of the country may be at stake.

The world of the spy is murky as well as honourable. The spy code means that you must take the whole package and keep silent about it all. Anyone who doubts this should simply look at the recent cases of David Shayler of MI5, Richard Tomlinson of MI6 and Katharine Gun of GCHQ, all of whom alleged that their services were involved in illegal activities. The essence of the case against them was not whether they were right or wrong, but that they tried to speak out at all. Are you prepared to sacrifice that freedom as part of the price of being a spy?

Mental Pressure

Being a spy is lonely work. You can't trust anyone, even your colleagues, as the cases of Kim Philby, George Blake and Aldrich Ames have emphasised. Being involved in this secret world will change you – there are very few well-adjusted spies. Richard Tomlinson quoted Carl Jung on this: *'Maintenance of secrets acts like a psychic poison, which alienates their possessor from the community'*. Constantly looking over your shoulder for surveillance, trying to second guess the motives of your agents and your recruitment targets, watching your personal security every second of every day can become an obsession. Markus Wolf, the former East German spymaster, tells of Andrei Grauer, a former Russian NKVD officer who was special adviser to the East German intelligence service. He was a hero to the younger officers with his tales of past operations, yet he became a paranoid schizophrenic suspecting everyone around him, especially the head of the Service whom he became convinced was a Western spy. Eventually he was recalled to Moscow as a hopeless mental case. As Wolf put it: *'The watchfulness that had once made him a top intelligence officer had taken him over'*.

It is not just being privy to secrets which causes this pressure. There are other strains which don't become obvious until you start doing the job. One is that much of the job is boring. Once you have got over the excitement of seeing the word 'SECRET' stamped on everything, you will begin to realise that much of the work requires huge amounts of painstaking research. Yes, there are moments of great excitement, sometimes more thrilling than you can imagine, but the groundwork for those moments is thousands of hours of paperwork, routine meetings, reports and more reports. The financial rewards are not great either – spies are considered to be civil servants and paid as such. As you watch your contemporaries climbing other career ladders and receiving considerable rewards it can become dispiriting. For this

Adam Kaczmarczyk was a twenty-eight-year-old communications clerk in the Polish Ministry of Defence. In 1967 he was recruited as an agent by MI6. He was a valuable agent, his access to high-level communications within the Ministry allowed him to supply a range of reports on both Polish and Soviet bloc military plans and capabilities. In fact he was too good. Polish counter-espionage officers became suspicious and placed him under surveillance. One day he was followed to a meeting with his MI6 handler who was living under diplomatic cover. The Polish security forces pounced and Kaczmarczyk was arrested together with his handler and a bundle of incriminating documents. The MI6 handler was expelled from the country for 'activities incompatible with his status', Kaczmarczyk was interrogated and shot for treason.

His handler went on to become a senior and very successful MI6 officer. But it is likely that he never forgot Kaczmarczyk and perhaps he wondered if there was some way he could have been saved, through better training or by not being used so intensively perhaps. Those are the sort of thoughts a spy has to live with for the rest of his life. Not everyone can handle it and of those who can, many are too unfeeling to ever make good intelligence officers.

reason some intelligence services have a considerable problem retaining staff after the first five years. The divorce rate for spies is probably higher than almost any other profession.

Then there are the risks involved. Very few intelligence officers get killed. Most of the risks are run by their agents. But losing an agent on an operation can scar an officer for life. The 'Great Game' is never the same again. For some the sense of guilt has been so bad that they have left the intelligence services. No matter how closely you work with agents, no matter how careful you are, sooner or later you may have to put them in harm's way. This may be someone with a spouse and children. If they get caught the whole family may suffer. You have to be prepared to live with that. This risk was something the ex-spy and novelist John le Carré explored in one of his earliest novels, *The Spy Who Came in from the Cold*. If you want to understand the type of guilt you may have to live with, read that book and see how it affects its hero, Leamas. Le Carré definitely knew what he was talking about.

The other extreme is almost as bad. What happens if you get to the stage where the plight of the agents who work for you no longer affects you, when they become, in the manner of the old cliché, simply pawns on a chessboard? For some people that can be worse.

A Caring Service?

And what about your partner and children? How will they react to having a spy in the family? Your children have the choice of being taken around the world, often to some rather bad places or being sent to boarding schools. Spouses have to share many of the mental strains which their partner suffers and yet they get little support and no reward. It is almost impossible for them to follow their chosen career (though some do). Once spouses were supposed to simply put up with this treatment, but times are changing and in the 1990s problems had reached such a state that MI6 set up a 'spouses' committee' to deal with grievances and offer support. Other agencies have done the same but it hasn't necessarily solved the problem. In an article in the *Guardian* in October 2002, the former wife of an MI6 officer told how badly her husband had been treated when he was diagnosed with cancer. She also gave an indication of strains in the job generally:

> When you need them, they let you down. It starts at the school gate, collecting your toddlers. You have to say to your friends, 'I'm not sure where George is just at the moment.' You go home alone but you can't talk to others about it. I never told my mother. He never told his parents.

She also told of their poor quality housing when abroad and their exclusion from some of the more glittering diplomatic occasions for the same reasons.

Of course that is just one woman's view and if everyone were treated like this, spies would be jumping ship left and right. But it does highlight some of the issues which both spies and their partners have to consider: you don't join for the money or the fame, your cover life may be tiring and uncomfortable and you both have to live with the strain of the fact that you can't tell others what is going on. The intelligence services are at base military services – in time of war its officers hold military ranks. And like members of the armed forces, families are expected to make sacrifices.

Are the Intelligence Services Worth Joining?

There is one final issue you may wish to consider before deciding if you want to become a spy in Britain today. Are our intelligence services any good?

It could be argued that they didn't predict:

- The invasion of the Falkland Islands by the Argentinians in 1982.
- The invasion of Grenada by the Americans in 1983.
- The collapse of the Soviet Union in 1989.
- The invasion of Kuwait in 1990 leading to the First Gulf War.
- The terrorists attacks of 9/11.
- The absence of weapons of mass destruction in Iraq.
- The whereabouts of either Osama bin Laden or (for some considerable time) Saddam Hussein.

Analysts looking at the intelligence services from outside have often reached the same conclusion. The foreign affairs and defence specialist Mark Urban in his book *UK Eyes Alpha* claims that in the 1980s MI6 had 2,400 staff and a £100 million budget yet could produce only one decent Soviet agent and that Government Communications Headquarters could not crack Soviet codes. The indications are that things haven't changed. Of all the terror suspects recently arrested following a massive intelligence effort, less than twenty per cent have been charged with terrorism offences and more than half are released without any charge at all.

Foreign intelligence services do not seem to fare much better. The failure to find weapons of mass destruction in Iraq is well documented, but there is a long history of similar intelligence failures. In the 1980s the US intelligence services claimed that the Vietnamese were using a chemical weapon called Yellow Rain in Cambodia and that the Russians were using chemical weapons in Afghanistan. Neither of these claims turned out to be true.

But of course this is only one side of the argument. The intelligence services claim that they cannot reveal their greatest successes. In 1994 Stella Rimington, head of MI5, was able to claim that intelligence was preventing four out of five terrorist operations and it is certainly true that the organisation was enjoying considerable success at this time. The revelations of MI6 agent Oleg Gordievsky about the thinking at the highest levels of the Soviet government had a profound effect on the response of the US government which had previously assumed the Soviets were far more bellicose. And even if as a spy you only took part in *one* operation which saved hundreds of lives, wouldn't that be worth it?

No one knows where the truth lies because for better or worse the intelligence services are shrouded in secrecy. The most important thing is that no one should apply to join an intelligence service believing that they are some sort of elite. They are large organisations and prone to the same faults as any other. Some officers are very good, others less so. If you are going to apply at least do so with your eyes open.

Oleg Gordievsky (1938–)

A senior KGB officer and Britain's most valuable Cold War agent. He was recruited by MI6 in 1974 during his posting to Copenhagen and was run successfully by them until he became Deputy KGB Resident (deputy head of station) in London in the early 1980s. His reports are known to have been highly influential in affecting the thinking of the US administration towards the Soviet Union at that time. MI6 arranged to have the Resident expelled so that Gordievsky could be moved into the top spot. This may have led to suspicion against him or it may have been information from a defector but Gordievsky was recalled by Soviets in May 1985. He was arrested and interrogated, but his accusers lacked conclusive proof. Gordievsky was allowed home under close arrest and was able to alert his MI6 handlers who put an exfiltration plan into operation. Gordievsky was hidden in a vehicle and smuggled over the border into Finland in July. He has since made a successful living in the West as a writer and TV personality commenting on espionage.

How to Apply to the Real Intelligence Services

By the end of the training course only one of our recruits actually still wanted to work for the real intelligence services. They had applied for the training believing that it would be all glamour and guns, but had found it to be something else: still a demanding and worthwhile job requiring staff of the highest calibre, but one which requires high levels of personal sacrifice, painstaking attention to detail and the ability to withstand considerable mental strain. It is a job which is occasionally exhilarating and challenging, but also at times dull and frustrating. A job which you will almost certainly never be able to tell anyone else about. If you still believe that the world of espionage is for you then you have the following options:

The Internet

Almost all of the major intelligence services now have websites with details of where to apply for recruitment information. For those that don't, a letter to their headquarters building will do just as well. If they think you are a potential recruit they will reply to you. Details for many of the major services are at the back of this book.

The Press

Most of the services openly advertise their vacancies in newspapers. It is a matter of keeping your eye open for the advertisements.

Talent Spotters

If you are at university you can ask a careers adviser. Many of them have quite open links with the intelligence services and will pass your details along.

Whichever route you take you should ideally have a degree-level education, be a national of whichever country you apply to and be under thirty years of age (some services may take older applicants, it is always worth asking). Women and people from ethnic minorities are particularly in demand as they are under-represented.

Sexual orientation used to be a reason to bar people from the intelligences, but that has changed in recent years and arrangements have even been made in MI6 (one of the most conservative of the services) for officers to take their same-sex partners on foreign postings.

Religion is not a bar. In fact it could be argued that the intelligence services desperately need members of other religious backgrounds to balance some of the dubious reporting on issues in the 'war on terror'. However, given current sensitivities, security vetting will be particularly strict so prepare for a long and thorough investigation.

Whoever you are and wherever you apply, **good luck**!

Max falls at the final hurdle. Thinking that he has been dismissed
from the course, he takes the tempting bait devised by PR guru
Max Clifford (*below*) and freely gives away compromising
information about Sandy.

APPENDIX 1   How the Recruits Fared on the *Spy* Training Course

Warning: This Section Contains Information which you should Not Access Unless You Wish to Know the Final Results

Psychological Pressure

From the very start of the course the recruits were kept under the maximum psychological and emotional pressure. First, they were given only four hours in which to pack and prepare a cover story for their journey to London. They were only allowed to tell one other person where they were going and they would only be allowed to contact that person twice during the next seven weeks under strictly controlled conditions. As soon as they arrived at their hotel in London various small tests were set to see if they could maintain their cover and on arrival at the *Spy* training school they were thrown straight into their first full exercise (the Balcony exercise) without any preparation or training. To cap it all, that same night, when they were almost dropping with fatigue, they were abducted and interrogated by a team consisting of former SAS soldiers. Although not as brutal as a full military interrogation, it was a traumatic experience for people who were still untrained 'civilians'.

This level of pressure was kept up throughout the course. The recruits never knew when they would be tested or filmed, sometimes even being woken at three in the morning for questioning on their latest cover. At the same time, they were never allowed to forget that they were in competition with one another and often they were asked to spy on each other to obtain particular pieces of information. There were no rest days at all and the recruits were in a state of almost constant exhaustion. It is hardly surprising that Suzi's health broke down after only a few days.

It's hard to imagine what it is like to be subjected to this sort of pressure twenty-four hours a day. A strong-willed person can cope for a week or so but after that fatigue begins to take its toll. Jennie was the strongest of the recruits but the phone call home which the recruits were allowed half-way through the course affected her very badly and she was never the same again. Simon was one of the most promising recruits, but was constantly homesick even though he probably wanted to be a spy more than anyone else on the course and the 'Follow Your Mum' exercise when he was close enough to touch his wife but wasn't allowed to speak to her, almost broke him. In the end his separation from his family overwhelmed him: he became confused, performed poorly on several exercises and was actually relieved to finally leave the course. Reena seemed to deal with the pressure by just not taking part to the best of her ability, always holding something back. This meant that she didn't get as badly stressed as the other recruits, but also led to her being evicted from the course at an early stage. The last four recruits were so exhausted and drained by the last week that the trainers had to ease the pressure on them to give them time to recover. Even so, by the end of the course Jennie and Gabriel both said independently that, although they now had greater respect for real spies, it made them realise intelligence work wasn't something they wanted to do for real.

This state of constant apprehension replicates one of the most important aspects of a spy's life: a spy must constantly be on guard because if he gets it wrong for even a moment he could be killed or his family could suffer. At the same time a spy is responsible for all his agents, many of whom are running great risks. It is always possible that one of them might be imprisoned, tortured or killed. A spy has to be strong enough to deal with the guilt of that and still keep working effectively with the rest of his agents. If our recruits were to be tested effectively we had to replicate that constant fear and sense of threat.

Overall Assessment

As stated in the Introduction, one of the purposes of the course was to determine if only Oxbridge types are suitable to become spies or whether there is room for a broader spectrum of recruits to face our new enemies in the twenty-first century.

The eight recruits on the course only had one chance at demonstrating most of the skills required to be a spy and this sometimes made them look weaker candidates than they really were. On a real training course, recruits repeat the same type of exercise again and again until they get it right. Recruits with very good degrees from top universities often show an appalling lack of common sense at first and some of the early exercises can be quite embarrassing. But they are given the time to learn from their mistakes and move on. This is a chance our recruits did not get.

All the recruits had potential, some of them might have made it as spies, but one thing was clear to all of the trainers – the modern intelligence services need to broaden their recruitment net. There is a lot of talent out there which isn't being used.

Suzi was the first recruit to be dismissed. She succeeded in the balcony mission and did extremely well on the building-entry mission where she kept staff busy for more than thirty minutes without them becoming suspicious. But small details seemed to upset her performance. She often appeared to worry too much about the equipment or other minor details. She did not bond well with others on the course who felt that she did not really want to be there. It was felt that she never fully settled at the school, which was disappointing because as a representative of the 'older generation', we had high hopes for her.

Reena was the second to go. She had never settled on the course and was almost first to go because of her poor performances, but some of the trainers felt that she deserved a second chance. Things did not improve. This was disappointing as she was clearly a young woman with ability. But she never fulfilled her potential. The general feeling was that she was more interested in being on television than in learning how to become a spy. She and Max failed their building-entry mission and she did not perform well in any of the cover missions. Her attempt at an approach was such a disaster that the target ended up interrogating her and assumed she was some sort of journalist. In the end she had to go.

Simon and Austin were the next two dismissed. Both started the course strongly, but as Max improved, they both suffered a run of poor performances. Neither had any complaints. **Simon** had initially started as one of the strongest recruits. He has a quick mind, a charming personality and a very good eye for small details. But his nerve tended to fail him at vital moments: on the office-entry mission all the work was left to Jennie and on the Millennium Bridge surveillance exercise he failed to move when Austin was in trouble. As the trainers became more and more concerned, his performances on missions seemed to go to pieces: he blew the OP mission when, having planted the bugging device, he opened the door to a concerned neighbour. More significantly, it was his weapons notes which were found left behind in the house – on a real operation under hostile conditions that might have been enough to lead to the death or imprisonment of the OP keeper. He was too laid back. His test scores were not high enough for a man of his intelligence and when challenged to find a DLB he claimed that he just couldn't do it. He missed the DLB in the pub garden on the last major exercise when the whole mission hung on his efforts. Finally he was caught red-handed breaking the rules of the school for a third time by keeping pictures of his family. He had been repeatedly warned about how dangerous this could be, but was dreadfully homesick and just didn't seem able to bring this element of his character under control.

Austin was a more marginal decision than Simon. He had a great deal of promise and had done very well on certain exercises. He had succeeded on the balcony exercise against all expectations and he came up with a risky but successful approach in the café exercise. He was always willing to put himself forward on surveillance missions and was team commander for two of the final missions. It was these that finally killed his chances: on the first it was Simon's poor performance which really let the team down, but Austin was responsible for the planning. As the lookout, Nicola was too far away and the failure to make sure there were communications meant that the bugging device was put in the wrong position. He failed to fully include Nicola (probably the strongest member of the team) in the planning. She felt that it became a 'lads' mission'. Finally, as

242

commander, it was his responsibility to make sure the OP was cleared. The discovery of equipment and papers was largely because the evacuation was rushed and poorly planned. In the last major exercise, Austin was given a chance to redeem himself. To a considerable extent he was let down by Jennie who didn't give him as much support as she should have. But the exercise was his second outright failure and as Austin said himself, 'If you don't produce the results, you don't deserve to stay.' However, Austin was a bright and popular recruit, at his best when he used his natural authority. The trainers felt that, given more time and training, he could have made a good intelligence officer.

Max was one of the weakest recruits at the start of the course. He had a tendency to lie about everything and this caused friction with several members of the *Spy* school, particularly Gabriel. He made it to the last four because of the improvement in his performances in the middle of the course. He was successful in the approach mission and in the 'Meet the Family' exercise where he successfully gained access to Nicola's house. He performed well in the OP mission and in the final selection exercises. The trainers admired the fact that he was always willing to put himself forward even though he made mistakes and he was especially good in the mission where he had to 'recruit' a member of the public over four days where he achieved complete success. He fell at the final hurdle when the recruits' loyalty was tested just before the team were sent abroad for the last mission. Although he didn't pass any sensitive information to Max Clifford, he did say, 'I'd love to give you something on Sandy. I hated her.' That was enough to fail him.

Gabriel had a tendency to arrogance which he needed to keep a careful eye on as it irritated some of the recruits and the trainers early in the course. He was clearly intelligent and scored well in the written tests, but his complete loss of composure on the balcony exercise almost had him removed from the course straight away. Still, his performances improved and he showed in exercises such as the approach and informant recruitment that he could turn on the charm when required. His failure to gather evidence against Max on the investigation exercise marked the high point of Max's performance and at that stage it was possible that he was going to overtake Gabriel. But Max's failure on the loyalty mission was enough and

Gabriel made the final three for the overseas mission. Unfortunately his work abroad was poor, particularly in surveillance and, against two strong performances by the girls, he was first to be eliminated.

Jennie was the star of the course from day one. She had the intelligence, the charm and the nerve the trainers were looking for. She succeeded in almost all of her missions and her written work was always of the highest standard. Her work in the building-entry mission was especially good – she not only got access to the restricted part of the shop but also persuaded a member of staff to help her. On the informant recruitment mission when she had to work under cover for four days the success of the mission was never in doubt. But then things started to go wrong. The constant strain of the work and the emotional shock of hearing that she would have to betray Simon pushed her to breaking point. Her performances suffered and Austin's departure from the course was largely because of her failure to support him as commander. At one stage it seemed that she would take herself off the course. But then she pulled it all back together and having made the final three she performed excellently with some first-class solo surveillance work. Only on the final day did it all go wrong: first she performed poorly when her task was to stop the target from returning to her room where Nicola was copying information. Her work was clumsy and almost alarming. Finally, when arrested by local police, she blew her cover in a very short time. The trainers believed that the strain of the course had ultimately caught up with her and that, as with Simon, her attachment to her family had proved to be her Achilles' heel.

Nicola was the find of the course. It was always clear that she had charm and she easily succeeded in early exercises such as the balcony mission, the building-entry exercise, 'Meet the Family' and the approach missions. But her written test results were poor and it was felt that she was too much of an intellectual lightweight to succeed at the later stages of the course. By the midway assessment, she was doing as well as most of the men, but still way behind Jennie. The upturn in her performances came when surveillance exercises began. Some people have just got it and Nicola performed excellently at a time when Jennie was starting to falter. The targets never spotted her and when she carried out counter-surveillance she was the only recruit to spot a member of the surveillance team. In her written

The final mission

Nicola had to work fast because Jennie failed to think of a cover story convincing enough to delay the target

Nicola keeps her nerve in the final exercise, breaking into the target's room, and collecting the vital intelligence with only seconds to spare.

Only a very few are good enough to be real spies. On the foreign exercise in North Africa, Nicola stuck to her cover story, was released and made it to Spain with the secret information. Jennie's cover story was broken and she remained in jail.

work she put in hard effort and raised her scores markedly. She was soon considered the second strongest recruit next to Jennie and made the final three easily. She started poorly on the foreign mission, but some of this was felt to be Gabriel's fault. Once he was eliminated her performance improved and she was superb in the hotel mission, gathering the information under severe time pressure. Finally came the interrogation by local police and, unlike Jennie, she held her nerve and stuck to her cover story. The interrogators were impressed. Nicola was the winning student and deservedly so.

The Real Selection Process

For the real intelligence services training is expensive – they can't afford to waste it. In Britain the drop-out rate from training courses for MI5 and MI6 is lower than ten per cent because the selection process before training is designed to weed out the weaker candidates and only those who have a really good chance of making the grade get through. The British system of selection is primarily based on interviews and paper tests aimed at evaluating intelligence. A range of outside interests as well as good academic qualifications are seen as important because they demonstrate social skills, areas of possible expertise (such as linguistic aptitude) and give clues to possible areas of difficulty for the candidate: for instance, a candidate who held very strong political views and worked for the youth branch of a particular party might not want to work for a government led by a party of the opposite persuasion.

In Britain several thousand people apply to the intelligence services each year. A hundred or so will be accepted into administrative posts. Of those who will run agents, effectively the officer class of the intelligence services, less than fifty are likely to make the grade. Both MI5 and MI6 are currently undergoing periods of expansion, but they are limited in the number of people they can recruit by the number of training places they can offer. In Britain a basic training course lasts approximately six months, in the United States it is almost two years. However, one thing is certain, the intelligence services in Britain are not receiving enough applications from women and members of ethnic minorities and the services are particularly looking to recruit people from these groups.

APPENDIX 2   Intelligence Agencies

United Kingdom

MI5

Aka:	The Security Service, Box 500 (its Whitehall postal address)
Current Head:	Eliza Manningham-Buller
Responsible for:	Domestic security and counter-espionage
Staff:	c. 1,900 but expected to rise to c. 2,900
Website:	www.mi5.gov.uk
	www.mi5careers.info
E-mail address:	Messages can be sent via the website
Postal address:	The Enquiries Desk, PO Box 3255, London SW1P 1AE
Phone number:	020 7930 9000 (for passing information, not for general enquiries)
Notes:	Originated in 1909 when the Secret Service Bureau was created and divided into domestic and foreign espionage duties. The section responsible for the UK was headed by Captain Vernon Kell and had a staff of just ten. The main target was the threat of German agents. In 1916 the section became part of military intelligence

and was designated MI5. By the end of the First World War the number of staff had risen to 850. Although officially renamed the Security Service in 1931, MI5 remains the Service's most recognised designation. In recent years it has been expanding its influence in Whitehall: the Security Service Act 1989 allowed the Service to work on 'economic well-being' targets as well as threats to undermine the security of the state. In 1992 it became the lead agency in gathering intelligence against terrorism replacing Special Branch and in 1996 it became responsible for assisting in the fight against organised crime. It recently announced plans for another thousand officers and its political influence is likely to continue to grow.

MI6

Aka:	The Secret Intelligence Service, SIS, Box 850 (its former Whitehall postal address), 'the Friends' – nickname in the Foreign Office. Their very unclandestine headquarters building in London is often referred to as 'Legoland' because of its blockish appearance.
Current Head:	John Scarlett
Responsible for:	Foreign intelligence and counter-espionage
Staff:	c. 1,800 but expected to rise to c. 2,500
Website:	www.fco.gov.uk/sis
E-mail address:	None public
Postal address:	The Secret Intelligence Service, PO Box 1300, Vauxhall Cross, London SE1 1BD
Phone number:	None public
Notes:	Originated in 1909 when the Secret Service Bureau was created and divided into domestic and foreign espionage duties. The section responsible for foreign intelligence gathering was headed by Captain Mansfield Cumming and to this day the head of the Service is known as 'C'. In 1916 the section became part of military

intelligence and was designated MI6. Like MI5, it has consistently sought to expand its influence. In 1988 as the threat from the Soviet Union decreased it set up the Counter-Narcotics Section. It has recently announced plans for a substantial increase in staffing levels. Its garish new headquarters building on the banks of the Thames at Vauxhall within sight of the Houses of Parliament is seen by many of its critics as a statement of political power by this supposedly secret organisation.

GCHQ

Aka:	Government Communications Headquarters
Current Head:	David Pepper
Responsible for:	Sigint collection and analysis
Staff:	c. 4,500
Website:	www.gchq.gov.uk
E-mail address:	recruitment@gchq.gsi.gov.uk
Postal address:	GCHQ, Priors Road, Cheltenham, Gloucestershire GL52 5AJ (Employment enquiries should be directed to: The Recruitment Office, Room A1 108)
Phone number:	01242 232 912/3
Notes:	In 1919, various military experts involved in deciphering enemy codes were assembled as GC&CS, (the Government Code and Cipher School). In 1922 this school came under the control of the Foreign Office. During World War II the GC&CS based at Bletchley Park had several major successes including, of course, cracking the top secret Nazi Enigma and Lorenz codes. To assist with this they developed the world's first programmable electronic computer, Colossus. The organisation was renamed GCHQ in 1946 and moved to premises in Cheltenham in 1952 where it claimed to be part of the Foreign Office. Its existence was formally acknowledged to Parliament in 1983. The 1994

Intelligence Services Act brought it onto a formal legal footing. In 2003 the organisation moved into new accommodation at Cheltenham, a massive purpose-built circular building known as 'The Doughnut' which cost £330 million.

DIS

Aka:	Defence Intelligence Staff
Current Head:	The Chief of Defence Intelligence
Responsible for:	Gathering and analysis of military intelligence
Staff:	c. 4,500
Website:	www.mod.uk/aboutus/keyfacts/factfiles/dis.htm
E-mail address:	None public
Postal address:	Old War Office, Whitehall, London SW1A 2EU
Phone number:	0870 607 4455 (MOD general enquiries line)
Notes:	Started life as the Joint Intelligence Bureau. Renamed the DIS and amalgamated with the three single-service intelligence organisations in 1964. The DIS comprises two main parts: the Defence Intelligence Analysis Staff (**DIAS**) which provides defence intelligence assessments and the Intelligence Collection Staff (**ICS**). The ICS comprises two main sections: the Defence Geographic and Imagery Intelligence Agency (**DGIA**) which deals with imagery and other geographic support and the Defence Intelligence and Security Centre (**DISC**) which provides intelligence training for armed-forces personnel.

United States of America

FBI

Aka:	Federal Bureau of Investigation, the Feds, the Bureau
Current Head:	Robert S. Mueller III
Responsible for:	Domestic security and counter-espionage
Staff:	c. 27,000
Website:	www.fbi.gov
E-mail address:	None public
Postal address:	J. Edgar Hoover Building, 935 Pennsylvania Avenue, Washington DC 20535–0001
Phone number:	202–324–3000
Notes:	Originated in 1908 when the US Attorney General appointed thirty-four officers (including no fewer than twelve accountants) to investigate crimes such as slavery and land fraud. This concept of federal enforcement of laws across state lines was seen as new and by some disturbing. The group was formally named the Federal Bureau of Investigation the following year. By 1924 the Bureau had 650 staff, rising to 1,800 by the outbreak of World War II. The war against Communism under Director J. Edgar Hoover (who was Director for forty-seven years) led to a rise in the FBI's numbers to more than 17,000 by the end of the 1960s. The war on terror has seen a similar explosion in numbers and a budget which is now in the region of $2 billion.

CIA

Aka:	Central Intelligence Agency, the Agency
Current Head:	John E. McLaughlin (Acting Director)
Responsible for:	Collection and evaluation of foreign intelligence
Staff:	Supposedly classified, but at least 16,000
Website:	www.cia.gov www.cia.gov/employment/apply (for employment opportunities)

E-mail address:	Messages can be sent via the website
Postal address:	Central Intelligence Agency, Washington DC 20505
Phone number:	703–482–0623 (CIA Office of Public Affairs)
Notes:	Intelligence during and after the First World War was the responsibility of various military departments. In 1942 an attempt to form a single foreign intelligence agency was made in the shape of the OSS (Office of Strategic Services). It wasn't a tremendous success and was opposed by the military and the FBI. In 1947 the CIA was formed as part of the National Security Act. It has been growing in power and influence ever since. Its main headquarters is in Langley, Virginia. Executive Order 12333 issued in 1981 by President Ford supposedly forbids operatives from engaging in or conspiring to secure assassination. Some have expressed doubts about whether this Order is still in force.

NSA

Aka:	National Security Agency
Current Head:	Lt. General Michael V. Hayden, USAF
Responsible for:	Sigint collection and analysis
Staff:	Undisclosed but believed in excess of 15,000 worldwide
Website:	www.nsa.gov
E-mail address:	nsapao@nsa.gov (media enquiries) careers@nsa.gov (employment)
Postal address:	9800 Savage Road, Fort George G Meade, Maryland 20755–6000
Phone number:	301–688–6524 (Public affairs)
Notes:	The Armed Forces Security Agency (AFSA) had been established in 1949 to bring all military departments responsible for cryptography and sigint under one umbrella. However, it quickly became clear that the organisation needed a wider remit and in 1952 all military and non-military departments with a similar responsibil-

ity were amalgamated into the new NSA. In 1984 the NSA was additionally given responsibility for computer security throughout the USA.

NRO

Aka:	National Reconnaissance Office
Current Head:	Peter B. Teets
Responsible for:	Designs, builds and operates America's spy satellites
Staff:	Undisclosed
Website:	www.nro.gov
E-mail address:	None available
Postal address:	Office of Corporate Communications, 14675 Lee Road, Chantilly, Virginia 20151–1715
Phone number:	703–808–1198
Notes:	In operation since the 1960s, the NRO was publicly acknowledged by the US government in 1992.

NGA

Aka:	National Geo-Spatial Intelligence Agency
Current Head:	Lt. General James R. Clapper Jr. USAF (Ret.)
Responsible for:	Imagery and geographic intelligence
Staff:	Undisclosed
Website:	www.nga.mil
E-mail address:	None available
Postal address:	NGA General Help Desk, Mail Stop L-52, 3200 South Second Street, St. Louis, Missouri 63118–3399
Phone number:	314–260–5032
Notes:	Dates its origins to the geographic expeditions of the US Army's Lewis and Clark but really has its modern origins in 1961 and the establishment of the National Photographic Interpretation Centre (NPIC) to handle output from spy planes and satellites. All imagery and mapping was brought under one organisation, the National Imagery and Mapping Agency (NIMA) in 1996. This was re-designated the NGA in 2003.

Details of other Foreign Intelligence Agencies

France

DGSE

Aka:	Direction Générale de Surveillance de L'Extér-ieure, Les invisibles
Responsible for:	Foreign intelligence gathering
Website:	www.dgse.org

DST

Aka:	Direction Surveillance de Territoire
Responsible for:	Domestic security and counter-espionage
Website:	www.interieur.gouv.fr/rubriques/c/ c3_police_nationale/c335_dst /

Germany

BND

Aka:	Der Bundesnachrichtendienst, the German Federal Intelligence Service
Responsible for:	Foreign intelligence gathering
Website:	www.bundesnachrichtendienst.de

BfV

Aka:	Bundesamt für Verfassungsschutz, the Office for the Protection of the Constitution
Responsible for:	Internal security
Website:	None available

Australia

ASIO

Aka: Australian Secret Intelligence Organisation
Responsible for: Domestic security and counter-espionage
Website: www.asio.gov.au

ASIS

Aka: The Australian Secret Intelligence Service
Responsible for: Overseas intelligence and counter-intelligence
Website: www.asis.gov.au

DSD

Aka: Defence Signals Directorate
Responsible for: Sigint collection and analysis
Website: www.dsd.gov.au

DIGO

Aka: Defence Imagery and Geo-Spatial Organisation
Responsible for: Imagery collection and analysis
Website: www.defence.gov.au/digo

Russia

SVR

Aka: Sluzhba Vneshney Razvedki
Responsible for: Foreign intelligence gathering
Website: www.svr.gov.ru

FSB

Aka: Federal'naya Sluzhba Bezopasnosti, the Federal
                      Security Service
Responsible for: Domestic security and counter-espionage
Website: www.fsb.ru

BIBLIOGRAPHY

The recruits in the *Spy* training school had access to a library of relevant material. Below is a selection of the titles they had at their disposal.

General History

Allen, Martin *Hidden Agenda: How the Duke of Windsor Betrayed the Allies* (London: Macmillan, 2000)

Andrew, Christopher and Vasili Mitrokhin *The Mitrokhin Archive: The KGB in Europe and the West* (London: Penguin, 2000)

Bailey, F.M. *Mission To Tashkent* (Oxford: Oxford University Press, 2002)

Breuer, William B. *The Spy Who Spent the War in Bed: And Other Bizarre Tales from World War II* (London: John Wiley & Sons, 2003)

Funder, Anna *Stasiland: Stories from Behind the Berlin Wall* (London: Granta, 2004)

Herman, Michael *Intelligence Power in Peace and War* (Cambridge, Cambridge University Press, 1996)

Hesketh, Roger *Fortitude: The D-Day Deception Campaign* (New York: Overlook Press, 2002)

Hoare, Oliver *Camp 020 MI5 and the Nazi Spies* (The National Archives, 2001)

Hood, William *Mole: The True Story of the First Russian Intelligence Officer Recruited by the CIA* (London: Weidenfeld & Nicolson, 1982)

Judd, Alan *The Quest for C: Mansfield Cumming and the Founding of the Secret Service* (London: HarperCollins, 1999)

Kahn, David *The Code-Breakers: The Comprehensive History of Secret Communication from Ancient Times to the Internet* (London: Simon & Schuster, 1997)

Kerrigan, Michael *The Instruments of Torture* (Lyons Press, 2001)

Knightley, Philip *The Second Oldest Profession: Spies and Spying in the Twentieth Century* (London: Pimlico, 2003)

Lorenz, Marita and Ted Schwarz *Marita: One Woman's Extraordinary Tale of Love and Espionage from Castro to Kennedy* (London: Bloomsbury, 1993)

Page, Bruce, David Leitch and Philip Knightley *Philby: The Spy Who Betrayed a Nation* (London: Penguin 1969)

Philby, Rufina, et al *The Private Life of Kim Philby* (London: Little, Brown & Co., 1999)

Singh, Simon *The Code Book: The Secret History of Codes and Code-Breaking* (London: Fourth Estate, 2000)

Stafford, David *Churchill and the Secret Service* (London: John Murray, 1997)

Stafford, David *Secret Agent: The True Story of the Special Operations Executive* (London: BBC Consumer Publishing, 2002)

Tarrant, V.E. *The Red Orchestra: Soviet Spy Network Inside Nazi Europe* (London: Cassell Military, 1998)

Taylor, Peter *Brits: The War Against the IRA* (London: Bloomsbury, 2002)

Urban, Mark *The Man Who Broke Napoleon's Codes: The Story of George Scovell* (London: Faber & Faber, 2002)

Volkman, Ernest *Espionage: The Greatest Spying Operations of the 20the Century* (London: John Wiley & Sons, 1998)

Volkman, Ernest *Spies: The Secret Agents Who Changed the Course of History* (London: John Wiley & Sons, 1994)

Wires, Richard *The Cicero Spy Affair: German Access to British Secrets in World War II* (Westport: Greenwood Press, 1999)

From the Inside

Corbett, David *Both Sides of The Fence: A Life Undercover* (London: Mainstream Publishing, 2003)

Dorril, Stephen *MI6: 50 Years of Special Operations* (London: Fourth Estate, 2001)

Foot, M.R.D. (ed) and Brian Harrison (ed) *Secret Lives: Lifting the Lid on Worlds of Secret Intelligence* (Oxford: Oxford University Press, 2002)

Ford, Sarah *One-Up: A Woman in the SAS* (London: HarperCollins, 1997)

Henderson, Paul *The Unlikely Spy* (London: Bloomsbury, 1993)

Hollingsworth, Mark and Nick Fielding *Defending the Realm: Inside MI5 and the War on Terrorism* (London: Andre Deutsch, 2003)

McGartland, Martin *Dead Man Running: The True Story of a Secret Agent's Escape from the IRA and MI5* (London: Mainstream Publishing, 1999)

Mendez, Antonio *Master of Disguise: My Secret Life in the CIA* (New York, Perennial, 2000)

Rennie, James *The Operators: Inside 14 Intelligence Company – The Army's Top Secret Elite* (London: Century, 1996)

Rimington, Stella *Open Secret: The Autobiography of the Former Director-General of MI5* (London: Arrow, 2002)

Tomlinson, Richard *The Big Breach* (Cutting Edge, 2001)

Urban, Mark *UK Eyes Alpha: Inside Story of British Intelligence* (London, Faber & Faber, 1997)

Wolf, Markus, *Memoirs of a Spymaster* (London: Pimlico, 1998)

Wright, Peter *Spy-Catcher: The Candid Autobiography of a Senior Intelligence Officer* (New York: Penguin, 1987)

Handbooks

Barham, Debbie *The Real Life Scenario Survival Handbook* (Chichester: Summersdale, 2002)

Borgenicht, David and Joe Borgenicht *The Action Hero's Handbook* (London, Chronicle Books, 2003)

Chesbro, Michael *Wilderness Evasion: A Guide to Hiding Out and Eluding Pursuit in Remote Areas* (London: Paladin, 2002)

Jernkins, Peter, *Advanced Surveillance* (London: Intel Publishing, 2003)

Mack, Jefferson *Running a Ring of Spies: Spycraft and Black Operations in the Real World of Espionage* (London: Paladin, 1996)

Minnery, John *Pick Guns: Lock Picking for Spies, Cops and Locksmiths* (London: Paladin, 1989)

Mitrokhin, Vasili *KGB Lexicon: The Soviet Intelligence Officer's Handbook* (Frank Cass Publishers, 2002)

Ostrovsky, Victor and Claire Hoy *By Way of Deception: Making and Unmasking of a Mossad Officer* (London: Arrow, 1991)

Parker, John *Total Surveillance: Investigating the Big Brother World of E-spies, Eavesdroppers and CCTV* (London: Piatkus, 2001)

Piven, Joshua and David Borgenicht *The Worst Case Scenario Survival Handbook* (London: Chronicle Books, 1999)

Polmar, Norman and Thomas B. Allen *Spy Book: The Encyclopedia of Espionage* (London: Headline, 1996)

Rapp, Burt *Serious Surveillance for the Private Investigator* (London: Paladin, 1992)

Seaman, Mark *Secret Agent's Handbook* (The National Archives)

Treverton, Gregory F. *Reshaping National Intelligence for an Age of Information* (Cambridge: Cambridge University Press, 2003)

Worick, Jennifer and Joe Borgenicht *The Action Heroine's Handbook* (London: Chronicle Books, 2003)

The Psychology of Spying

Benson, Ragnar *Ragnar's Guide to Interviews, Investigations and Interrogations: How to Conduct Them, How to Survive Them* (London: Paladin, 2001)

Berne, Eric *Games People Play: The Psychology of Human Relationships* (London: Penguin, 1970)

Buzan, Tony *Master Your Memory* (London: BBC Consumer Publishing, 2003)

Buzan, Tony *Use Your Head* (London: BBC Consumer Publishing, 2003)

Caro, Mike *Caro's Book of Poker Tells* (Cardoza Publishing, 2003)

Cava, Roberta *Dealing With Difficult People: Proven Strategies for Handling Stressful Situations and Defusing Tensions* (London: Piatkus, 1990)

Cizek, Gregory J. *Cheating on Tests: How to Do It, Detect It, and Prevent It* (Lawrence Erlbaum Associates Inc., 1999)

Cox, Tracey *Superflirt* (London: Dorling Kindersley, 2003)

Ferris, Stewart *Je t'aime: How To Say 'I Love You' in 100 Languages* (Chichester: Summersdale, 2003)

Gudjonsson, Gisli H. *The Psychology of Interrogations, Confessions and Testimony* (London: John Wiley & Sons, 1996)

James, Judi *Bodytalk at Work: How To Use Effective Body Language To Boost Your Career* (London: Piatkus, 2001)

Johnson, Dr Spencer *Who Moved My Cheese: An Amazing Way to Deal With Change in Your Work and In Your Life* (London: Vermilion, 1999)

Lorayne, Harry *Page, A Minute Memory Book* (New York: Ballantine, 1996)

MacInaugh, Edmond A *Disguise Techniques: Fool All of the People Some of the Time* (London: Paladin, 1984)

Neenan, Michael and Windy Dryden *Cognitive Behaviour Therapy: An A-Z of Persuasive Arguments* (London: Whurr, 2002)

O'Brien, Dominic *Learn To Remember: Transform Your Memory Skills* (London: Duncan Baird, 2000)

Quillam, Susan *Body Langugage Secrets: Read the Signals and Find Love, Wealth and Happiness* (London, HarperCollins: 1997)

Vrij, Albert *Detecting Lies and Deceit: The Psychology of Lying and the Implications for Professional Practice* (London: John Wiley & Sons, 2000)

Wainwright, Gordon *Teach Yourself Body Language* (London: Hodder Arnold, 2003)

Weekes, Dr Claire *Self Help for your Nerves: Learn to Relax and Enjoy Life Again by Overcoming Stress and Fear* (London: HarperCollins, 1995)

Spy Novels

Buchan, John *The Thirty-Nine Steps* (London: Penguin Modern Classics, 2004)

Childers, Erskine, *The Riddle of the Sands: A Record of Secret Service* (London: Penguin Popular Classics, 1995)

Conrad, Joseph *The Secret Agent* (London: Penguin Modern Classics, 2000)

Davies, Robertson *The Cornish Trilogy* (London: Penguin, 1991)

Deighton, Len *The Ipcress File* (London: HarperCollins, 1994)

Deighton, Len *Game, Set and Match* (London: Century, 1986)

Fleming, Ian *Casino Royale, Live and Let Die, Moonwalker* (London: Penguin Modern Classics, 2003)

Fleming, Ian *From Russia With Love* (London: Penguin Modern Classics, 2004)

Greene, Graham *Our Man in Havana* (London: Vintage Classics, 2001)

Harris, Robert *Enigma* (London: Arrow, 1996)

Higgins, Jack *The Eagle Has Landed* (London: Penguin 1998)

Kipling, Rudyard *Kim* (London: Penguin Modern Classics, 2000)

le Carré, John *Smiley's People* (London: Sceptre, 1999)

le Carré, John *The Little Drummer Girl* (London: Sceptre 2000)

le Carré, John *The Looking Glass War* (London: Sceptre 1999)

le Carré, John *The Spy Who Came in from the Cold* (London: Sceptre, 1999)

le Carré, John *Tinker, Tailor, Soldier, Spy* (London: Sceptre, 1999)

le Carré, John *A Perfect Spy* (London: Sceptre, 2000)

Ludlum, Robert *The Janson Directive* (London: Orion, 2003)

Moulton, Doug *The China Files* (First Books Library, 2003)

Porter, Henry *Empire State* (London: Orion, 2004)

Seymour, Gerald *Harry's Game* (London: Corgi, 1999)

Silva, Daniel *The Mark of the Assassin* (London: Orion, 1999)

SPY TOP TENS

Spy Movies

Dr. No, 1962, Dir., Terence Young
Lady Vanishes, 1969, Dir., Alfred Hitchcock
Patriot Games, 1991, Dir. Philip Noyce
North by North West, 1959, Dir., Alfred Hitchcock
The Bourne Identity, 2002, Dir. Doug Liman
The Ipcress File, 1965, Dir., Sidney J. Furie
The Conversation, 1974, Dir., Francis Ford Coppola
The Spy Who Came in from the Cold, 1965, Dir., Martin Ritt
The Thirty-Nine Steps, 1935, Dir., Alfred Hitchcock
Spy Game, 2001, Dir., Tony Scott

Fictional Spies

James Bond (Ian Fleming)
Harry Brown (Gerald Seymour)
Neil Burnside (Ian Mackintosh)
Francis Cornish (Robertson Davies)
Richard Hannay (John Buchan)
Kim (Rudyard Kipling)
Harry Palmer (Len Deighton)
George Smiley (John le Carré)
Mr Verloc (Joseph Conrad)
Jim Wormold (Graham Greene)

Real Life Spies

Sir Paul Dukes
Oleg Gordievsky
Odette Hallowes
Jean Moulin
Michael Oatley
Oleg Penkovsky
Kim Philby
Francis Walsingham
Markus Wolf
Sir Richard White

INDEX